M.C. Vaughan is a contemporary romance ri want to giggle throughout You'll root for her characters as they fall for their perfect people...and you'll simultaneously shake your head as they stumble along the way. M.C. grew up in a house crowded with family, friends, books, music and the occasional ghost. Currently, she lives in Maryland with her husband and three delightful kids.

Also by M.C. Vaughan

Romancing Miss Stone

Discover more at afterglowbooks.co.uk

DESTINATION WEDDINGS
and Other Disasters

M.C. VAUGHAN

afterglow BOOKS

All rights reserved including the right of reproduction in whole or in part in any form. This edition is published by arrangement with Harlequin Enterprises ULC.

This is a work of fiction. Names, characters, places, locations and incidents are purely fictional and bear no relationship to any real life individuals, living or dead, or to any actual places, business establishments, locations, events or incidents. Any resemblance is entirely coincidental.

Without limiting the author's and publisher's exclusive rights, any unauthorized use of this publication to train generative artificial intelligence (AI) technologies is expressly prohibited. HarperCollins also exercise their rights under Article 4(3) of the Digital Single Market Directive 2019/790 and expressly reserve this publication from the text and data mining exception.

® and ™ are trademarks owned and used by the trademark owner and/or its licensee. Trademarks marked with ® are registered with the United Kingdom Patent Office and/or the Office for Harmonisation in the Internal Market and in other countries.

First Published in Great Britain 2025 by
Afterglow Books by Mills & Boon, an imprint of HarperCollins*Publishers* Ltd
1 London Bridge Street, London, SE1 9GF

www.harpercollins.co.uk

HarperCollins*Publishers*
Macken House, 39/40 Mayor Street Upper,
Dublin 1, D01 C9W8, Ireland

Destination Weddings and Other Disasters © 2025 Mary Vaughan

ISBN: 978-0-263-39753-6

0625

This book contains FSC™ certified paper and other controlled sources to ensure responsible forest management.

For more information visit: www.harpercollins.co.uk/green

Printed and Bound in the UK using 100% Renewable Electricity
at CPI Group (UK) Ltd, Croydon, CR0 4YY

To David,
for proving every day that I made the right choice
when I asked you on our first date.

This book contains references to a deceased parent.

One

Carson Miller winced as he eased his SUV through his father's Sherman Oaks driveway gate. A half dozen cars already dotted the parking pad.

Damn.

In a perfect world, he'd have arrived at the engagement party early and discreetly cleared the air with his dad's fiancée's daughter. What could he do, though? On his way here this afternoon, his operations manager had alerted him to a significant menu change at a high-profile event. She'd assured him she had it under control, but as CEO of Limitless Events, his number one responsibility was overseeing their transition from start-up to scale-up. Word of mouth was crucial, and their pop-star client's autobiography launch included big industry names.

So he'd turned his SUV around to help his crew.

Now, he'd be forced to surprise Julia Stone, his soon-to-be-stepsister and former tutor/crush, in front of everyone. He had no idea how this would go. For ten years, she'd avoided him here in LA and on social media. The last time they'd spoken in the lemon-scented hallway of Bronson Alcott High School, she'd clearly hated him with a supernova's intensity.

After the rumors he'd spread about her, he'd deserved it.

He'd been *such* a tool, especially while she was tutoring him senior year. Most of their classmates let his antics slide, eager to be in his well-to-do, raucous, future-so-bright circle.

Not Julia, though. Focused, determined, and whip smart, she was two years younger and twenty times more mature than he and his friends had been.

And really, *really* cute.

His heart rate kicked up a notch. She was in there, right now, and didn't know he was about to pop back up in her life. From what he could tell, in the six months their parents had been dating, she and her sister hadn't clocked that *he* was Jim's son. The second he'd realized they were Michelle's daughters he'd planned to offer a private, heartfelt apology. Groveling was best done in person, so he'd figured Thanksgiving would be his shot.

Instead, their face-to-face reunion would be at this party.

She'd have to give him a chance to apologize if their parents were getting hitched, wouldn't she? They'd both be part of the rehearsals, ceremony, toasts, dancing. And after the wedding, he'd be around for the World Series and holidays. Would she refuse to pass him dinner rolls? Kick him under the table?

If she was the same Julia she was in high school…maybe.

He blew out a long breath.

Please let her give him a chance.

Carson checked his reflection in the rearview, then ran his hand through his hair. Older, humbled, and carrying scars from the car accident that grounded his college baseball career before it launched. He gave his father all the credit for helping him through his darkest days, which was why he wanted to help the happy couple with their wedding planning. It was his chance to repay Dad for helping him get on his feet after his accident.

From the passenger's seat, he snagged a chilled Veuve Clicquot and ambled into the house through the back door. The caterers he'd booked worked their magic, and the aroma from the heavy appetizers made his stomach rumble.

"Hey, Andrés," he greeted the chef. "How's it going?" He jerked his head toward the party chatter outside the kitchen.

"Good." Andrés straightened as he yanked a disposable chafing dish from the professional-grade oven. "Been wanting to try this baby out since your dad had us all over for Labor Day. But if you're asking about the service, the waitstaff's circulating. You just missed the daughter. She was in here asking if she could help."

"She was?" He angled toward the doorway.

"Yeah. Said she works in hospitality." Andrés peeled the foil from the chafing dish, then plated the apps. "Told her no, obviously. Can't put a guest to work."

"What's she wearing?" He tried to sound casual, but his nerves had spiked the moment he'd entered the house. He couldn't let her sneak up on him and preempt his chance to steer the potentially prickly conversation to a private space.

Andrés lifted a shoulder. "I don't know, man."

"Yes, you do."

"She's your family, bro." He avoided Carson's gaze as he spiked toothpicks into maple bacon–wrapped scallops. "You'll stop hiring me."

"Tell me. Even if we weren't Phi Gamma Titan brothers, I'd keep booking you because you're the best in town. Now, what's she look like?"

"Red dress that hugs her curves in all the right places." He added a floral sprig to the platter. "Your sister's hot, man. I might ask for her number. I've got a thing for blondes."

Whereas Carson had a thing for one specific blonde who'd relentlessly pushed his buttons back in high school. But that ship had sailed, so he'd ignore this tight feeling in his gut. He had no right to be jealous.

"Stepsister. To be. Our parents aren't married yet, and she's only in town for this party."

But he hoped Julia stayed longer. Michelle had given him the impression her daughter was at loose ends. If she extended the visit, he'd have a chance to siphon the awkwardness from this situation.

Andrés twisted a short stack of cocktail napkins, then set them on the platter. "A short stay? Even better. I'm a lotta fun for a night."

"You're a real gentleman."

"Never claimed to be."

Carson picked up the tray. "Do me a solid and leave her be. My dad's the happiest I've seen him in ages. I don't want anything or anyone to fuck this up for him, which includes my friends messing around with Michelle's daughter."

Andrés arched an eyebrow. "That's a wordy way to say back off 'cause you're into her."

Carson's heart skipped a beat. Into Julia? Not possible. Especially with their parents getting married.

"I'm not. I'm protective—that's all."

"Okay, okay." Andrés held up his hand. "We'll leave it there, Mr. Protective. Now get out there with those apps. They're best served hot."

He raised an eyebrow. "You're telling the CEO of the fastest-growing event company in town how to handle an apps tray?"

"I sure as hell am. If it's food, it's my domain." Andrés shooed him away. "Now go."

Carson backed through the swing kitchen door without a word. The biggest pro and con to working with his frat brothers was they'd witnessed each other's epic failures and successes since they were eighteen and relentlessly called each other out on their shit.

Good guys, all of them, but it didn't mean he'd let them hit on Julia. She was going to be his stepsister, after all. Even if they were both fully adults, overly protective big brothers were normal.

And Julia was...where, exactly?

Not in here. Guests drifted from the living room to the pool area through the open sliding-glass walls. October was plenty warm in LA, but some people wore wraps to combat the slight chill in the air. She could be out there, somewhere.

Ready to pounce and confront him.

Jesus, what a rookie mistake to allow a potentially explosive moment happen in a crowd. As guests eagerly snagged bites from his proffered tray, a musical giggle from the pool area cut through the low conversational thrum.

He'd recognize her laugh anywhere.

Several people parted, and there she was, talking to his father on the patio. Andrés's description hadn't done Julia justice. Her sexy-yet-somehow-appropriate snug red dress with a fluttery skirt would be at home in Marilyn Monroe's closet. It contrasted sharply with her low ponytail, her shiny blond hair curling between her shoulder blades like a ribbon.

After handing the tray to a catering staffer, he adjusted his tie. No sense delaying the inevitable. He'd figure this out. Life threw plenty of punches, and he always found his feet.

Halfway to Julia, someone grasped his elbow.

"*Carson,*" Michelle trilled. "It's about time."

She stood with another woman who...yes, he'd met her before. At the Labor Day barbecue. Michelle's sister. She was taller than his future stepmother, but the same gleam shone in her eyes.

"Minor emergency at work. You're Mary, right?"

"Well remembered," she said. "Can you believe these two plan to get married in Belize?"

He nearly choked. "You *are*?"

This would ruin his plan to coordinate their wedding.

"Yes!" Michelle beamed. "Won't it be fun?"

Mary rolled her eyes. "If you ask me, destination weddings are a not-so-subtle way to cut the guest list."

"You're such a downer." Michelle bumped shoulders with her. "Especially about the date, but that's out of our hands. When I called the resort I *adore* in Azul Caye this afternoon, they said they had a last-minute cancelation. So we booked it."

The bacon-wrapped scallop he'd sampled wasn't sitting well.

How could Dad not call before they'd settled on a date to make sure his only child could be there? Carson would move mountains if he had to, wouldn't complain because he'd never steal any joy from a celebration.

But it stung that he was finding out like this.

"How last minute?" Carson's current event schedule was booked out six months, but he could rearrange coverage.

"Next weekend," Michelle said.

Carson wobbled on his feet. *Next weekend?* Clearing his schedule that fast would be tough but doable. His crew would rise to the occasion. The management tier he'd carefully hired over the past few years had said they wanted to shoulder more so he could focus on strategy. And last week his COO had straight-up told him he was overdue for a vacation.

So what if it was a working vacation?

But damn, Dad. A heads-up would've been nice.

"You'll need an event planner," he said. "Timelines are tight."

Michelle waved a hand. "Only if you're fussy. All we want is to exchange vows on the beach and have a nice meal. Easy breezy."

This was the problem with people who didn't work in event management. *Easy breezy* was only achieved through diligent behind-the-scenes work.

He cleared his throat and adopted the tone he used with challenging clients. "I love that attitude, but you and Dad should put someone else in charge so you can enjoy the day."

Mary nodded. "He's right, Michelle. Wouldn't it be nice to soak up the sun and be cruise-directed for your wedding weekend?"

"That *does* sound appealing." She pressed her fist to her chin. "Especially since I've never had a head for details."

"Or much else." Mary giggled into her champagne flute.

"That's enough from you," Michelle said.

"I'd like to plan the wedding and reception," Carson said. "As my gift to you and Dad."

"That's sweet, but things operate differently in Belize." Michelle widened her eyes. "Oh wait, light bulb! Julia can do it. She's mostly unemployed right now, and this would be a *real* confidence booster. Let's go tell her the good news!"

Michelle dragged him outside. This was it. A moment ten years in the making. Which was unfortunately scored by Dad's favorite sappy yacht rock.

"Jim," Michelle called breathlessly. "Your son had the *best* idea."

Julia's back straightened. "Do I finally get to meet my stepbrother-to-be?"

He swallowed hard. "Hi."

Her skirt flared as she spun on her wedge espadrilles. He regretted that they had an audience while Julia discovered her high school bully was Jim's son, but he couldn't fix that. Just… please let her not knee him in the balls.

Her gorgeous brown eyes widened as she locked in on him.

"*You,*" she accused.

A firework shot through him. Her sparkly hair clip…the flush in her cheeks…the tantalizing peek at her cleavage… He shouldn't think this about his future stepsister, but Julia Stone was breathtaking. He'd known she would be the moment she'd ordered him to crack a book during their first tutoring session all those years ago. Didn't take a crystal ball to see that in her future, but sometimes he hated being right.

Because this blaze of attraction? This would be a problem.

"Do you two know each other?" Jim asked.

"We..." Julia dragged her lush lower lip between her teeth. "Went to high school together. Carson was two years ahead."

"Listen to this." Michelle squeezed her daughter's arm. "*Julia* can handle the logistics for our whirlwind wedding! Isn't Carson brilliant?"

"I can?" Julia asked.

"I assume so. Why spend all that money on a master's in hospitality management at a fancy college if you can't whip up a small destination wedding?"

Julia flipped her palms upward. "Scholarships paid for half."

"More proof you're the right person for the job." Michelle threaded her arm through Dad's. "Give me some sand, surf, and a warm sunset breeze with the man I love, and I'll be a happy camper. It's absolutely low stakes, so if everything goes sideways on you, it doesn't matter."

"Nothing would go sideways." Julia muttered the last part under her breath, but Carson caught it. "It's the rainy season, Mom. A beach wedding might not pan out."

"Whatever will be will be, but I'd like an unforgettable moment exchanging vows with Jim and I'd like our children to be present."

Dad lowered his brow, then cleared it, fast. Hmm. Last time he'd seen that expression, the Dodgers had been down five runs to the Yankees during Game Five of the World Series. Tonight was not the place, but he'd ask him if everything was okay.

Dad planted a kiss on Michelle's cheek. "Whatever my bride wants, she gets."

Julia thinned her lips, then backed away. "Will you excuse me for a moment?"

Her skirt swished as she sashayed into the house.

"Something we said?" Jim asked.

"No, that's our Julia," Michelle said. "When she hasn't eaten, her hangriness takes over. She'll be back to my sunshine girl after dinner."

Carson rocked on his heels. Guaranteed he was the cause of Julia's hasty flounce. Her mother didn't understand the grace and control her daughter displayed after being surprised by the jerk who'd teased her mercilessly in school.

Not that he'd shed a light on that this minute.

"I'll see if I can help," he said and chased after Julia.

Two

Julia marched straight toward the bar tucked into the living room.

Hoo-fucking-ray, there was no line.

"What can I get for you?" the bartender asked.

Liquor never solved any problems, but a friendly beverage sure could take the edge off a shitty surprise. Like her nemesis sidling close enough for her to feel his body heat, and the split second she'd enjoyed it before realizing it was *him*.

The snarky comments he'd made when she was sixteen came rushing back.

Nice pants.

Love the way you eat that banana.

You're cute for someone who diagrams sentences for fun.

He was supposed to stay in her past. She'd avoided him and his friends on social media, and once she'd graduated high school, she'd left this side of the country behind. But here he was, live and in person. Worst of all, the stupid zing that she thought was dead and buried woke right the hell up the second she locked eyes with the worst person she'd ever met.

Carson Fucking Miller.

"What do you recommend?" she asked the bartender.

"Champagne?"

A natural suggestion for a celebration, but she couldn't stomach the stuff. A magnum of Cook's Brut, a booze funnel, and a college dare had ruined bubbles for her.

"Actually, could I have a white wine or…" She noted the standee advertising a specialty cocktail for the evening—A Perfect Pear. She pointed to the sign. "I'll have that. Make it a double?"

"You've got it. I'm supposed to top it with champagne—want me to leave it out?"

"Yes, please."

As the bartender prepped and shook her drink like a maraca, Julia drummed her fingers against the bar's granite surface. This did not compute. Four million people in Los Angeles, and her mother was engaged to the father of the most annoying meathead she'd ever met.

How? She could already tell Jim was a sweetie.

When he and Mom had picked her up from the Burbank airport earlier today, he'd insisted on handling her bags. After some pleasant chitchat in the car, a tour of his lovely home—who knew home contracting paid so well?—and a power nap so she wouldn't fall asleep during the party, she'd rushed to get ready, then headed downstairs.

The chef good-naturedly rebuffed her attempts to help circulate the food, so she'd wandered out to the living room and found Jim alone. Not surprising. Mom was always fashionably late, even to her own parties. But it was a good chance to learn more about her future stepfather. As she and Jim talked, she was struck by déjà vu. The set of his shoulders, the way he cocked his head toward her to show he was listening… She'd seen that somewhere before.

Now she knew where.

This salt-of-the-earth guy, who seemed to *get* her mother and love her quirks, had spawned Satan. Unlike Carson, Jim was great and she genuinely got good vibes from him. Like when his eyes lit up because his son had arrived. Charming, right? That's how a father *should* react to his kid.

Unless that kid is Carson Fucking Miller.

"Here you go. A Perfect Pear. Since it's a double, I used a bigger glass." The bartender eyeballed the hurricane glass typically reserved for piña coladas. "Might be more like a triple."

"Even better." She collected her deliciously chilled cocktail and snuck out the side entrance. At least she hoped it was the side entrance.

For all she knew, it led to the garage, a storage closet, or Narnia.

Score. This *was* the side entrance. She faced a faded play set nestled within a secluded patch of fragrant flowering bushes. Florals were one hospitality topic on which she lacked a firm grip. She knew the basics. Roses, plumeria, lilies, sunflowers—crowd-pleasers that brought freshness to otherwise impersonal lobbies and meeting rooms. The gorgeous bloom into which she stuck her nose, however, was unknown to her.

Her grad school mentor *had* advised her to spend time at lawn-and-garden shows to bone up on her greenery. Better add that task to her personal-growth project in her Positively Productive app. Ah, the comfort of logistics. If she buried her brain in plans, she'd distance herself from the icky, less-than feelings swirling around inside her right now.

Alcohol might help with that, too.

Unhealthy? Yes. But she'd worry about that tomorrow.

Gingerly, she sat on the wooden swing dangling from the play set. As she typed out the task with one thumb, she sipped her cocktail. Tasty. Fresh pear purée, gin, and elderflower liqueur. She swished it around in her mouth. Lemon juice to brighten it up. Even without the champagne, it was an excellent choice for a fall engagement party.

She tipped her head back. Los Angeles's light pollution and

smog erased the stars from the sky. Ithaca's stargazing was better, especially via Cornell's Fuertes Observatory's public-observation Fridays. But most night skies paled in comparison to Belize's.

When they were kids, her dad had taken her and her older sister, Alex, on overnight camping trips. Away from civilization, the star-thick night seemed textured, touchable, dense. Under Belize's skies, she almost felt her father's presence. Which was probably why she'd been avoiding her favorite place in the world.

The hole in Julia's chest, the one her dad's death carved three years ago, widened.

Sigh. Now she'd be flying to Belize for the wedding. This must've been why Mom had insisted Julia pack for two weeks.

This engagement may seem sudden because you've only just found out about Jim, but I'm desperate for you to be here for the party and meet him. I'm planning lots of events and excursions, so pack loads! And your passport in case we daytrip to Mexico.

Why hadn't she just *said* so?

She'd been excited that her mother invited her here for her engagement party. Sure, this was Mom's fourth marriage, but love was worth celebrating. And maybe, possibly, they could invite Alex to fly in and they could spend time together as a family. Something they hadn't done since Julia was in high school and Alex moved back to Belize.

Instead of a celebratory vacation, though, Mom was putting her to work.

She sipped her drink.

Locating her wedding in Belize was an obvious ploy to get Alex to attend. It wasn't Julia's job to play peacemaker between them, but she couldn't help it. After Dad died and Alex took her grief out on Mom, Julia panicked that her fractured family would fall completely apart. She'd spent the last three years showing up for both Mom and Alex, hoping they'd listen to her and hash out their differences.

From the shadows, a dashing figure emerged. "Julia?"

Fuck my life.

Had she known he'd seek her out, she would've hidden in the play set's fort. Too late now, though. The swing next to her creaked as Carson eased into it, all suave, handsome confidence.

"Hey," he said.

Age had chiseled away Carson Miller's smidge of teenaged softness. In the ten years since they'd last spoken, he'd become unfairly broader, thicker, and…well, he'd become a man. Had she met him for the first time today, impure thoughts would've streamed through her brain.

Lucky for her, though, she had context.

She wasn't fooled by his attractive packaging. Nope. He hadn't pulled the wool over her eyes in high school, either. Her lack of fawning had confused him and triggered his ceaseless taunting. Back then, she couldn't always handle his snarky attention. Sometimes it had frozen her.

The older, wiser Julia, however…

Still froze, damn it.

Three

The swing's frayed rope roughed Carson's palms. He could smooth talk any situation, but Julia Stone threw him off his game. Always had.

When he was a teen, his sports-agent mom had insisted charisma and looks were just as important as his athletic ability. College scouts—and eventually MLB scouts—would make him an offer over equally talented players if he was likable. So he'd adopted an overconfident persona 'til he became that guy. The adulation from his buddies and girls proved he was the clever, funny, handsome ballplayer his mom pushed him to be.

Not Julia, though. She hadn't fallen for any of it.

She'd been hired as his English tutor when his grades teetered on the edge of student-athlete GPA requirements. So he couldn't exactly pretend to be a genius. And when he'd cracked tried-and-true jokes other girls had said were *hilarious*, Julia ignored him and continued quizzing him on the English Romantic poets he'd constantly mixed up.

As for handsome? Julia hadn't seemed to notice.

So he'd settled into just being himself instead of the jock everyone expected him to be. He'd liked that guy better, looked forward to their afternoons together. Enjoyed them more than time on his own because her company kept him out of his head.

Still no love from her, though. Eventually, her cool detachment drove him wild.

Sitting with her tonight was bizarre. She was a time machine to his younger, asshat self. A time machine who'd said nothing to him in the last hour. Instead she coolly sipped on the cocktail he'd designed for the party this evening, while he sat here with nerves pinging around his body like he'd shotgunned Mentos and Pepsi.

"Hope you like the Perfect Pear. I figured you for a champagne girl."

"Woman. Champagne doesn't agree with me. I usually partake of crisp white wine or the fruitiest drink possible for events like these." She held up her enormous glass. "Voilà."

Their swings groaned under them.

Over the past ten years, he'd learned that if he wasn't sure what to say, keeping his trap shut was the better choice. Otherwise, he'd spew something he'd regret.

Julia sighed. "Here's the thing, Carson Miller. I don't like you."

Wow, she was direct. "I get that, but—"

"This is a good time for you to listen." As she glared at him, the light from inside the house caught her helix earrings. "I don't like *you*, but I love my mother and Jim seems nice. You and I live on opposite coasts, so it'll be easy for us to keep our distance. I'd rather family events not be hella awkward."

He blew out a breath. "We can agree on that."

"Good. Then let's be honest. You and your richie-rich friends were jerks to me. What did I ever do to you besides help you with your English papers?"

The stiff rope fibers dug into his fingers.

She'd done nothing wrong. It had all been him.

Her moxie, her humor, her superhuman ability to cut through bullshit... Julia was tantalizing, always had been. But she hadn't been the type of girl he'd normally have asked out in high school. Her family had no money, she'd dressed in granny-style vintage clothes, and she'd been a studious ballbuster. There was also the small matter of him never being sure she'd actually *liked* him. For example, out of the blue one day, when he was talking about the epic party his buddy Caleb had thrown over winter break, she'd said his friends were clout-chasing fakes.

That makes me one, too, he'd said. *'Cause I'm just like them.*

She'd shaken her head. *No, there's more to you. Something vulnerable you hide.*

When he'd laughed, she'd said his circle would drop him like a dead ball if he wasn't Bronson Alcott High School's golden boy. That had frozen him cold. She couldn't have known that was his number two fear. His number one? That his mom loved that he was a star center fielder more than she loved him.

So again, he'd laughed. But that August, he'd found out how right she was.

"Carson?" she asked. "Hello?"

"You did nothing," he said. "It was all me, and I'm sorry. I was an insecure asshole. I zeroed in on you, said your glasses were too big, your clothes came from thrift stores, harped on you for going to dances with friends instead of—"

"Okay, okay." She held up a hand. "I was there. No need to list the grim details."

The ruby, sapphire, and diamond tattoos inside her forearm were vivid against her pale softness. What was the story there? She had no other visible ink.

"Sorry. I wanted to prove I know what I did wrong. Rest assured, I'm a changed man."

For a woman with eyes the color of molten-chocolate-lava cake, Julia's gaze sure was icy.

"I'd love to believe that." She sipped the Perfect Pear. "Fool me once, and all that jazz. I have another question."

He braced himself. "Yeah?"

Julia twisted toward him. If he wasn't slightly terrified, he'd have salivated at the way her ponytail curled against her breast.

"When our parents started dating…did you know Michelle was my mother?"

Ah, hell. He'd hoped this wouldn't come up. From her tense shoulders to her twisted red lips, he suspected Julia wanted the rawest truth possible.

Yeah, he knew.

When he met Michelle, her eyes lit up like diamonds when she talked about her daughters, Alex and Julia. Upon hearing the names, he thought…maybe? Michelle's last name was different, though, so he didn't put two and two together until he saw a pic of Julia and Alex. By the time he did, his dad was happier than he'd been in years.

So, to not mess things up for his father, he said…

"No, I didn't. Not until later."

There—that was honest enough.

She sipped her drink again. "I take it, then, you didn't tell our parents we have history."

"No," he said.

"Good."

The atmosphere around them shifted, calmed. A light breeze carried the evening primrose's scent. For the umpteenth time that evening, Carson noticed Julia's naked shoulders.

"Do you want my jacket? It's chilly."

A giggle bubbled from her. "Chilly? It's in the sixties."

"Which is chilly."

"Not when you're coming from Ithaca, New York." She gestured toward the night. "People are still wearing shorts and sundresses back home."

"Uh-uh." He shook his head. "I don't accept it when former Californians change regions and then make fun of those of us who are still acclimated to the weather here."

She lifted a shoulder. "Not my fault you're soft."

He was anything but soft, but he'd let it slide.

"You're in Ithaca for school, right?" He gestured toward her now-empty glass. "May I?"

She handed him the empty, and he sat it on a rung of the fort's ladder.

"I was. In Ithaca for grad school, I mean. But I graduated in May." She shrugged. "Now I'm job-hunting. Soon as I land a job at a five-star resort, I'll move."

"What's the holdup?"

She pointed at him. "That is information reserved for friends and family. You're neither."

"Yet."

She nodded. "Yet."

"So," he said. "About planning our parents' wedding. Shall we partner up?"

Another laugh escaped her. This one was less bubbly but more sarcastic.

Could laughter be sarcastic?

"Uh, I'm not sure if you heard, but my mother's super-excited to throw cash at her unemployed daughter. Not you, her soon-to-be husband's hotshot son."

"Hotshot?" he asked.

"I'm guessing." She flourished her fingers at him. "You have hotshot vibes."

He wrinkled his forehead. "Events are what I do for a living."

"Hospitality is what I'm trained to do, and that includes events. I can handle this. You're welcome to punch out. Besides I grew up in Belize. What do you know about the country?"

"Not much, but—"

"I rest my case." She pushed back and off the ground. As she sailed past him, her skirt fluttered around her legs.

"Let me help," he said. "Pulling this off will be tough."

"No. I can't trust you. People don't change."

Ouch, but he didn't blame her.

No, what he'd *like* to do is go back in time to kick his own ass.

After spring break senior year, he'd been tired of wrestling with his unrequited crush on her. His buddies were doing the promposal thing, so he'd figured, fuck it. He'd ask Julia to prom. Hell, she'd probably be so delighted she'd fall backward with joy and open her legs in gratitude.

But she'd turned him down, and his hurt pride had morphed into something ugly.

Boneheaded negging, ghosting, and a smear campaign. Classic tactics to fool himself into thinking he still had the upper hand. To force her to keep her distance so he wouldn't be reminded that she saw him, the *real* him, and had rejected him all the same.

And it worked like gangbusters. Was still working, since she didn't want his help.

"People grow," he said as she arced past him. "Mature. Their priorities change."

"What are your priorities these days?" she asked. "Torturing kittens?"

"Work hard, play hard, laugh hard." It was his company's tagline, stolen from his frat's informal motto. "Mostly, I like to make people around me happy."

"On that, we can agree."

"So you'll let me help?"

"Hard pass," she said. Her dress fluttered as she curved through the air. The smooth plane of her thigh flashed him.

He chewed the inside of his lip. "Why?"

"Because, Carson Miller, life—especially you—gave me a bunch of lemons, and I learned to make lemonade. I don't need your help. I operate best flying solo."

He didn't like being compared to tart fruit. "I hate that saying. It's disingenuous."

"How so?"

"Without sugar, you can't make lemonade. Otherwise, you're making lemon juice."

She sailed past him again. "Buzzkill."

He leaned back against the ropes as irritation prickled his scalp. His whole deal was making sure people had a good time. He'd invented six legendary cocktails that were *still* in rotation at Phi Gamma Titan. At last count, twenty-three marriages could be traced back to parties he'd thrown during his tenure as social chair.

"The *last* thing I am is a buzzkill. I literally have industry awards for my parties."

"I don't know what to tell you." She pumped her legs again. "I was enjoying a light buzz, you came out here, and *bam*. Buzz killed."

This conversation was going nowhere. Time to swing for the fences with an offer she couldn't blow off.

"I have a counteroffer."

"You can't *counter*offer," she said. "There is no offer."

Once again, the tantalizing glimpse of her thighs under the rippling fabric distracted him. Negotiations went better when he wasn't distracted by supple flesh.

"Could you stop for a second?"

"Nope." She glanced backward. "It's in physics' hands."

He tightened his grip on the swing's ropes. "I have contacts in LA, Vegas, New York, the Riviera, and Cabo San Lucas."

She dragged her toes through the grass. "I'm listening."

"If you agree to work with me, I'll put you in touch with my hotelier network. You're guaranteed to land a job with one if I put in a good word."

She searched his gaze.

"*Why* wouldn't you make those professional connections since I'm your future stepsister? You owe me one. Scratch that—you owe me, like, six."

Easy. He wanted to spend time with her. To give him a chance to make amends for the bastard he'd been. Bonus, he'd also be able to exorcise her from his imagination. She'd gotten under his skin all those years ago, and he'd liked the guy he was during those tutoring sessions with her. Ever since, despite never even having kissed Julia, he'd compared his—*relationships* was too strong a word...*situationships*?—to the dynamic he'd had with her.

"I never make professional recommendations unless I have direct experience with the individual. I can't risk tarnishing my reputation."

That had the benefit of being true. Like a month ago, when his aunt Charlotte had asked him to serve as a job reference for his cousin Danny for a job. Instead, he'd offered Danny a probationary gig with Limitless Events so he could vouch for him in good faith.

"How dare you?" Julia spluttered. "I graduated with honors from *the* top-ranked hospitality management master's program in the country."

He lifted a shoulder. "That doesn't make my original point untrue. I can't make recommendations without working with you."

She hopped from the swing, then lasered her glittering gaze on him. "Fine. We'll work together. If you meet my one demand."

With her hands on her hips, dress fluttering in the breeze behind her, she gave off superhero vibes. This view of her standing over him was one he could get used to.

"What's that?" he asked.

"You'll put in as much blood, sweat, and tears as me. Deal?"

She stuck out her hand.

Carson rose from the swing, then wrapped his grip around her extended palm. A jolt rocketed through him, lighting up his brain, his heart, and dove straight to his cock.

Oh no, no, no.

That flame of attraction should never show up at a family party. Working closely with Julia was dangerous. He'd back out. Right the fuck now. Graciously give her the gig and hope for the best for their parents' wedding.

Instead, he heard himself say, "Deal."

Four

Julia wiped shower steam from the guest bathroom mirror. *Hello*, dark circles. She woke up, like, eleventy billion times after last night's Carson encounter. She'd been rude to him, yes, but for once, that wasn't what spiraled in her uncooperative brain.

Nope, he deserved zero politeness from her.

The thing that kept her spinning was the question her mother'd asked him as Julia melted away from the party.

Why don't you stay in the pool house tonight?

Carson Fucking Miller was *right* there. Twenty yards away. She shouldn't care, but tell that to her twisted brain that had allowed him and his tempting smile and bright green eyes to invade her dreams. During her 2:00-a.m. wake-up, she'd set up a finsta to stalk his profile undetected. Yep, as suspected, the pics were proof that he was still a huge dudebro player.

Argh.

After the stalking, she'd turned to wedding research, then whoops, it was sunrise. With her hair wrapped in a towel turban, she read the Positively Productive app's affirmation for today out loud from her phone.

"I let go of my fears, anxieties, and negative thoughts."

She'd embraced cacti more easily than this affirmation.

It was corny, but her grad school mentor recommended she say nice things to herself in the morning. To speak to herself the way her best friend would. Her older sister was as close as she came to having a bestie, but she wouldn't talk to herself in Alex's voice. Alex usually offered stellar affirmations like, *Are you bleeding? No? Then get the fuck on with it.*

Negativity was Julia's default mode, which was what made her good at her job. Anticipating problems and resolving them before they became catastrophes was a good thing. Nobody wanted to be around a constant bummer, though. She was working on it.

Julia roughed the towel around her head, slipped on a casual sundress and a light cardigan, then padded down the stairs and into the kitchen. Mom sat at the island, scrolling through her phone.

"Morning, Mom. Any coffee?"

"Plenty in the pot." Her mother clicked off her phone. "I picked up the yogurt you like, and there's fruit in the bowl. Did you sleep well?"

"Eh." She yawned. "It takes me a day or two to acclimate to the time zone."

"Belize will be easier since it's Central time."

Julia slid onto a rattan-topped stool at the island. "We're *really* doing this in Belize? You could have a great wedding here in LA."

"And invite everyone we know?" Her mother sipped her coffee. "No thanks. An intimate wedding in Azul Caye is what I want. I hear Carson will help with the details. Isn't he a sweetheart?"

No, he's a jerkwad.

Julia clutched her mug. "I don't know him well enough to say."

Her mom grinned as she sipped. "That'll change while you two handle the wedding details."

No it fucking won't.

"About the details..." Julia opened the Positively Productive app to capture the details for this event. "Are we talking menus or flowers or favors...photography?"

Her mother nodded. "Yes. Exactly."

"Yes, which?"

"Yes, all of the above." Mom lifted a shoulder. "I'm not a planner, but things always seem to work out."

Julia's neck stiffened. Things always worked out because everyone else picked up after Mom. As the person who became the planner in the family at the age of twelve, the do-er who was desperate for everyone to relax, hospitality was an inevitable career choice. If she handled the logistics for everyone else's good time, she might as well get paid for it.

"Does Alex know we're about to descend on her?" she asked.

Mom rolled her eyes. "We're not descending. We're her *family*."

"Well?" she prompted.

"No, she doesn't." Mom avoided eye contact with her. "She'd take the news much better coming from you."

Mom was right. Big fucking sigh. Julia hated being in the middle of her mother and sister, but she'd do it if it meant keeping her remaining family connected.

"I'll call her after breakfast," she said.

"Thanks. We've been talking more lately, and I'd rather not set us back. I always put my foot in my mouth." Her mother rose from the island. "Sure you don't want breakfast? I could whip up scrambled eggs and toast. You're grumpy when your tummy's empty."

"Mom, I'm not a toddler." She *was* kinda snacky. Last night, after talking to Carson, she'd lost her appetite and missed out on the delicious nibbles circulated at the party.

She slid off the stool to pluck a yogurt from the fridge.

"No one said you were, sweetheart. By the way, I booked

our flight for tomorrow. It's early, but that'll give us more time with Alex if she can tear herself away from work."

The yogurt in Julia's spoon wobbled. "Tomorrow?"

"No time like the present. Boots on the ground will be best."

Julia jabbed her spoon into the yogurt. "If I'm planning this thing, you can't make big decisions like this without talking to me first."

"Don't be silly, Julia. The flight was available, so I bought the tickets."

Goddammit. Her whole life, Mom had dropped decision bombs on her like they were no big deal. *Guess what? Dad and I are splitting up. Big news! We're moving to the US. See that man over there? We're getting married!*

Surprises were unwelcome. Discussions and plans were preferred.

"What if I had a hair appointment tomorrow?" she asked.

Her mother raised an eyebrow. "Do you?"

"*No*, but I could have."

"And you could also book an appointment in Belize. Oh, that's a good idea." She jotted a note on the pad attached to the fridge, right next to a picture of Julia and Alex from Julia's high school graduation. "I should freshen my color before the big day. If that's okay with you, my darling daughter?"

Sarcasm ran deep among the women in her family.

"That's fine. Your hair, your clothes, your song—those are up to you. Everything event-related is strictly my domain, okay?"

"And Carson's."

Julia's eye twitched. "Yes, and Carson's. Promise me you won't make any wedding or reception decisions without talking to me first?"

Mom leaned against the counter and swept her gaze over Julia. "That grad school turned you into Ms. Bossy Pants."

"I've always been like this. Grad school helped me see it's a soft skill prized in hospitality." She finally swallowed a mouthful of yogurt. "Now promise."

"Okay, okay." Her mother held up her hands. "I won't do anything without checking with you first. You're in the driver's seat."

Exactly where she preferred to be. "Thank you."

She scraped the yogurt tub.

"So." Mom leaned forward. "Are you seeing anyone?"

"What?" Julia coughed. *That* was out of left field.

"Alex seems quite happy with her boyfriend. Have you met him?"

"Over video chat."

"Me as well. I can't get a sense of who he is, but your sister seems smitten. What about you? Should *your* invitation include a plus-one?"

Time to shut that shit down.

"Nope. Too busy with my master's, working, internships, and networking."

That was the truth. But even if she was dating someone, she'd rather lop off her pinky finger than discuss her love life with her mother. Mom had a tendency to ask graphic and tactless questions about circumcision and whether Julia had ever heard of tantric sex and edging.

Things Julia never wanted to talk about over yogurt. Ever.

Mom shook her head. "I swear, the way your generation prioritizes your careers…"

Julia rinsed the yogurt container. "Oh, you mean gaining financial stability to live my life independently instead of relying on men's generosity?"

Shit. She'd barfed that right out, hadn't she?

When she'd moved them back to the States, Mom's full-time job and personal-shopper side hustle had earned enough to cover the basics. Her romantic partners' financial support determined the style in which she lived. And Mom liked to live well.

"Sorry," Julia said. "That was rude."

"But not wrong." Her mother winked.

This was Mom's best and worst trait—criticism didn't stick. It used to rile Alex that Mom had no shame about her love of money in her romantic relationships. Secretly, Julia admired that her mother gave zero fucks about what other people thought.

"Perhaps it's for the best you don't have a boyfriend," Mom said. "Other single young people will be at the resort."

Julia tossed her yogurt container into the recycling bin. "Great. I'll have a vacation fling. Mind if I call Alex to warn her about our impending invasion?"

"It's less of an invasion and more of a surprise party. Would it hurt you to look on the bright side of life, Julia?"

She was trying to be an optimist, truly. Well…more like a realist. She pursed her lips. But what was so wrong about acknowledging no one sprinkled pixie dust to make life magically pan out the way she wanted?

"I'll work on it," she said.

Julia took her coffee to the back patio, then carefully settled herself into a poolside upholstered lounger. Brr. The early-morning air was cold enough to cause a little nippage. She tugged her cardigan around her, then called her sister.

"Hey, Jules," Alex said. Something loud thumped in the background. "Shit."

"Oh my gosh, are you okay?"

"Fine. A kayak slipped out of the tow trailer." Alex grunted, clearly multitasking while they chatted. "How was the party?"

"Nice." Except for the presence of Carson Fucking Miller. She'd skip that part, lest it inspire a big-sister lecture on what she should do, say, or feel. "Jim's nice. He might actually stick around for a while."

Because that was how her life worked.

None of Mom's other boyfriends came as a package deal with her high school nemesis, so naturally the one who did would be her mother's forever and always person.

"Mom does seem pretty happy these days. We're fighting less. Bummer her happiness is dependent on her relationship status, but that ship has sailed. Mom's gonna Mom."

Julia wouldn't get a better doorway to deliver the destination wedding news to Alex.

"Along those lines…" She sighed. "Don't shoot the messenger, but Mom spontaneously booked the wedding at a resort in Azul Caye. Next weekend."

She braced herself for a prolific number of *fucks*.

Alex answered with a simple, "Yeah, I know."

"You do? How?"

More grunting. "Some dude named Carson called this morning. He said he was Jim's son and he's helping plan the wedding."

"He…called you?"

She cut her gaze to the pool house. Anger boiled in her gut. Her family was *her* goddamned turf. Was she not handling things fast enough for him?

"That's what I said. He called, like, an hour ago."

Alex sounded weirdly unbothered that Carson Fucking Miller had phoned her with intimate details about Mom's wedding. Did she not remember him? Julia had gone to great lengths not to involve her family when he was at his worst, but she didn't think she'd done *that* good a job.

"How did he get your number?"

"I assume Mom gave it to him. Don't stress that she picked Azul Caye. It's for the best that everyone's coming here. I can't get away from work, and it'll give me a chance to officially introduce you to Bo."

Good for Alex for seeing the upside, but, unlike Julia, she

wouldn't be working with her least favorite person on the planet.

"Anything else, Jules? Not to be rude, but I'm about to pick up a family to climb Nim Li Punit, then kayak down the river."

Longing tugged at Julia's insides.

Nim Li Punit were her favorite ruins. Nestled in the lush jungle, the place exuded more peace than La Prairie Spa at the Waldorf Astoria Beverly Hills, where she'd worked before grad school. The nearby museum was excellently curated, too.

"Are the dates okay for your schedule?" she asked.

"Yeah, fine. I'm taking advantage of the rainy season to train another guide. You remember Espy's son, Luca?"

Julia parked her hand on her hip. "You're busy enough to take on additional staff?"

"Just tour guides for now. Business is *booming*. The secret's out about Belize."

Excitement bubbled in her belly. "Does that bump up the timeline on the resort?"

"Possibly, but we talked about this. You need more experience."

She tightened her jaw. "I *have* experience. I interned every summer and winter break."

"You know that's not the same as running the show, Jules. Look, I *want* to do this with you, but you need a full year, minimum, managing a hotel department before we think about you developing a whole-ass resort. This is a business decision. It isn't personal."

It fucking felt personal.

Her pessimist…realist…self fully got that no one handed a potential world-class resort's development to an untested twenty-six-year-old. But she'd offered to help with the tour side of the business, too. Alex had pushed back and said Julia needed to build up her resort-operations experience so they could gut-check anyone they hired.

Why? Because last year, Alex had been fleeced by her ex-boyfriend/accountant, and it had nearly cost them the tour company.

"Maybe Mariele's hiring?" Alex suggested. "Her resort's expanding. I could ask."

Mariele, Alex's best friend, was chill. But living in Belize and *not* working with her sister would hurt worse than stepping on a long-spined black sea urchin. Julia and Alex had been Dad's adventure tour copilots. When he'd died, they were supposed to run things together.

Instead, Alex was trying to fob her off on someone else.

"Not necessary," Julia said. "I've got prospects."

By "prospects" she meant she'd sent her résumé to two dozen resorts.

"Anyway, I've gotta run, too. I just didn't want you to be shocked when we show up on your doorstep tomorrow."

"I appreciate the heads-up." Something clunked in Alex's background. "Text me your flight info. Let's get dinner—without Mom—so you can meet Bo without a three-ring circus."

"I will. Have a good tour."

She ended the deeply unsatisfying call. *Can you believe Mom did this* conversations had been classic bonding moments between them, but her sister was too busy to wallow in the ridiculous with her. This left-behind vibe sat like an unhappy ball in her stomach.

Fortunately, a convenient target for those raw emotions lurked inside the pool house.

"Carson!" She knocked insistently, like a woodpecker. "You called my sister? We can't do this together if you go behind my back."

She didn't like how shrill her voice sounded. Deep breath.

The door cracked open. "Behind your back? I called the other must-haves on your mom's guest list—your sister and your aunt—to give them more time to plan. Since you were deep in your drinks last night, I didn't know when you'd call. You're welcome."

Her cheeks flushed. "Deep in my drinks? I had *one*."

"Which was the size of your head, so I thought you'd sleep late. Look, what's the problem? I just want our parents to have their dream wedding."

"That's what I want too!" she threw her hands into the air. "Let me in. I've been up researching for hours. Let's have a planning session so you don't go rogue again."

Carson's playful smile crinkled the corners of his glimmering emerald eyes. Like he'd been hoping she'd pound on his door before 9:00 a.m.

"If you insist." He opened the door.

And…wow. He wore nothing but a pair of low-slung sweat pants. *Nope, nope, nope, not looking.* She snapped her attention back to his lightly stubbled face. *Maintain eye contact.* If she dipped her gaze she'd inventory the details of his half-naked body. Like his rounded shoulders or the broad plane of his bare chest and its light dusting of chest hair. Also the tidy bumps of muscle that marched straight toward his waistband.

Adulthood had been unfairly good to Carson Miller.

As he padded into the kitchenette, he called over his shoulder, "Want coffee? Or scones? Your mom dropped off fresh-baked ones an hour ago."

He even had those dimples above his ass, like his body was smiling at her.

Wait, what did he say about scones?

Julia frowned. "My mom doesn't bake. Or eat gluten."

She wasn't allergic, but she liked to try any specialized diet that made the news.

Carson shrugged. "Maybe she does now? My dad has a sweet tooth. Glazed orange. Pretty tasty, actually."

Carson Fucking Miller should not know more about her mother than she did.

"No thanks." She waved him off.

"What about coffee?" He lifted a pot toward her, causing his muscles to ripple. Oh whoa, he also possessed one of those vee-shaped situations that she read about in romance novels.

"Julia?" he prodded with a smirk. "Something wrong?"

She mentally slapped herself.

This was what Carson did. He charm-bombed and distracted her with his playful grin, fit body, and flirty wit. Then, eventually, *blammo*. She'd reestablish boundaries, and he'd ice her out with "jokey" feedback that was like a razor to the heart, unreturned texts, and back-channeled rumors.

She wouldn't be blammoed again.

Especially not when her mother was marrying his father. Carson wasn't going anywhere, at least not for a while, and they needed to work together. Ogling him was *not* okay.

"Could you put a shirt on or something?" She waved her hand in his general direction. "I can't work with your man flesh staring at me."

He spluttered his coffee. "Man flesh?"

"What do you call it?"

He peered at his chest. "I mean, I guess *man flesh* works, but I prefer *sculpted abs*. If you need me to cover up, so be it."

As he disappeared into the bedroom, she drummed her fingers. Her foolish attraction to Carson could go nowhere. Underneath that beautiful exterior was a Grade A asshat. At sixteen, she'd been too innocent to clock his manipulation tactics. At twenty-six, she knew better. Yet butterflies *still* flapped in her stomach when he came near. Ages ago, she'd unpacked why she couldn't simply switch the attraction off. It boiled down to one simple truth.

He'd *seen* her.

Lots of kids shined at Bronson Alcott, home of the fighting

Avocados. She was not one of them. Studious, yes. Disciplined, absolutely. But shiny? No, she was happy to let Alex have all the attention while she sat in a corner with her books.

One day in AP English, Dr. Temple had asked for volunteers to tutor Carson Miller, star of the varsity baseball team. A forest of hands went up around her. Then Dr. Temple mentioned it was a paid position, and she raised her hand.

Carson picked her.

During their first sessions, his attention was like a spotlight. He'd laughed at her jokes, complimented the sapphire studs she'd picked out for her sixteenth birthday, and asked her questions, like what was a small, everyday thing that made her smile? (Answer: her sister's random funny and encouraging messages in her notebook.)

She'd loved his irreverent critical thinking, too.

Carson had joked Lord Byron's poem "She Walks in Beauty" should be titled "Lemme Smash That Ass" because the short poem was "horny AF." They'd googled it, and sure enough, Byron had written it about his eventual wife, who'd left him after a year of tumultuous marriage because he couldn't keep it in his pants.

See? he'd said. *Dude was a fuckboy. Game recognizes game.*

After spring break, in the middle of baseball season, he'd sarcastically asked her to prom. She'd laughed and turned down his joke invitation. The next day his focus felt more like a rifle scope than a spotlight. He sounded different—more like his friends and less like the surprisingly considerate and warm boy she'd gotten to know. This changed Carson was aloof, wouldn't look her in the eye, said she was weird for asking if something was wrong.

Then, the personal details he'd hoarded about her became his arsenal.

He'd teased her about her taste in movies and jewelry—whatever, she could ignore it. The worst, though, was what turned out to be their last tutoring session. After waiting for a response to her text for fifteen minutes, she'd gathered her stuff and left the library. Just in time to hear him tell his cousin she looked at him with sad puppy eyes, that she pawed at him while they were studying. That it'd be different if she was hot, but this was pathetic. He'd only picked her for his tutor because she was a creepy nerd so he'd be able to focus on the work.

Her heart had deflated like a leaky balloon.

She'd headed straight to Dr. Temple's office to quit, but Carson had already fired her. He'd gotten his grades up for baseball season, so they were done. Rumors were already swirling that she'd flung herself at him. For people who were supposed to have squirrel-sized attention spans, a whole fucking lot of them called her Sad Puppy, SP for short, until she graduated.

So no, she would *not* be falling for Carson Fucking Miller's shit a second time. She'd keep her walls up. Even if he flipped switches inside her she'd super-prefer not to acknowledge.

"What's taking you so long?" she called.

"I didn't pack a bag, so I had to dig through my old stuff. This better?"

He reappeared in an ancient Dodgers shirt that had been washed so many times it hugged his defined chest and shoulders like his number one fan. She recognized it immediately. It was his post–practice and shower shirt, the one he'd worn to at least half their tutoring sessions.

"Yes." She sat on the lone firm gray couch. "We have a *lot* to do."

He sat next to her, his thigh dangerously close to brushing hers. "Couldn't agree more."

Sweet fucking Christ, this would be a long two weeks.

Ah, hell. He'd practically sat on Julia. In ordinary circumstances, he would've flipped the mistake into flirtation. *My aim's off, but your lap seems like a better place to sit than the couch anyway. Unless you want to sit on mine?* These, however, were no ordinary circumstances. Aside from the fact that she barely tolerated him, she was off-limits.

Because stepsister.

But not yet, whispered an unhelpful, bordering-on-evil voice.

"Actually." Carson popped up from the couch. "I think best when I'm on the move."

He grabbed a baseball from his stash on the kitchenette's counter, then rolled it up his forearm and bounced it off his biceps.

"Where'd they book the site for the wedding and reception?" he asked.

"Azul Caye Resort," she said. "It provides a private beach for the ceremony, an indoor event space, and the meal. I built a prioritized list of TBDs."

"Great. Hit me with it." Lightness filled his chest. Maybe things would work out. This could be an excellent working partnership. They'd build on each other's knowledge, volunteer for tasks, and probably get so in sync they'd finish each other's sentences.

Julia scrolled her tablet. "We need to select the menu, and…"

He filled her pause with the next logical task. "Outline guests' dietary concerns."

She shook her head. "Not what I was about to say."

"Oh." He rolled and popped the ball again. "Dessert? Dad hates lemon, FYI."

"*Carson.* Not that, either. Let me speak."

He caught the ball and paused. "Sorry. Go on."

"The Azul Caye Resort is undergoing renovations. Not sure if that's why there was a cancelation, but we'll check it out first thing to confirm it won't be a problem. Like, make sure guests won't have to hoof it a mile to get to the bathrooms."

He grinned as he pointed at her. "That's what I'm talking about. Excellent instincts."

She glared at him. "Stop it."

"Stop what?"

"This dynamic where you're in charge and I'm your eager assistant." She shot up from the couch, then popped her hands on her hips. "We're doing this *together*."

"I know." He squeezed the baseball.

Julia took the ball from him. "Then write things down and stop with your patronizing 'Great job, you spunky kid' tone."

She was so hot when she was annoyed with him. The pink spots high on her cheeks, the flash in her eyes, the heave in her chest… She obviously felt something about him besides apathy. An unhealthy thought, but he could work with annoyance.

"Who says *spunky*?" he asked.

"Not the point." She circled the ball between them. "And let's not fawn over every good idea we have. We're professionals. We're *supposed* to have good ideas. Save the compliments for the exceptional ones."

He stared at her. "Who hurt you?"

"You," she said.

Daggers in his heart. She was right, though.

"Jules, I'm sorry. I'll say it a million times to make you believe me."

"You don't get to use that nickname." She pinched the bridge of her nose. "You get I'm not your executive assistant, right? You should take more notes."

"I take notes." He tapped his temple. "Up here."

"Not good enough. Back in high school—"

"We've probably both changed, haven't we? I had to write everything down back then, but today my process is to talk things through. The conversation locks the plan in my memory."

"Doubtful." She tossed the ball back to him. "I've worked with self-described geniuses who got details wrong because they refused to take notes." She retreated to the couch and picked up her tablet. "I use an amazing event-management app to keep my brain from exploding."

His ears perked up. "What's it called?"

"Positively Productive."

Oh, he knew it well.

She tapped her tablet's screen. "What's your cell number?"

As he recited it, he couldn't help grinning. She'd *loathe* what he was about to tell her. A second later, his phone pinged with a text from her that contained a link. He clicked on it, and it opened the project she'd shared on his phone.

"See that?" She leaned into his personal space, then pointed to the project list. Her scent was intoxicating. Like spicy apples. "That's organized chaos. I'll grant you edit permissions once you take the tutorial."

He was so buzzed on her closeness he *almost* missed the last thing she said.

"I don't need a tutorial," he said.

"I *highly* recommend it. If you don't, you'll miss out on the amazing features."

Glad she thought they were amazing. "So I, uh... I actually created the app."

Julia's eyes widened. She glanced at her tablet, then back to him, and repeated that cycle a few more times. A flash of awe peeked through, the kind of admiration he used to see from the girls who'd flocked to him during his ballplaying days. He'd be a fool not to register the look on her face when she was close enough to kiss.

Not that he would. Yet.

Shit, buddy. Slow down. That was *not* in the cards.

She hugged her tablet to her chest. "Say that last part again."

"I created the app." He jammed his phone into his pocket. "Cocreated, actually, with my buddy Aadi. I don't write much code."

She clutched her tablet to her chest. "Stop it. You did not."

"Why would I lie about this? But you can check the app's credits."

"Positively Productive changed my life during my master's program." She scanned him like she was meeting someone new. "I tried using other tools, but they didn't relieve my 'Did I remember to do that?' anxiety like this one. I love the celebratory animations when I check things off. And the daily affirmations."

"Your sister's random notes inspired those. They always gave you such a kick." He clicked through to the credits on the About page. "See? That's me. I was the social chair for my frat, and one of my brothers, Aadi, was a computer science major. We took rinse-and-repeat event basics out of my brain, Aadi wired up a prototype, and I shared it with the other Greek houses. Everyone started using it, so we launched it."

"I can't believe I'm part of my favorite app's history." She drummed her fingers on her tablet. "I should've guessed you're a tech bro."

He laughed. "No tech bro here. I sold my rights to Aadi and used the profits to start Limitless Events. Parties, celebrations—that's where my heart is."

He meant it, too. The world was full of dark shit. Celebrating the good stuff was important, and he loved being the guy who helped everyone have fun.

Julia stared at the brightly colored lists on her tablet. "The person who made this *can't* be someone who shirks responsibility. In high school—"

"*Again* with high school?" He crossed his arms.

She was silent. And, unless he was mistaken, ogling his forearms. For fun, he drummed his fingers to make the muscles dance.

Yep, she was definitely staring.

She licked her lips. "For my peace of mind, I need to say

this out loud. *Back in high school*, you convinced girls to do your homework."

Carson curved toward her. "I never convinced *you* to do my homework."

She held her ground. "The only way you'd build confidence was to do the work. Far be it from me to steal that opportunity from you."

"I'm pretty confident about a lot of things."

"I'll bet." Julia rolled her eyes. "I'm just saying, I won't do all the work for you."

"You never did. Why would that change?"

"You make an excellent point. Let's keep that divide-and-conquer energy going, 'kay?"

She tapped him twice on the chest.

Yep, that definitely made his cock twitch.

"Agreed," he said.

Julia's take-control demeanor *did* something to him, exactly like it had during their tutoring sessions. These days, *he* was the one who took control. His staff, friends—hell, even his dad—followed his lead because they respected him, liked him, trusted him.

Not Julia, though. Not yet.

He got why. If he was her, he wouldn't like him, either. But if he could prove to her, his most reliable and accurate critic, that he'd changed and that she'd been right when she'd said there was something vulnerable about him...

Then maybe he could finally convince himself he'd changed, too.

Five

As they finished dinner, Julia mentally ran through this evening's task list. Shower, pack, charge devices, download a book… call Alex for an emergency consult on why she'd been unable to resist patting Carson's chest this morning.

No, wait, scratch that. She'd keep *that* embarrassment to herself.

"Now that we've eaten…" Mom twisted her wineglass's stem. "We have a slight change of plans with our departure time."

Argh. Finalizing logistics with her mother was like nailing Jell-O to the wall.

"Define *slight*." Julia forked up the last bite of swordfish Jim had grilled. "Direct flights are at dawn or early afternoon. If you miss the later one, you're bumped to the next day."

"Which is okay," Carson said. "We built slack into the schedule. Day one is menus and dessert, which we can handle."

Julia hid her surprise. He was right about the itinerary. Maybe he was *actually* good at event planning and this wasn't smoke-in-mirrors bullshit? Annoying he hadn't taken one note and simply memorized the plan.

Although…*annoying* wasn't the right word.

Hot, the unhelpful voice in her head whispered.

"My project went sideways," Jim said. "Materials are on back-order, and the client's unhappy. It's too high profile to delegate."

"Jim needs to stay to smooth things over at the site, and I'll stay, too." Mom squeezed his hand. "We don't want to travel separately, so we'll be there in a few days."

"But..." Julia rucked up her forehead. "You need to be there seventy-two hours before the ceremony to get a license."

"We'll be there in plenty of time." Jim leaned back in his chair. "By the way, I emailed the budget to Carson earlier today. Whatever you don't spend you can consider a bonus."

She clutched her fork. Sent to Carson? Who hadn't sent it to her?

"Hey, Julia." Carson scooted back from the table. "Help me with dessert in the kitchen?"

"Sure thing." The tips of her ears burned, but she pinned on a smile and definitely didn't notice his ass in his well-worn jeans as she followed him into the kitchen.

Alone together, she whirled on him. "What the hell happened to radical cooperation?"

Her whisper contained a tenth of the heat she felt, but their parents were twenty feet away.

"Calm down." He opened the oven door, and a sweet-but-somehow-savory aroma enveloped them. "Dad seemed off last night, so I stopped into his office this afternoon. He said the Costello project was behind schedule and overspent. I suggested he stay and let us handle things in Belize. Then we got to talking about the wedding budget. He sent it before dinner, but I don't have your email address, so I saved it to the app. Maybe don't assume the worst of me?"

Hmph. He was making some points. Also, dessert.

"When did you make a pie?"

"I didn't make it, I ordered it. It's a pear almond tart that'll change your life."

The crumbly dessert dusted with sugar *did* look delectable.

"What's with you and pears?"

"It's a pun. They're a pair. Get it?" Carson padded toward the freezer. "Also, I like pears."

"Me, too." She parked her hip against the counter. "Why are you so unbothered? We've got *such* a tight schedule."

He freed the cap from the pint of vanilla ice cream and tossed it onto the island.

"I'm all about the upside. This is an impossible situation. If we succeed, we're heroes. If we don't…well, it was an impossible situation. My dad's easy. He'll be happy no matter what. Your mom seems like someone who changes her mind a million times."

"That's accurate. How do you know that?"

"We've been out to eat a few times. She waffles among four different options, then eats half of Dad's. She's even called the waiter back because she saw another person's dinner and wanted to change her order."

"Oh my." Julia pressed her palms to her heated face. "Major secondhand cringe."

"Why?" He sliced around the tart's roasted pear halves.

"Because I work in the service industry." She opened a cabinet. "It's mortifying that my own mother treats waitstaff badly. Where are the dessert plates?"

"Top right cabinet, next to the stove." He gestured with the pie server, and *ooh*.

His inner biceps were defined, like a sculptor had lingered for weeks over the muscles' ridges. Smooth and curved, she'd bet his skin was warm and—

Shit. He'd caught her staring.

"She didn't treat the waitstaff badly." He smirked, then lifted a slice. "Even if she did, she's not a reflection of you."

Julia disagreed, which was why she'd walled Mom off from school.

Back then, she couldn't risk damaging the good impressions

she'd made on her guidance counselors, teachers, and club advisors for Distributive Education Clubs of America, aka DECA. A rude comment from Mom—and those happened often—could tank their willingness to write her recommendations for colleges, prestigious internships, and scholarships. So she'd studied, volunteered, smiled, and raised her hand frequently to impress her teachers.

Eventually the hustle had become a habit.

An exhausting, smiley habit.

She set a small stack of dishes next to Carson, and he plated four tart wedges. Fast, efficiently, and without spilling a crumb.

"Them arriving late is a good thing," he said. "We can move faster if they aren't there to question our decisions."

Hmm. He was right. These two would slow everything down.

"I hadn't thought of it that way. That's freeing, actually."

As he dropped smooth vanilla scoops next to the tart slices, his lips tipped up in a smile. "Happy to help you shift perspective."

She didn't want his help—with anything—but she was stuck with him through the wedding. After that, they'd go their separate ways and *maybe* see each other around holidays. Might as well make the best of it while keeping him at arm's length.

"Help me bring these in?" he suggested.

They grabbed the same plate, and their fingers brushed. Heat rushed up her arm, like he'd dragged a match from her wrist to her shoulder.

"Sorry," he said and let go.

His touch echoed on her skin.

Yes, distance would be crucial.

Carson didn't remember how he and Julia ended up in the pool, but he was pretty fucking glad they had. The curves he'd been admiring since their parents' engagement party were on full display in her tight white suit.

The underwater lights winked and rippled in the pool's surface as he cut through the water toward her like a shark. She splashed at him like a flirty teenager. He wouldn't be deterred. Not when he was finally about to get the armful of Julia Stone he'd been craving for a decade.

Whoa, was that an earthquake?

"Carson," she snarled. "Wake *up*."

Wake up? What did she—

Water smacked him in the face.

"We're late."

He bolted upright in bed.

"Finally," Julia said.

The hallway light loaned her an otherworldly glow.

"What the fuck?" He scrubbed his eyes with the heels of his palms. "Did you pour water on me?"

"No, I flicked it." She snapped on the bedside lamp. "Then you knocked into my hand and I dropped the cup. Sorry."

His chest was soaked. "What time is it?"

"Two thirty."

No wonder it was dark. "In the morning? Jesus Christ, *why*?"

"Our flight's at six, and we're thirty minutes from the airport."

"Thirty minutes at rush hour. Right now it'll take us fifteen. My alarm's set for three."

"*Three?* We should *be* there at three."

He desperately wanted to stand—bickering with Julia required commitment to the bit—but his typical morning wood hadn't actually waited for morning. Probably his dream about Julia in a tight, white, wet bikini.

"Only masochists want to go to LAX three hours early."

"FAA regulations recommend arriving three hours early for international flights. As it is, we'll be lucky to get there two and a half hours early. Please tell me you've packed."

"Yes, warden, I've packed." He gestured vaguely to the suitcase he'd thrown together when he'd dipped back into his apartment last night after dessert. His dad's place was closer to the airport, and he and Julia could Uber together, so it made sense to bunk in the pool house again.

He hadn't, however, expected a wet wake-up.

"Could I have privacy while I get dressed, please?"

Julia sighed. "Yes, but hurry."

"Faster you leave, faster I can get ready."

"I'll be out by the pool." Her sneakers squeaked against the floor as she made her exit.

Carson flipped back the covers. She'd lose her shit if he took a shower, but oh well. It was either that or rubbing one out. He twisted on the water and shampooed while the cold water took effect on his stubborn hard-on. Dream Julia had been sexy as fuck but didn't compare to the real deal hovering over him with her pink cheeks and their kissable constellation of freckles. He low-key loved to fluster her—it mirrored the way she drove him to distraction.

It also proved he had her attention.

Five minutes later, he rolled his bag out to the patio, where the glow of Julia's phone lit her serious face. As he shut the door behind him, she rose from the poolside lounger. Her travel outfit—a black jumpsuit, jean jacket, and white slip-on sneakers—was adorably practical.

Like her.

"Our Uber's almost here," she whispered.

As they exited the front gate, a sedan arrived at the curb.

"That's us," she said.

The driver popped the trunk. Carson reached for her suitcase, but she waved him off.

"I've got it." She hefted the large bag with surprising ease.

"Impressive." He snuggled his bag next to hers.

"My first internship rotated us through the resort's workstations, including bellhop. I learned to handle bags."

He held the rear passenger door open for Julia. As they

buckled themselves in, his knee brushed against hers, sending a sizzle up his leg.

That cold shower had been an excellent idea.

"Good morning. Which airline?" the Uber driver asked.

"United," they both replied.

The driver nodded, then peeled away from the curb. The directions on his dashboard screen estimated they'd be there in seventeen minutes. No matter how tempted he was to give Julia a taste of her own Type-A medicine, gloat, and point out this morning's fire drill was unnecessary, he'd be a mature, dignified adult.

On the 101 North, Julia jiggled her knees. "You'll be hot when we land in Belize."

He winked. "I'm hot now."

She couldn't set up gold like that and expect him not to knock it down.

"Sweaty hot." She rolled her eyes. "It'll be eighty degrees today. You're wearing jeans, a long-sleeved shirt, and a jacket."

"I'll be fine," he said through a yawn. "Layers."

"I'm amazed you could sleep. I was up all night researching and planning. Were you seriously not gonna wake up until three?"

He lifted a shoulder. "I've never missed a flight."

"Your loose relationship with punctuality makes me question your event skills."

Her assumption of his incompetence was astounding.

"You're basing that on the me from ten years ago. I run my own business, remember?" He relaxed into the seat. "I respect the clock, but event management is more than devotion to a schedule and a checklist."

"Obviously. Nothing ever goes a hundred percent according to plan, but you go through the planning effort to mitigate those risks."

"It's too early for conversations about risk mitigation." He ran his hands through his damp hair. "We shouldn't plan all the contingencies before we're in Belize. A perfectly executed event can still be a dud if you don't leave room for spontaneity, serendipity, kismet."

"You sound like a romantic."

"I *am* a romantic."

"Not with me, you're not." She scrolled through an unending task list on her tablet. "We're having dinner with my sister tonight, by the way."

He ran his hands along his thighs. "What about your dad?"

"Um." Julia dragged her lower lip between her teeth. "I guess my mom didn't tell you? He doesn't live there. Or anywhere. I mean…my dad died three years ago."

His chest tightened. "Jesus, I'm sorry. I didn't know."

"That's okay. Mom should've said something."

"You don't get along with her, I take it?"

"We…mostly get along." She slipped her tablet into her bag. "Listen, not to be rude, but can we not talk during the ride? I meditate before flying, and I'd rather not do it at the airport."

"Be my guest," he said.

"Thanks." She plugged her ears with fuchsia wireless buds, then closed her eyes.

He sank back into the seat to enjoy the ride. More importantly, the view.

Julia's style was impeccable. She'd pulled her hair into a pinup girl updo, complete with a kerchief tied around it to pull it in place. Despite the early hour, she'd also given herself a subtle cat-eye with her eyeliner and painted her luscious lips a berry pink. Lips he'd bet were soft as cherry panna cotta, and just as sweet.

Damn, she was cute.

And bossy.

Which ramped up the cute.

Six

Julia breathed deeply. The scent of a fresh spring evening the moment before it started to rain filled the air. What was that word? She'd read it once and liked the way it felt on her tongue. *Petrichor.* This plane smelled like petrichor.

Something clicked in her muzzy brain. That wasn't the air. That was *Carson.*

As understanding dawned, her stomach curdled with embarrassment. She'd fallen asleep on him during the flight. Planted her face against his rounded shoulder and tumbled deep into dreamland.

There was no graceful way out of this.

She opened her eyes, snuck in one more deep breath, then peeled herself up. "Sorry for making you my pillow."

"I didn't mind." He dog-eared the page of his paperback, then dropped it onto his tray. "Glad you caught up on some sleep."

He draped his forearm along their shared armrest, then leaned toward her. His closeness sent up warning flares.

A thin gray blanket covered her lap and legs. "Where'd this come from?"

"Thought you might get cold, so I asked the flight attendant for a blanket."

Bet it was the brunette with the wide smile. "The one you were flirting with when we boarded? Just want to make sure I thank the right person."

"You can thank me. And I was chatting, not flirting."

She was sure the flight attendant would say otherwise. You'd have to be dead not to be mesmerized by Carson Miller. His honeyed tones, his well-developed sense of humor, and the way his full tractor-beam attention pulled you in as he asked deeply personal questions.

Which single emotion would you eliminate from your roster? he'd asked while they were waiting to board at the gate. Who asks questions like that before sunrise? Anyway, she'd lied and said fear, but her real answer was shame. Then she'd be off the hook for worrying what everyone thought of her all the fucking time.

Anyway, anyone would hope he was flirting.

"And..." He gestured toward a coffee and a packet of chocolate chip cookies. "If you're done busting my balls, those are for you."

"Your fucking balls?" She almost clapped a hand over her mouth. She cursed like a fucking sailor in her head but rarely swore aloud.

She must've been jet-lagged.

"No, you weirdo." He chuckled. "The coffee and cookies. If you want them, better dig in. They announced we're descending."

"I've never wanted anything more." She sipped, and oh, the coffee was *perfect*. Extra cream and sugar. Her favorite way to drink it after many an all-nighter. Lucky guess on his part? She tore open the cookies, then held it out to him. "Want one?"

"Nah, already ate mine."

Thank God. She mowed through the crunchy sweet goodness as Carson leaned closer to stare through the window. She popped the last one into her mouth, crumpled the trash into the empty coffee cup, then held the tidy package out to the passing flight attendant.

"The water's *so* blue." Awe threaded Carson's voice.

An inadequate description. She *adored* this view. A tapestry of otherworldly shades of blue colored the flight path from LA to Azul Caye, waters that Dad, she, and Alex had sailed every time he'd borrowed a boat. The area where mangrove forests met the sea gleamed aqua, as did the many coastal lagoons. The open ocean rolled with undulating sapphire currents. Both gorgeous, but her personal fave was the shallow waters' turquoise.

Turquoise meant they were close to land and she was almost home.

This moment enthralled her every time.

Oh, fuck. The cookie stuck in her throat. She was *such* a jackwagon.

"Oh my gosh." She delved under the blanket for the seatbelt buckle. "Switch with me. You should have the window."

"Stop." He rested his hand on hers. His commanding pressure rocketed a thrill through her. "Don't sweat it. I don't fit under the overhead anyway."

She gulped. She should *not* think about Carson and size. At all.

Despite the cool air streaming from the spout directly overhead, Julia was roasting. If this was how she reacted every time he got close, she wouldn't make it through this week. She peeled the blanket from her legs, folded it into a neat square, then tucked it into her seat back pocket.

"When's the last time you were in Belize?" Carson asked.

A trickle of grief iced her giddy homecoming feels.

"Three years ago." For Dad's funeral.

He'd never been a part of her life in the States, so when she was there, it was easier to ignore his absence. But her father never felt more real—and more permanently gone—than when she was in Belize.

Seriously, fuck cancer.

First, its withering havoc came for his energy, then for his smile, and last his personality as he withdrew into the pain. The grief counselor at school had assured her that someday, she'd be able to remember Dad without crying. That she wouldn't ache for his hug or his reminder that his Julesy-girl was tough and bright as the sapphire for which she was named.

But today was not that day.

She swiped away the tear that had threatened to fall. No one in Belize had seen her cry since the funeral, and she refused for Carson to be the first.

"Three years is a long time," he said. "Are you excited to be back?"

As the pilot swooped the plane around, nauseated fluttering erupted in her stomach. Julia closed her eyes. Landing would be another gut punch. No one to meet her at baggage claim with a caramel-and-pecan cluster because *it's been too long since you've tasted Belizean chocolate, the food of the gods.*

This was not the homecoming Julia envisioned.

The threatening tears dissolved, replaced by irritation. A homecoming that made sense centered on Alex inviting her to help run Stone Adventures, to fold her into their father's dreams. Not this. Planning her mother's fourth wedding with Carson Fucking Miller.

"*Excited*'s not the word for it." She gripped the armrests. Whoops. Her right hand grabbed Carson's wrist. She let him go faster than she'd let go of a poisonous frog.

"What is the word?" he asked.

"*Frustrated.*" Was the pilot barrel-rolling this jet?

Carson shifted his arm until they were holding hands. "*Frustrated* is not a happy word."

"I'm not a happy person right now." She breathed deeply

through her nose, choosing to ignore the warmth of his hand and the reluctant comfort she took from it. She refused to freak out during this landing, even if she was desperate to collapse with fear.

"Why?" Carson asked.

She glared at his big dumb smiling face "What's with the questions?"

"Promise me you won't get mad." He squeezed her hand.

Dammit, that actually soothed her. "No, but tell me anyway."

"Your mom said you're a nervous flyer—"

"I am not." G-forces tugged at her insides as they descended.

This was it. This was the moment where the engines could conk out. They were still high enough they'd die in an explosive fireball instead of crashing straight into the pavement below.

"She said you hate the landings, and the best way to help you through it—" the plane jerked as the wheels hit the runway "—was to distract you with conversation."

Julia exhaled.

She resented her mother for sharing her vulnerability with this asshole. As though she was a person to be managed. *She* was the manager of people and things and situations, not Carson Miller.

She opened her eyes, and oh my God, his face was *right* there, his green eyes searching her expression.

"I'm fine." She leaned away from him.

His grin was addictive. "Good."

The plane efficiently sidled up to the airport. She didn't protest when Carson grabbed her bag from the overhead bin. His height was an advantage. As his shirt raised above his belt, she caught a tantalizing slice of his abs.

Stop that, she chastised herself.

As they descended the air stairs, familiar tropical humidity walloped her. She breathed deeply. Underneath the jet exhaust she caught the familiar mix of rich earth, native flowers, fragrant citrus, and a hint of the salty ocean. This was the perfume that had rolled through her childhood home's open windows. Tears pricked her eyes.

She'd forgotten that this was what home smelled like.

Three years *was* a long time.

Before her feet touched the tarmac, something shifted inside her. One of Dad's stipulations when her parents split was that she and Alex visit Belize twice per year, minimum. He wouldn't have cared that Mom wanted to marry Jim here. In fact, he would've loved the bonus time with his girls.

Regardless of the reason for the trip, *this* was where she was meant to be today.

After a deep breath, she said, "So, bags, then the rental car."

Compared to LAX, Belize International Airport was adorably bijou. What it lacked in size, it made up for in efficiency. Their suitcases lay on the carousel at baggage claim, and the line for rental cars moved quickly. She'd selected a local company, because tourism dollars spent with them funneled directly back to the community.

As the clerk entered her information, Carson asked, "Do you need my license?"

"Spouses are entitled to drive," she answered.

Julia coughed. "He's not my spouse. He's my..."

She faltered. Frenemy? Competition? Questionable fantasy?

"Stepbrother," he said.

That word was full of *ew*. It landed wrong in her ears.

"Not yet," she interjected. "Our parents are getting married."

The woman shifted her gaze between them. "In that case, if you're unrelated, I'll add you to the contract. That'll cost an additional two dollars per day."

"That's fine." Carson dropped his license and credit card

on the counter. "I'll pick this up and reconcile the expenses with Dad later."

"Be my guest." It was a godsend not to charge big expenses to her meager credit limit.

"There you are." The clerk folded a printout into a paper folio. "Take this to the parking lot across the street there and select a minivan. The keys will be waiting in the vehicle."

"Thank you." Julia collected the folio.

"A minivan?" Carson asked as they headed to the parking lot.

"Yes. We'll be carting stuff and people around, and my mom had knee surgery a few years ago. It's easier for her if the car's lower to the ground. What's the problem? Minivans not cool enough for you?"

"Even when I'm married with kids, I'd rather chew off my own hand than drive one." He pointed to a silver minivan. "That's not terrible. It's got more room than those other three."

That caught her by surprise.

When he was married with kids? High school Carson Miller had a reputation for smashing and dashing. The number of senior girls who'd never been in the library but were suddenly casually perusing the World War II–nonfiction section near their tutoring table helped solidify the reputation in her mind.

She didn't *care*. It was interesting information, that's all.

"Works for me if it means we get on the road," she said.

He opened the lift gate and grabbed her giant suitcase. This time, she didn't argue. If he wanted to heft bags, he could go for it.

"Thanks." She dropped her weekender bag beside it. "We'll head to your hotel first."

Carson closed the gate. "Then dinner with your sister?"

"That's right." She ventured to the driver's side…as did Carson. "What are you doing?"

"You said you were up all night."

"Then I napped on the plane. I grew up here, Carson. It makes more sense for the person who knows the roads to drive."

He flashed his palms. "We've got GPS, but okay. You're in charge."

Finally, he was beginning to understand their dynamic. She should've remembered that it always took him a minute to catch up.

Carson nervously tapped his knees as Julia drove them from the airport to the Azul Caye Inn. Since the car accident that stole his baseball career, he rarely trusted anyone else behind the wheel. One bad turn could mean disaster. But Julia was right—she knew these twisty, busy roads better than he did.

And if anyone took driving seriously, it was Julia.

Since she'd insisted they drive with the windows down, salty-ocean-and-pine-scented air whipped through the minivan. The warmth prickled the back of his neck, and he rolled up his sleeves. He was hot, but he wouldn't give Julia the satisfaction of being right. From now on, when checking the weather, he'd look at the *humidity* as well as the temps. Eighty degrees in LA was pleasant. Here in Belize, where it was eighty-three percent humidity? Eighty degrees felt liked wearing a hot wet sweater, then being wrapped in cling film.

It sure was beautiful, though. Happy sunlight beamed overhead, barely acknowledging the wispy clouds feathering the azure sky. Bright yellow-and-black birds with rainbow beaks circled above the dense green trees flanking the main road.

"What are those?" he yelled over the rushing wind as he pointed to the swooping birds.

"Keel-billed toucans," she shouted. "Belize's national bird."

Looked a lot more fun than the American bald eagle. Like nature had mixed a rack of disco lights with a tropical bird.

The thick wall of trees thinned, revealing bright white beaches and beyond them, a calm silvery ocean. The shore was like nature's Xanax. As soon as he was within earshot of crashing surf, he always lowered his shoulders an inch, evened his breathing, and slowed down. Digging his toes into the sand, the cool waves lapping at his ankles, then untethering from gravity and bobbing in the ocean's vastness... It brought peace.

In LA, it took thirty minutes to get to the sand.

"Hey," he yelled over the rushing air. "When can we check out the beach?"

"Tomorrow," she shouted. "During the Azul Caye Resort tour."

"No, to swim, nap, frolic. C'mon, I *have* to swim in the Caribbean while we're here."

"Before the wedding will be tough." She tapped the steering wheel. "If we get through tomorrow's list, maybe we can squeeze in a twilight visit."

"I'll take it." Carson leaned back in his seat.

He poked the top of the door frame. The last time he'd taken a proper vacation was...sophomore year? Maybe this time in Belize was the forced break he needed.

Every day was a new opportunity in which to excel, but starting up Limitless Events his senior year of college and pushing it to the growth stage this year had been exhausting. The grind was necessary, though. He'd had no choice but to pour himself into it and prove baseball wasn't his *one* thing, that he'd succeed at whatever he put his mind to.

Maybe someday his mom would believe it, too.

This section of town was more heavily developed, riddled with cantinas, restaurants, churches, and marinas. Beyond them, the ocean glistened.

"How does anyone get anything done with a view like that?" He gestured toward the endless horizon of blue. "It's hypnotic."

"That's what causes island time." She eased into a parking space in the lot, then popped the lift gate. "FYI, to maintain a schedule, embrace telling everyone things are happening an hour earlier than they actually are. Why are you staying at this inn, by the way? Wouldn't it have been better to book a room at the resort?"

He hauled his suitcase from the back. "It was fully booked until the wedding block takes effect. There's a music festival in town, so this was the best I could do."

"One of the many reasons I'm grateful my sister kept my dad's house—a free place to crash when I'm in town."

"Are you two close?" he asked.

He'd always wanted siblings. Not in the cards, but he'd found brothers in the fraternity. Those dudes always had his back. Checked his ego, too, which was something he'd lacked in his childhood. But he wished he had someone growing up in the same house with him to witness shit and tell him he wasn't off base. He might've figured out Mom was a conditional-love hard-ass sooner or that Dad rarely spoke up about what he wanted.

"We were close, once. The past few years have been busy. She's running the tour company and I've been in school, but we'll figure it out when I relocate."

"I'm sure you will."

It was obvious that Julia worshipped Alex in high school. Her weekend plans had always involved her sister. Not to mention all the times she'd cackled when she'd found messages like *When in doubt...don't. Doubt's for basic bitches* in her notebook. He'd meant it when he'd said her reactions had inspired the daily affirmations in the Positively Productive app.

He hustled to open the door for Julia. Inside the cathedral-ceilinged lobby lay several different service desks and guests lounging in the comfortably squashy couches.

"Oh, clever." Julia appraised the welcoming interior. "The office is next to registration, and the bar's right there. If people have food and entertainment, they're less likely to complain."

"Who'd complain? This place is perfect."

Low lights, lazy overhead fans, and a bustling bar area. It gave off five-star-luxury-Caribbean vibes without being fussy. No worries, no stress. If anything went sideways, an army of staff would set it to rights while the guests sipped piña coladas. Plus, the temperature was perfect. The air-conditioning blissfully siphoned the humidity from the air.

"You'd be surprised at what people complain about. Too few towels, the sheets don't have a high-enough thread count, the remote isn't responsive, the restaurant offerings aren't varied, the neighbors two doors down are having outrageously loud sex."

"You sound like you're speaking from experience."

"Oh, I am." She lifted a shoulder. "The thing is I get it. People scrimp and save to set aside a pocket of time for relaxation, and I want them to have that. So I send extra towels, dip into the fancy linens, swap out batteries, ask the chef to craft a special order meal, and send complimentary room service to interrupt the sex-a-thon. People should feel welcomed and cared for. Like they belong."

He easily pictured her in gracious problem-solver mode. Elegantly moving through the back-of-house areas like a dancer, collecting the things her guests needed, coordinating staff to deliver it, and doing it all quickly and with a smile. God, competency turned him on.

But it made him wonder…

"Who does that for you?"

She pursed her lips as they approached the counter. "What do you mean?"

"Everyone needs to feel like they belong."

Julia rolled her eyes. "I'm not taking life advice from the guy who once made fun of my thrifted vintage dresses."

His gut clenched. He'd earn her forgiveness if it was the last thing he did. "Again, I'm sorry. But just so you know, sometimes I was curious because your clothes were unique."

She squinted. "Sure you were."

Forgiveness would come easier if she believed he was sincere. He'd work on that, too.

"Can I help you, sir?" the registration clerk asked.

"Yes. I have a reservation for Carson Miller."

"Thank you." She clicked rapidly on the keyboard. "Ah, yes, I see you here. Welcome to the Azul Caye Inn, Mr. and Mrs. Miller."

Julia laughed. "I am *not* Mrs. Miller."

Damn. She didn't have to laugh *that* hard.

"My apologies," the clerk said. "Sir, I'll need your identification and a form of payment."

"Be back in a second." Julia nipped toward the expansive veranda off the lobby. She cut an adorable figure. As soon as they'd touched down, she'd shed her jacket, exposing the smooth shape of her naked shoulders. She must've been dying in that jumpsuit, though.

He pinched his T-shirt away from his abdomen.

Unless he wanted to strut around shirtless, this was as cool as he'd get. The sticky air brushed against his skin, like he was swimming through soup. No, not soup. Spiderwebs.

"Are you in town for the music festival?" the clerk asked.

"No. Should we check it out?"

"Oh yes, sir, if you like punta, soca, reggae, dancehall, and or Latin beats. You'll see Belize's megastars. Even if you don't go to the main stage, acts are popping up all over town."

He tracked Julia, who was now inspecting the stand holding trifold tourism pamphlets. With her hair twisted and pinned up, he had a perfect view of the delicate column of her neck. She returned to the registration desk, head tipped back to gaze at the ceiling.

"You look like a tourist," he said as the clerk handed him his keycards.

"I look like a hotelier checking out the competition."

He rolled his suitcase toward the elevators. "This place isn't competition until you're working somewhere else."

"*Yet*. And ouch." Julia slowly rotated as she followed him, scanning the wicker furniture with muted patterns, the ceiling fans with the palm-frond blades, the walls painted with a palette that matched the beaches behind the hotel and villas. "But I'm talking about when my sister and I open up a boutique resort. My market research shows tons of dive inns around here—places that opened up ages ago during the original tourism wave in the eighties. Youth hostels, too. Then behemoths opened in the last decade, but there's an underserved middle population."

"Like who?" he asked as they entered the elevator.

"Our customers would be people who can afford a nice Airbnb but prefer hotel amenities. A place where they don't have to be their own cruise director, like this place. I'm scoping out potential differentiators." She hovered her finger over the number pad. "Floor?"

"Six." Carson's belly dropped as the elevator tugged them upward. "You've put lots of thought into this."

"I'm not just a pretty face, you know."

He knew all too well that she also possessed a beautiful brain.

In school, he'd been a little embarrassed that his tutor was two years younger. But her grasp of the subject matter was firm, and she had intense study skills. She'd mapped out a plan to make sure they covered the right amount of material during each session. He'd actually borrowed her principles for his college classes and the frat events he hosted. Eventually, they made their way into Positively Productive app's workflow structures for its initial release.

"I refine the Stone Adventures & Resort's business plan when I'm not at work or doom-scrolling for new jobs."

"See, the job thing confuses me. You've got the credentials and strike me as competent."

She clutched her chest. "I may swoon."

"I don't understand why someone hasn't snapped you up."

"Story of my life, actually." She grinned, but the smile didn't reach her eyes.

The world was sleeping on Julia Stone.

He wouldn't. Not any longer.

They strolled the hallway together until they arrived at room 612. After holding the card against the reader, the lock *thunked*. He opened the door and gestured for Julia to enter.

She giggled as she surveyed the small room. "I see you booked the Presidential Suite."

"It's what they had left," he said.

The room was *this* close to being cramped. If there was one bed, the space situation would've been better. With two full-sized beds and the table and chairs in the corner, he had barely enough room to drag his massive suitcase to the luggage rack.

She whipped open the curtains that led to the pocket-sized balcony. "The view's unbeatable, though."

Beyond them lay the impossibly blue Caribbean. He flipped the lock and opened the sliding door. The breeze carried the scent he'd huffed at the airport. Earth, spice, citrus, and salt.

"The view's probably what I paid for."

"Definitely not the square footage," she said. "Although I like the paintings. I bet they buy from local artists."

"I hadn't noticed." Mostly because the way her top molded against her breasts was distracting him. "What should we do first? Check out the resort? Choose the cake?"

She shook her head. "Belize doesn't do business after six p.m."

"Room service? This seems like a nice backdrop for a cocktail."

She checked her watch. "No can do, sir. I don't want to be late to my sister's."

He nearly protested, but he didn't want to repeat this morning. She was clearly a *five minutes early is ten minutes late* person.

"Got it," he said. "Let me change my shirt."

Never good to meet family when you've sweated through your clothes. His suitcase sighed as he unzipped it, then flipped the top open and coaxed a nearly identical blue T-shirt from the stack. He tugged at the back of his shirt.

The brisk air-conditioning was heaven on his heated skin.

"I can give you privacy," Julia squealed.

"For what?" He twisted toward her and caught her eyeing him. Well, how about that? If she was looking, he'd give her a show. Carson flexed his pecs, and the interest that flashed in Julia's eyes made him feel about ten feet tall.

"That." With her gaze averted, she vaguely gestured toward his naked torso.

"Didn't figure you for a prude."

"I am *not* a prude. Far from it. But I don't hang out in hotel rooms two feet away from half-naked strangers."

"Not a stranger." He dragged on the shirt. "We've known each other for a decade."

"That's technically true. If you've changed as much as you say you have, though, I don't know anything about you. Ergo, strangers."

"You don't like to lose arguments, do you?"

"Are we arguing?" She popped her hand on her hip.

"Sure feels like it." Not that he was complaining. Arguing with Julia was more entertaining than peace with anyone else. He opened the door. "After you."

"Why do you keep doing that?" she asked from the hallway.

He tugged the door closed. "Argue with you?"

"No, open doors and handle my bags. I don't know what to do with casual assistance."

"You must hang around dopes. I'm a gentleman."

She snorted.

"I know," he said. "I wasn't, once upon a time. But I grew

up. Now I'm helpful. I open doors, pull out chairs, top off beverages. Gentleman stuff. You deserve that kind of attention."

She poked the elevator's Down button. "I don't like to make work for other people."

Something about that left a dissatisfied feeling in Carson's chest. They'd handle the wedding, which wouldn't be easy. They'd spend a ton of time together, and Julia'd produce a successful event. But that comment, right there, was the moment Carson decided he'd use this trip to Belize to convince Julia that she was worth the work.

Seven

Julia zigzagged through the unmarked streets on which her father had taught her to drive. Officially, not until she was eighteen, the legal driving age in Belize. Unofficially, the lessons had started when she was fourteen and didn't let up until he was convinced she could handle the roads with the skill of an F1 driver. If she were alone, she'd go faster, eager to see her sister for the first time in three years.

"Are you paying attention?" She made a hairpin turn, an immediate lane switch, and another left. "This part's tricky, and GPS apps get it wrong. I don't want you to get horrifically lost on your way back to the hotel."

"Yes, I'm paying attention." Carson's big frame overflowed the passenger seat. "Are you okay? You seem edgy."

"Fine," she said tightly.

Since she wasn't actively vomiting, she'd call that the truth.

Scarlet Macaw Lane hadn't changed much. The happy yellow house in which she spent her childhood, however, was now turquoise. Alex had enclosed the front porch, too. Minor changes, but enough to deepen Julia's disconnect from this place.

She glided to a stop. Time's obvious passage stung.

This was Alex's home now. She'd bought Julia out of her

half, and the windfall paid the grad school tuition not covered by scholarship or loans. Eager to put distance between herself and Belize, Julia had taken the money and run to Ithaca.

"This it?" Carson asked.

"No, I like stopping at strangers' houses."

"I'll take that as a yes." He unbuckled his seat belt.

She squeezed the steering wheel. That was rude. Carson seemed unbothered, but still. Snippy bitch wasn't who she wanted to be. It wasn't Carson's fault she was operating on an adrenaline, coffee, and cookie cocktail. And he'd been helpful and kind on the plane, so she should attempt to be a little nicer. She checked her reflection, swiped on more gloss, then met him outside.

"The door's up the side stairs," she said.

He unlatched and held open the front gate for her, and for once, she didn't argue. Might as well enjoy the princess treatment. Rich aromas emanated from the house, and her stomach audibly rumbled.

"I'm hungry, too," Carson said. "Smells good."

"Stewed chicken, rice, and beans, I'd bet. It's a traditional meal in Belize, but don't get your hopes up too high. Alex is a terrible cook."

A light breeze swirled around them. Like a ghost saying hello, her father's wind chimes jingled against each other. She paused as the reminder of him—and his absence—clawed at her most tender parts. She wished she could talk to him about things—Alex's boyfriend, the pandemic, the mangrove-protection legislation that made it harder to give up-close-and-personal tours. Hear his laugh as she told him about the guest who'd requested she build a pillow fort. Simple stuff, but the simple stuff was everything.

"Forget something?" Carson asked.

"No. The wind chimes…" She massaged her hands.

Grief made her fingers tingle like she'd slept on them and cut off the circulation. Her doctor had diagnosed her with anxiety numbness and prescribed deep breathing and distraction.

Distraction, however, was a tall order when everything reminded her of Dad.

"What about them?" Carson asked gently.

"My dad brought them home when I was little." The unvarnished truth spilled from her. "My mom said they were melancholy, but Dad loved them. We played dolls out on the porch, did homework, watched the sunset, hid from their arguments while the chimes played."

That was *way* more than she meant to share. Carson brought out her most authentic self, warts and all. Petty snark, bummer memories, impatience, hangriness… Probably because she didn't like him, so she didn't make an effort to hide her flaws.

"It must be nice to still feel connected."

His voice tickled her ear, and his chest warmed her back. His solid presence was confusingly reassuring, like he'd catch her if she fell.

She wanted none of it.

"Can you back off? You're crowding me." She rushed up the stairs, then knocked twice before entering the house. "Hello?"

The aluminum door slapping into its frame was another echo from her childhood.

Alex was a blur as she rushed from the kitchen. "You're here!"

She sank into her sister's outstretched arms. "I'm here."

"Don't stay away so long next time," her sister murmured.

She wouldn't go anywhere if Alex gave her a job, but hey, no need to ruin a nice family moment by pointing out reality. She'd indulge in this hug as they rocked back and forth.

"Turquoise?" Julia asked.

"It was on sale." Alex peeked over Julia's shoulder. "Carson?"

"That's me. Hi." Carson stuck out his hand, but she went straight for a hug.

Since when had Alex become a hug machine?

"Hello, stepbrother." Alex released him, then cupped her hands around her mouth. "Bo! They're here!"

A bespectacled man with a slanted smile came through the door, wiping his hands on a dish towel. Her sister's boyfriend seemed sweet and attentive to Alex during their occasional video chats. She hoped he liked her. He'd been around for six months now and seemed like he'd be sticking around.

"Julia! Nice to see you outside of a computer screen."

"Hi." She hugged him, then gestured toward Carson. "This is Carson, and this is Bo, my sister's boyfriend."

Alex hid a giggle behind her fist as Bo shook hands with Carson.

A *giggle*?

Alex Stone didn't giggle. She chuckled, chortled, guffawed, and occasionally slapped her knee. Her entire tomboy life, she'd never done something so girly as giggle. Girly was Julia's territory. Styled hair, makeup tutorials, clothing chosen because of trends, not because it had deep pockets and could survive a tropical storm. Something was up. Alex was grinning at Bo like he'd simultaneously solved world peace and given her an orgasm.

"What's up with you two?" Julia asked.

"Bo's not my boyfriend." Alex slipped her arms around his waist. "He's my fiancé."

For the second time in ten minutes, Julia went numb.

She barely knew Bo's name, and her sister was *marrying* him? They'd always rolled their eyes when Mom announced a sudden engagement, and here was Alex, doing the same thing. What was *wrong* with the women in her family? And why hadn't Alex called her immediately to share the news? Julia forced herself to breathe. Her mother and sister were happy, thriving, glowing, moving on while she was floundering.

This was terrible.

She zeroed in on her sister's hand. "You don't have a ring."

"I don't need one. I have this necklace." Alex drummed her fingers against the gorgeous pendant hanging against her breastbone. "We have a lot to catch up on. Most importantly, though, will you be my maid of honor?"

Well, fuck.

"Yes!" She awkwardly looped her arms around her sister and future brother-in-law.

The hug gave her a chance to hide her face. Her big sister was getting married to a guy Julia didn't know at all. She squeezed them, like she could reduce the itchy distance between herself and Alex by gripping just tight enough.

Their embrace was interrupted by a tabby cat prancing from the kitchen.

"When did you get a cat?" Julia stepped back.

"When I got Bo." The cat buffed Alex's ankles. "Her name's Lorelai, and she's a Stone through and through. Gets hangry."

"That's my cue." Bo backed toward the kitchen. "I'll feed her and finish up dinner."

"He cooks?" Julia asked.

"Like a demon."

"Lucky." Neither she nor Alex could make anything beyond the most basic meals. They were too impatient to let things simmer. Both Mom and Dad had enjoyed cooking, so they'd never recruited her or Alex to help, preferring to do it themselves.

Just as well. Julia preferred eating to cooking every day of the week.

"I can cook." Carson squatted to scratch the cat's ears.

"You can?" She twisted toward him. "Color me surprised. You give off big frat-bro energy. Like your idea of a meal is dinosaur chicken nuggets and a pound of spaghetti."

He swept his hand down his midsection. "I contain multitudes. Frat bros eat, too."

"Does Mom know?" Julia asked.

"That Carson can cook?" Alex scrunched her forehead.

"No, about the engagement, you goof."

"Ah." Alex relaxed her face. "Not yet. I wanted to tell her in person. Either of you care for a drink? I made sangria."

Carson nodded as she said, "Yes please."

A barrel of rum wouldn't sand the edges off this rough evening, but sangria was tasty.

"Dinner's ready," Bo called from the kitchen.

"You go help yourselves, and I'll bring out the drinks." Alex opened the doorway to the now-enclosed porch, where their father's minibar lived.

"This way." Julia led Carson to the kitchen as Bo set a tureen on the counter. The concentrated aroma of stewed chicken, rice, beans, and—oh wow, he'd fried plantains?—made her mouth water. "Bo, this smells amazing."

After they heaped food onto their plates, Julia led Carson to their parents' dining table. As busy as her parents had been with work—Dad giving tours, Mom ringing up sales at Belizean Bliss Boutique—they'd always eaten a late dinner together as a family. This was also where they'd breakfasted and drawn pictures of their adventures with Dad.

Rather, it had been.

"You got rid of our table?" Julia's voice caught.

"Had to." Alex set down glasses of sangria. "Hurricane Lisa ripped the screening off and smashed the table to the street."

"You didn't tell me that."

"Didn't want to be a bummer. Hey, why does your name sound familiar, Carson Miller?"

"Oh, you remember him." Julia sipped her sangria. "You gave me tips for how to deal with his snide comments about my clothes, about living in the cheap apartment buildings near school, and that I'd probably never have sex. He's *that* Carson."

"That's *you*?" Alex laid her cutlery on the table.

Carson sighed. "Yes, but I promise I'm a changed person."

She touched Julia's hand. "I've got a tranquilizer gun and a shovel."

Bo sat next to Alex. "The tranq gun's locked up at the office."

"Which is a two-minute walk away. Are you okay, Jules? This—" she gestured in Carson's direction "—is a lot."

"I'm fine," she said through a smile.

Despite the awkward circumstances, Julia's heart was full. Alex was her ride-or-die. She'd doubted it for a beat, but offering to bury a tranquilized Carson was her version of sweet.

"My sister's nicer than me." Alex pointed her fork at Carson. "Why were you such an asshole to her? This better be good because I hold grudges, and I refuse to pretend to like you."

"I can attest to that," Bo said. "She didn't like me at first."

Alex returned her attention to Carson. "Spill."

Julia couldn't wait for this.

"I…" He cleared his throat.

Was Carson Fucking Miller nervous?

"I don't have a good reason," he said. "But maybe an explanation? See, my mom's a sports agent, and she put pressure on me to be the next A-Rod. When she failed to land Chase Whitaker—"

"The center fielder for the Orioles?" Bo asked.

"That's right."

He whistled. "That had to hurt."

Ugh, boys. Julia exchanged a look with Alex, who shrugged.

Bo explained, "He was the American League's Rookie of the Year, and the center-fielder Gold Glove. It's really hard to get both. He's got one of the best batting averages in the league and has a ton of merch and endorsement deals."

She had no idea what a rando baseball player had to do with Carson being an ass.

But she'd keep listening.

"That's right," Carson nodded. "Other agents said she'd lost out on Whitaker, because she got distracted by being a mom. So she quit and started her own agency. Once I showed promise, I think she saw me as validation. Like, she could be a mom *and* a talent developer. I wanted to be the best, for her. But the pressure got to me. I took it out on easy targets. It didn't help that my ego was the size of Dodgers Stadium. I was an asshole."

Julia felt itchy in her skin. "I was an easy target?"

"Not because of anything about you personally." He touched her shoulder. "You were paid to be around me. So you'd… take it."

"The fuck she would," Alex said.

"No, I did." Julia pressed her fingers to her forehead. "But this makes an awful kind of sense. You got moody when baseball started. And the kinesiology tape—you strained your rotator cuff during spring training. I said you should take a break from baseball."

Unless Carson was a fabulous actor, he looked genuinely sheepish. "And I snapped at you. Which you didn't deserve, of course. But I was hurting."

She would *not* listen to the inner voice that wanted to pat his hand.

"All that's tragic," Alex said. "And somewhere in there you said you were an asshole, but I'm not hearing an apology."

Julia tried to fight her smile but…nope. She couldn't. Alex rarely acted as a protective older sister, and this exchange was the verbal equivalent of wrapping Julia in a cozy serape. But Carson *had* actually apologized to her directly.

"He apologized, Alex. Multiple times. On different continents."

"Good—you deserved that. But I want one from him, too, because I talked you off ledges and coached you through anxiety attacks."

Julia shot daggers at Alex with her eyes. For fuck's sake, let her keep some dignity. He did *not* need to know about those. "I haven't had one in years."

"Oh, Jesus." Carson clutched his glass. "Anxiety attacks? Alex, I'm sorry, but Julia, I'm *really* sorry. Do you want me to go?"

No. No part of her wanted him to leave, which was something she'd unpack later.

She tilted her head, considering him.

Everything he'd said rang true, but most of it sounded rehearsed. A prepared apology. Which was nice in a way—he'd been worried enough about it that he'd practiced. Her anxiety attacks upset him, though. Like he finally got that yeah, it was ten years ago, but it was intense. Completely survivable, but helped shape her and how she approached the world.

"If we're voting, I'd like you to stay." Bo scooped up stew. "Otherwise we'll have leftovers."

"There's only one vote that matters," Alex said, staring at her.

Julia sipped her sangria. "I vote stay, on the condition you tell us why you changed. Because you seem like you're finally aware other people have feelings and you shouldn't stomp on them. But if you say you just…matured, I call bullshit."

"That's fair." He rotated his glass on its base. "It was a car accident after graduation. August. I lost it on Mulholland Drive on the way to a party and rolled my car."

"That road is the *worst*," Alex said.

Julia leaned back in her seat. "Was everyone okay?"

She'd heard he'd been in an accident. But she never asked for Carson Miller lore lest her interest trigger a fresh wave of Sad Puppy snickering. Without details, she'd assumed it was just a fender bender, not a life-altering, personality-shifting wreck.

"Mostly. The airbags did their thing, so my friends—do you remember Caleb and Jonas, from the team?—they walked away with scratches. My cousin Danny, too. But I broke my throwing hand and wrist to powder. Goodbye playing for Cal State, and goodbye MLB."

That was what caused the faint scars wrapping around his wrist. She'd seen them—and the ones on his shoulder—at the pool house but didn't want to pry.

"RIP my car insurance rates, too," he continued. "Caleb and Jonas sued me for more than my liability cap. My aunt repped me pro bono, 'cause I had no money. Luckily, the jury didn't award anything beyond what the insurance paid."

"Jesus, Carson, I'm sorry to hear that." Julia fiddled with her fork. She'd wished for Carson's comeuppance countless times, but not by having a dream ripped away.

"It's all good. The accident made me a better human. And you were right, you know."

She fumbled the fork. "About?"

"My friends were fake. After the accident, baseball was out the window and my life was surgery, physical therapy, and lawsuits. No one stuck around."

"I'm sorry." Her heart squeezed. She normally loved being right, but not like this.

"Don't be. Clearing them out made room for what's good for me. Life's been a genuine blast since then. A lot of hard work, but I wouldn't trade it."

The two of them locked gazes. How had she not noticed the change in his eyes? She'd been so distracted by the bigger, broader, thicker changes in his body, she'd missed the new-to-her softness in his green gaze.

"Fine," Alex dramatically cut in, "you can stay. How's the wedding planning? Has Mom made you want to jump out a window?"

As Julia said, "Yes," Carson said, "No."

"No?" Julia laughed. "She wants a wedding on the beach during the rainy season. *Nothing* is done besides selecting the venue for the reception. She keeps saying 'It'll work out,' but it's my job—"

"Our job," Carson interrupted.

"To make that happen," Julia continued without missing a beat. "She wants miracles, but we're mere mortals."

"Fortunately," Carson said, "mortals can work miracles. They're called saints."

"You're no saint."

He raised an eyebrow. "Agreed."

Alex pointed at her sister. "Don't do the thing you always do and bend over backward to accommodate her. Set boundaries. Decline her demand for a sandcastle replica of a Maya pyramid for her wedding."

Julia blanched. "Does she want that?"

She might be able to hire that random guy who sculpted Christ and the Ten Commandments in sand every night near the tourist areas. If she could just…

"That was a fictional example." Alex thumped her sangria on the table. "You *immediately* started figuring out how you could make that happen, didn't you?"

"No," she lied.

"Liar." Alex jabbed the table with her index finger. "The sooner you set boundaries, the happier you'll be. The best thing I ever did for myself was realize I wasn't everyone's cup of tea. It's okay if people—including Mom—don't enjoy me. I found people who did."

"Maybe *I* found *you*," Bo said.

"Please, who's the adventurer here?" Alex squeezed his hand again. "Maybe we found each other."

Barf. If she didn't interrupt, they might start making out.

"That's easy for you to say. Dad's friends are rooting for you, you've been besties with Mariele since you were eight, and now you've got Bo. I've got surface friends but no deep ones. I'm not risking my relationship with the only parent I have left."

Instant regret.

She'd spilled her biggest insecurity in front of the very man who used to catch these factoids and hurl them back at her like emotional dodgeball. In high school, she'd trained herself to be on guard around Carson. Since then, she'd avoided him, his friends, social media, and had successfully created a Carson Miller–free zone. Her walls went up in smoke, though, after two days of sleep deficit, a wonky eating schedule, and a minor existential crisis about her family.

Please let her instincts be right and he'd actually changed.

With concern etching Alex's face, she said, "You can tell Mom no, Jules."

Julia's appetite shriveled. "Can we stop talking about this?"

"Absolutely," Carson said. "Bo, this is outstanding. Are you a chef?"

Thank God he'd shifted the conversation.

"Nope." Bo nested Alex's empty bowl into his. "I'm an algorithm developer. I like it as a hobby, but coding's my passion."

Their conversation swirled around Julia. She kept her mouth shut to prevent yet another round of *Here's what Julia should do*, which was her sister and mother's favorite game. They were experts in offering guidance she didn't want, and the fucked thing was when she was actually at an emotional crossroads and came to them for advice, they shrugged.

For Alex, that made a certain kind of sense. Her gut was her compass, and she loved quoting Dad—*There's no point borrowing trouble from tomorrow.* Unlike Mom, who enjoyed teasing out all the different possible scenarios. Which actually made Julia more like her mother than her father, and that was *not* a thing she was prepared to ponder right now.

"Who's ready for dessert?" Alex asked.

"I'll help clear." Julia scooted back from the table.

She'd learned this trick ages ago. When she needed a moment to herself, she'd volunteer for a chore. No one questioned it, she got brownie points for being helpful, and she could catch her breath in private. Win-win-win.

"Nah, stay." Carson collected her bowl. "I've got it."

Dammit.

"Thanks," she said through tight lips.

Alex and Carson disappeared with the dishes, leaving her with Bo. The best way to preempt awkward silence and deflect more tunneling into her life was to ask *him* a personal question.

"Tell me about the necklace." She plucked an apple chunk from her empty sangria. "Why does it replace an engagement ring?"

Bo topped her off from the pitcher on the table. "It's a family heirloom. It goes to the eldest son to give to his forever person."

Julia sipped her drink. "Alex has worn it for months."

"I gave it to her after we'd known each other for a week." He adjusted his glasses. "Even if she wasn't there yet, I knew."

"Whoa, are you sure?" She swirled her glass. "I love my sister. She'll keep your secrets and bury the bodies. But she's also…a lot."

He lifted a shoulder. "She felt like home. From day one, I was myself around her. By day three, couldn't imagine life without her. By day six, I was brave enough to tell her that."

"Marriage is *such* a big step, though." Julia clapped her hand over her mouth. "I'm sorry. This is completely inappropriate on the day you've announced your engagement."

"It's fine." Bo laughed. "You two are actually a lot alike that way. If you're worried I'm a gold digger, Alex proposed to me. The last time I got the monthly stamp on my passport, the immigration office said I had to provide further documentation at six months to explain the long-term stay. There are more fees, too. Alex decided that was ridiculous since we'll be together forever, so we should get married."

"Man, she hates paperwork."

He laughed. "She does indeed."

"Dessert time!" Alex sang in her off-key voice as she and Carson plopped plates onto the table. The dishes contained deep orange squares topped with marshmallow-fluff dollops.

Happiness burbled inside of Julia.

"I haven't had sweet potato pone in *years*." Her appetite roared back as she eagerly spooned up the creamy dessert. Cinnamon, ginger, and the caramelized–brown sugar crust took her back to her childhood Christmases.

Alex smiled. "I found Dad's recipe. Bo baked it."

"It's...odd." Bo tapped his spoon against his chin. "It's like a dense flan sweet-potato casserole. Is it okay?"

She went back for more. "It's perfect. The best I've ever had."

"You're a dessert weirdo." Alex pointed her spoon at Julia as she said to Carson, "She doesn't like cake."

"Who doesn't like cake?" he said.

"Me." Julia shrugged. "Never have."

"She always insisted on this goop or rice pudding for her birthday dessert. The two worst desserts on any menu."

"Only if you have an uneducated palate."

"I've missed your highbrow insults." Alex surveyed the table. "Want another sangria to wash away the weird taste, Carson?"

"Nah, better not. I'll be driving back soon."

Julia laid her spoon on the table. "Let me grab my bags first."

"Wh— Oh, hell." Alex winced. "Oh, Jules, I'm sorry, but we don't have room."

Julia fought to keep the crushed feelings from showing on her face. "Why? When I come to Belize, I always stay here."

"Since everything's happening across town, I figured you'd stay there. Mariele's friend—Santi—is in town for the music festival. They couldn't get a decent rate on a room, so I said they could stay here months ago. We owe Mariele a huge favor. I can't kick them out."

"I get that." Plans shouldn't be upended because their whimsical mother decided *Hey, let's get married this weekend in another country.* "I can sleep on the couch."

Julia gestured toward the wicker love seat that looked less comfortable than sleeping on a pile of rocks. Surely Alex could meet her in the middle on this.

"Jules, stay at the hotel. To survive this week you need sleep, and it won't happen here. Not with me getting up before dawn for my tour groups and Santi coming in from the festival at all hours. They'll be gone in two or three days—you can have the room then."

The spare room.

Not her room. Not anymore.

Her big sister wasn't letting her stay in their childhood home. Cool. That didn't feel like doors slamming shut on her soul or anything.

She wouldn't show it, though. No, her customer-service smile took over, the one she deployed when guests asked for something outrageous, like if she could deliver a pedicure chair to their suite for girls'-night-out prep.

"No problem," she lied.

Eight

As they pulled into the hotel, Carson tapped his knees.

The drive back had been ticking-time-bomb tense. His one-sided attempts at small talk went nowhere. He got the sense if he turned on the radio, Julia'd snap off his finger. *This* was the Julia who kept him on task when he was working on his essays for English, the one he was low-key afraid of, and…the one he'd been hot for.

She cut the engine, then wordlessly slid from the minivan. He hustled to reach her bags first. "Can I get those for you?"

"I'm capable," she said.

"Never said you weren't, but I like to help."

"Don't need it." She stomped toward the hotel, sparks practically flying from her enormous suitcase's wheels.

The plate-glass doors swooped open, blasting them with that sweet air-conditioned chill. Julia marched toward the front desk. She obviously wanted nothing to do with him, but he didn't trust her to call him if this didn't work out. She'd probably try something ridiculous like sleeping in the lobby. He opted to lurk near the front desk.

"May I help you, miss?" the clerk asked.

"I'd like a room, please."

She sucked her teeth. "That may be a challenge. There's a music festival in town, and I believe we're full. Please wait as I check."

As the clerk typed, Julia rubbed the diamond tattoo inside her forearm. "Anything?"

He kept meaning to ask about those. Visible tattoos didn't match her vibe. She wanted to work at a five-star resort and was so worried about other people's opinions, he was surprised at her blatant ink.

"I'm searching," the clerk said.

The solution was obvious. "Julia, why don't you—"

"Ah, here we go," the clerk said. "We won't have availability for three days. However, our sister hotel—the Joys Costera—has a beachfront villa available."

The rubbing stopped. "How much is that?"

"That'll be fifteen hundred dollars US per night, plus room fees and taxes."

"Oh. Are you *sure* there's nothing else? I'll take anything. Broom closet? Bunkbed in a youth hostel? Haunted room?"

"I'm sorry, ma'am, I don't have access to all hotels in Azul Caye." She gestured toward the lobby. "You're welcome to use our lounge area to search for alternative accommodations."

Julia nodded. "Yes, thanks. I'll do that."

She made no sense. The clerk said there was a vacancy. Why didn't she— Whoops, she was already gone. Carson followed and sat next to her on the couch.

"Why didn't you take the villa? My dad'll pick up the tab."

"I hate spending money without good reason." Her tablet lit up her face as she scanned lodging options.

Annoyance fizzed through him. Sometimes she was her own worst enemy. That had been true in high school, too. Like she believed the hardest, most difficult solution was the right one, even though something easy was staring her in the face.

"Not having a bed seems like a good reason."

"You heard your dad. Whatever we don't spend is our bonus. It might not mean much for you, but I could use the money."

"You're stubborn, aren't you?" It'd be infuriating if it wasn't kinda sexy.

"I prefer *determined*. It's fine. I'll sneak into a beach cabana. The weather's lovely."

Yep, stubborn. Come hell or high water, she was taking his spare bed. The lone hitch was he'd need to squelch his urge to flirt with her. He could do that.

Probably.

"Do you smoke?" he asked.

"No." She poked dates into a hotel search engine. The search came up empty.

"Do you snore?"

"No." She wrinkled her brow. "At least, I don't think so."

"Then take the other bed in my room."

She laughed. In his face.

"Stay with *you*?" She shook her head and laughed more. "No."

"Julia, the hotel won't allow vagrants to sleep in their cabanas."

"I'm not a vagrant. I'm a pre-guest."

"That's not a thing." He ran his hand through his hair. "If you're worried, I don't snore."

"*That* is not what I'm worried about."

"Then what?"

"You're so very..." She circled her palm at him. *"Carson."*

She said that like it was an adjective. "What does that mean?"

"You, um, you fill a room. You're impossible to ignore. If you're not talking, you're throwing a ball...or flirting." She twisted her ponytail and avoided his gaze. "I like to rest at the end of the day."

She was a hundred percent correct, but he could dial that down. Like right now, every cell in his body was screaming at him to sit next to her, lean close, and ask her if she was sure the flirting bothered her *that* much. He'd seen how she'd looked at him in the room earlier. But because he was a master of restraint, he stayed put.

"I get that, but my dad would be pissed if I didn't look out for family. I promise I'll chill and give you headspace."

She returned to angrily poking at her tablet. "You can't. You're such an…an extrovert."

He grinned. Couldn't help it. "You say that like it's a dirty word."

"It isn't. The world needs extroverts. I, however, need to quietly recharge, and I'd bet a dollar you start asking philosophical life-and-death questions at midnight."

Guilty. Did she ever get tired of being right?

"Are you hungry?" he asked. "You seem cranky."

"Gasp." She narrowed her deep brown gaze at him. "Are you wondering if I'm on my period, too? This situation is legitimately annoying."

He tried not to laugh that she'd said *gasp*. "No, I—"

"Listen, Carson Miller." She shoved her tablet into her bag. "I'll take your extra bed because I don't have a choice. Thank you. But I'd like to work right now, so if you could give me a key and leave me be, I'd appreciate it."

"Duly noted. Here." He fumbled in his shorts pocket for the keys, then handed her the extra. "The number is—"

"612. I remember. We were there three hours ago."

Prickly. And, he still contended, hungry. Not that he'd say that out loud. He'd give her the space she wanted and use the time to find food.

"While you settle in," he said, "I'll do a little shoe-leather research."

As he pivoted away, he caught her murmuring, "Shoe leather?"

Nine

As Julia plotted their logistics for tomorrow and outlined the key points she'd cover in her maid-of-honor speech, she tracked Carson. He circulated through the lobby, chatting with the staff posted at various service points. Now he was at the concierge's desk.

What was he up to?

Never mind. She shook her head and returned her focus to her tablet. She had plenty of tasks to accomplish. Paying undue attention to Carson Miller was not one of them.

Five minutes later, he was still at the desk. The attractive concierge wore impeccably tailored clothing, waves of dark hair caught in a conservative low ponytail, and a friendly—but not flirty—smile. The poor woman was trying to do her job, and Carson was keeping her from it.

Julia should intervene. Not because she wanted to interrupt any bantering that might be happening. Not at all. She merely wanted to do a fellow hospitality worker a favor.

An unnecessary favor, actually, since he was headed back here, all smiles and loose-limbed enthusiasm. His predictable optimism both irritated her and made her laugh. This was actually golden-retriever energy, not frat bro.

"I have good news." He dropped onto the couch next to her.

Hope bloomed in her chest as she tidied her jostled notebooks. "You got another room?"

He knit his brows. "I thought we'd settled that. If you want, though, I'll go ask again."

"No. Tell me the good news." She caught his arm, then yanked her hand away like he'd shocked her. His thick muscle under her grip intrigued this future stepsister more than it should've.

"The hotel has a preferred vendor list for florists, photographers, DJs...basically everything we need for a wedding. The concierge emailed it to us."

Oh. He hadn't been flirting with her. Though their conversation might've been both an info mission *and* a flirtation. She had firsthand experience with his adept conversational skills. Not that his intentions toward the concierge were her business.

Get a fucking grip, Julia Stone.

"That's good. We have those covered, but alternatives are useful."

"Are you done for tonight?" Carson leaned closer. "Because the concierge—"

Did he have to sit so close? "What's her name?"

"Gayonne. She said the reggae café next door is fun. She's headed there when her shift ends. Want to go?"

Third-wheeling Carson's meet-cute with the concierge and her Disney Princess–size brown eyes and neatly bound brown curls was her idea of hell.

"I'll pass, thanks." Julia rose, then shoved her tablet into her bag, which she let slide to the crook of her arm. As she rolled toward the elevators, she called behind her, "Don't stay out too late. We've got an early morning."

"Sir, yes, sir," he boomed from the couch.

He didn't follow.

She wouldn't let that bother her. Not while she was on the

elevator, not when she unpacked her clothes and sprayed them with wrinkle release or when she showered in piping-hot water strong enough to scrub travel grime from her skin. She was still definitely not bothered when, an hour later, she sat cross-legged in an old concert T-shirt, loose PJ pants, and a towel wrapped around her head with her tablet in her lap. Still alone.

Noise from the hallway snagged her attention from the concierge's vendor list.

Earlier, the room next door had been blasting a blend of punta and Caribbean soul music. She enjoyed it, but wow, the walls in this hotel were thin. Unlike their future resort. Nope. At Stone Adventures & Resort, people could expect privacy, like they were in a bubble, and free to do whatever they wanted—parties, meetings, wall-shaking orgasmic sex—without worrying about unintentional spies.

The door's lock clunked, and the door slowly swung open.

"Hello?" she called.

Carson's ear-to-ear grin when he locked eyes with her made Julia's heart skip a beat. Most people emerged from night clubs a sweaty mess, but he glowed, glistened, effervesced.

Even more enviable? He was carrying a paper sack with telltale oil spots.

"I was hoping you'd be up," he said. "Guess what?"

There went that darn heart skippage again. The sleep deprivation and stress was fucking with her judgment. She yanked the towel from her head and tossed her tablet aside. "What?"

"I booked a reggae band for the reception." He handed the paper bag to her. "Here. You didn't eat much at dinner, and Gayonne said this was the best sandwich on the island. You eat chicken, right?"

"I eat everything." Warm air puffed in her face as she uncurled the crinkling bag. Oh, bless him. He'd gotten fries, too. "*Why* did you hire a band for thirtyish people?"

He withdrew two Belikin beers from the mini fridge.

"Because it's a destination wedding."

She ignored his forearm's sexy sinews as he held both bottles in one hand and uncapped them with the bottle opener, then handed her one. The effortless move sent a shimmer through her. Competency, attentiveness, and generosity was a surprisingly hot combination.

The beer bottle was perfectly frigid. "And?"

Carson parked his ass against the bureau. "The point of a destination wedding is to experience a different place and culture. Otherwise, why not host it in a hotel ballroom in Culver City?"

His frustratingly correct opinion would have chapped her ass *if* she weren't scarfing the world's most perfect chicken sandwich.

"Okay, fine, I agree. But can you check in with me before making big decisions? I'll want to talk before you book a clown or a petting zoo."

He pointed his beer at her. "You have my solemn vow that I'll never book a petting zoo. Goats scare me with their weird rectangle pupils. Aliens."

"Does that mean clowns are on the table?" The frothy beer bubbles scrubbed her throat, the perfect complement to the sandwich's mild spicy heat.

He lifted a shoulder. "Never say *never*."

"I'm saying *never* right now. Never book a clown for our parents' wedding."

"Feeling better?" His lips kicked up. "You were quiet after dinner."

Julia was too tired to deny it or be embarrassed.

"Sorry." She popped the last morsel into her mouth. After chewing, she said, "I know better than to splash my bad moods on other people."

"You didn't splash. In fact, I'd say you kept it tightly corked up. Which, in my experience, leads to explosions at inappropriate times. What's the deal with your sister? Friend? Foe? Frenemy?"

"There is no deal." She flipped her palms to the ceiling. "*That's* the problem. We *used* to be close, which meant our snarky opinions about each other's lives were well-informed and valid. But I don't know enough to have an opinion these days."

He lifted a shoulder. "You seemed pretty close to me. The way you're describing it sounds like you treat each other like adults now."

Julia sighed. "I wish. She still sees me as a kid who gets whipped up by gossip and doesn't do her chores."

Carson was weirdly easy to talk to. He projected a nonjudgmental air, like he understood any less-than-perfect thoughts or feelings she burped out weren't who she was at her core. When did he start to understand her so well? And why wasn't that making her lose her shit?

Speaking of being nonjudgmental…

"Should I clear out?" she asked.

One day, Julia's questions would cause him whiplash.

The last thing Carson wanted on God's green earth was for Julia Stone to leave. She gave good conversation, but also? Her tissue-thin shirt did nothing to hide her perky nipples. Wonder what color they were? Cherry, like her favorite lip gloss? Coral pink, like one of the dresses she'd hung up while he was gone? Or more of a rose, something that matched her cheeks when he caught her staring at his chest. Any other woman and he'd be shooting his shot, angling for a way to peel that Blondie T-shirt from her and find out.

Not his dad's wife's daughter, though.

"Clear out?" He wrinkled his forehead. "Why?"

She lifted a shoulder. "You chatted up the concierge and then met her at the bar, so… I'm not Sherlock Holmes or anything, but I can read signals."

Julia was terrible at reading signals. Because when she fiddled with her T-shirt's hem and tugged the material tighter against her breasts, he nearly groaned. In a perfect world, he'd show her exactly how much he didn't want her to leave this room.

Impossible. *That* was so far off the table, it was on the moon.

Julia would be his stepsister. Fuck this up, and he'd fuck up their blended family and his relationship with Dad.

"She's an informed source, Sherlock, not a vacation hookup."

"Oh, phew, okay, so you aren't about to kick me out. I'd understand." She knuckled her eye. "But I'm sleepy."

Affection washed over him. She was a perfect blend of sexy and cute. The few women he'd dated didn't admit they got tired or hungry or that they had any other basic human need. Might've been the fact that he'd met them in LA clubs and Las Vegas conferences, but they were sharks who didn't shed a tear when he ended things. Which had been mutually convenient, but he wasn't sure he wanted that for himself anymore.

"Your eight hours of sleep is safe," he said.

His, though, was shot to hell.

"Then I'll brush my teeth again."

As the bathroom door closed behind her, he popped open his suitcase. He traded his clothes for a fresh T-shirt and basketball shorts. Normally he slept shirtless and in boxers, but that didn't seem appropriate. Not when his dick would give his horny ass away. What *was* the etiquette for hosting your almost-stepsister, whom you'd fantasized about kissing since you were eighteen years old? Ah hell, the fantasies involved *way* more than kissing. Home runs.

Grand slams, actually.

He opened the dresser's top drawer to unload what he'd packed for this trip. Oh, *shit*. Julia had already filled this drawer with her bras and panties. Silky, satiny, lacy, sheer. Without touching them, he could imagine the textures, like phantoms on his fingertips.

Carson shut the drawer, then gripped the dresser's edge.

This was fine. They were two adults, splitting a room due to circumstances beyond their control. *He* hadn't planned a music festival or plunked a houseguest into her sister's home.

All the same, he was delighted the universe had worked this out.

This was his chance to prove to Julia he'd outgrown his high school persona. The man he was today was his authentic self, someone she might like and respect. Not the guy who froze her out because of his insecurities, which his therapist at Cal State helped him see were rooted in the fucked-up dynamic he'd had with his mother.

Ah, mommy issues. Always super sexy.

"About the concierge," Julia said.

He jumped. Jesus, she snuck around like a jewel thief in a heist movie.

"Oh, sorry." She laughed as she smoothed lotion along her arms. "Did I startle you?"

His heart knocked against his chest. "Yes, but it's fine."

As she sat on her bed, a coconut-and-pineapple scent wafted from her. Great. She smelled like piña coladas. And getting lost in the rain. She might've been into yoga and definitely had more than half a brain.

Wonder if she liked making love at midnight?

Stop that. Damn his dad's yacht-rock obsession.

"What about the concierge?" he asked.

"We should have a code word. In case one of us wants to, um…" She shifted her gaze back and forth. "Bring a guest back to the room."

"Julia Stone, are you carving time from your schedule for a hookup?"

She finished with the lotion, and God, he'd love to lick a trail up her pale arm, linger on her neck, then land on her cherry lips. Bet she tasted like a maraschino dipped in whipped cream.

With a sigh, she said. "In my experience, the hookups don't take much time."

"That's awful. I have so many follow-up questions." He dropped onto his bed. The lamps embedded into their headboards draped them in stark shadows.

"We're on vacation and might enjoy...company," she said. "We should be prepared."

Jealously clenched his gut.

"Don't be weird," she said. "You were all heart eyes at the concierge."

"You keep saying that and are *so* wrong, which makes me wonder if anyone's ever properly looked at *you*."

He gave her his best smolder.

She snapped off her light. "I know what heart eyes are, buster."

Buster? Where did she learn to talk like this?

She flipped back the covers and slid between them. "My suggestion is practical. It totally kills the mood when you have to be Captain Obvious." She dropped her voice an octave. *"Hey, Julia, this person and I want to boink. Can I have the room?"*

She was ridiculous.

"Is that supposed to be me? I promise I'd figure out a more artful way of describing the circumstances. I'd never involve the word 'boink.'"

"Good for you. I still recommend a code word, something you can casually work into conversation. Celebrities worked best for me and my roommates because you can always reference a movie or a concert. How about Beyoncé?"

"Veto. I don't casually discuss Beyoncé. How about Danny DeVito?"

Her body quaked with laughter. "Veto, for the same reason. I adore him, but in a lusty moment, do you want to invoke Danny DeVito?"

No, but if *she* were enjoying a lusty moment with a vacation hookup, he'd want to splash as much mental ice water on that situation as possible.

She snapped her fingers. "How about Paramore? It works on two levels—the band and the synonym for *lover*. Efficient."

"Paramore it is." He made sure his phone was plugged in, then snapped off his light. "Are you really okay? You seemed upset earlier."

She shuffled in her sheets for a moment, then, finally...

"I was, but I'm better now. I was mostly upset that Alex is getting married." She sighed. "Wait, that didn't come out right. I'm thrilled for her, but I had no idea she and Bo were ready to take the plunge. Being out of the loop hurt my feelings."

They sure seemed like an incredibly happy couple. "How long have they been together?"

"Only six months. It's not like they knew each other their whole lives and light bulbs suddenly popped on, so it's fast."

He felt *that* one in his gut. "Yeah?"

"Yeah. She was his tour guide for an insane trip that went sideways six different ways. They hated each other, which was a cover for wild attraction, and then they boinked, and then they fought again. But he saved some artifacts from the auction block, which is Alex's catnip, and chased *her* across the country to give them to her. The showy grand gesture won her over."

"Not your style, I take it?" The dark made it easier to ask questions. It hid his desperation to learn everything about what appealed to Julia Stone.

"Grand gestures are great for fiction, but they aren't realistic. Me, I prefer lots of smaller gestures. Consistency, reliability, awareness... Swoon with a capital *S*. I'd rather someone make my coffee for me every day, pick up my favorite sweet at the bakery, make reservations at my favorite restaurant... Things like that are *my* catnip."

Holy shit.

Most people didn't hand you an instruction manual like that.

"From where I sit, you and your sister seem pretty close."

"Not the way we used to be, and this space between us bums me out."

Despite the confessional feeling the darkness loaned the room, she was downplaying her hurt. Why? Because she didn't trust him enough to be vulnerable? He couldn't blame her, but he'd keep building that bridge.

He propped his head on his fist. "Can I ask you one more question?"

"You just did." Rumpling indicated she'd snuggled into the bed's downy softness.

He imagined her smooth skin under the blankets, sneaking his hand under her T-shirt…

"Oh my God, ask already so I can go to sleep."

Right. The question. "How many times did you Beyoncé your roommates?"

Through a yawn, she said, "Five, maybe six times."

He wished he hadn't asked, because now he couldn't stop picturing Julia in the throes of passion. As he tried—and failed—to squash those images, Julia's breathing deepened and steadied. In the dark, he smiled. She made these soft little contented sighs as she dropped off to sleep. If only she could be this unguarded in her waking life. Maybe he could help with that, too.

Also, she was a liar.

Because she definitely snored.

Ten

That beer last night had been a mistake, because Julia desperately needed to pee. She twisted toward Carson's bed. *Bet he's an annoyingly chipper person who wakes before dawn to seize the day.*

Oh good. Still asleep.

She could let her gaze linger on him, which she hadn't sufficiently done since he crashed back into her life four days ago. His bare-chested greeting at the pool house was a special struggle to start things off, but, like a goddamn professional, she'd avoided the linger.

Mere feet away, Carson slept on his back. Puffs of air rhythmically escaped his full lips, like a metronome. She was fascinated by the ways he'd changed. Firmer jaw line and longer, wavier dark hair that suited him. In high school he'd kept it short, a classic jock cut. Sometime in the night, he'd thrown off the comforter and shoved the sheet down to his hips. She was *sure* he'd gone to bed in a T-shirt.

Guess he ran hot while he slept and had taken it off?

She was glad he had. The morning sun shining through the sheer curtains loaned his exposed pecs and abs a golden glow. Stray blond hair glistened within the soft down of his body, especially his chest. He'd filled out there, and through his shoulders. What else had filled out? She could take a peek.

No, that was bad. She shouldn't. Wouldn't, because that'd violate all sense of—

Gasp.

He had a legit tent situation. An impressive one at that.

On a deep breath, his eyes fluttered open, and he twisted toward her.

"Morning."

Oh boy, his gravelly morning voice was sexy.

Oh man, his erection was now pointing directly at her.

"Morning," she trilled, then slithered from bed and dashed toward the bathroom, phone in hand. She didn't want to be there when he discovered his morning wood.

Morning timber, more like it.

As she scrubbed her teeth and face, the image of a sleeping Carson superimposed itself over everything. The sink's bowl—his square-jawed face. The shower curtain—his broad chest. Her reflection—giant erection.

Stop that. She pressed her palms against her closed eyes, and there he was again. She *knew* it was wrong to stare at a person while they slept, so she got what she deserved.

Pure, unwelcome, unadulterated horniness.

How could a man who irritated her *also* turn her on, especially with their history? When someone wronged her, no matter how hot they were, she dried up. Total turn-off, instant villain. Life was too short to pine for red flags.

With Carson however, her body spotted green flags on green flags on green flags.

Yeah, well, her body should hush.

Staring into the mirror, Julia twisted her hair into a high ponytail, the only acceptable hairstyle for running errands in Belize during the rainy season. Then she picked up her phone—7:45 a.m.? This was the latest she'd slept since... She couldn't remember. After swiping on lip gloss, subtle eyeshadow, and enough mascara to make her blond lashes visible, she opened the Positively Productive app.

She couldn't believe Carson had a hand in developing this tool. It was like he took all the organizational methods and project mapping she'd shared during their tutoring sessions and turned it into a digital version, only better. After double-checking the tasks that were on tap for today, she swiped to the daily affirmation.

She locked gazes with herself in the mirror. "Amazing opportunities exist for me. I am open to miracles in my life."

Miracles like Carson half-naked on the other side of the bathroom door.

Wait, was that a miracle? Or a curse?

Quietly, she opened the door and... Oh. He was sleeping again.

Good. She didn't need an audience as she selected a coral maxi dress for today's itinerary. She eased open the dresser's top drawer and selected a matching blush-pink bra and panties. Lingerie was her secret vice, a hidden confidence booster.

Back in the bathroom, she changed.

There. That was the version of herself she preferred. Styled, pressed, and a light daytime face. As she folded her T-shirt and PJ pants, a knock on the door startled her.

"Hungry?" Carson asked. "I ordered room service."

"Yeah, be right out." Her stomach cheered as she exited the bathroom and the aromas of bacon and her beloved Belizean coffee greeted her. "Impressive kitchen turnaround. You placed the order, what, ten minutes ago?"

"Nope." Carson turned from the tray on the small table in the corner.

Wow. This intimate peek of his sleepy eyes and stubble thrilled her.

"I ordered breakfast last night before I came upstairs. Figured you'd want to get a jump on today. It's light fare so we don't fill up before we sample the tasting menu. Take your pick, and I'll eat whatever's left after I shower."

It was nice not to be the default person thinking ahead.

"Thanks." She poured rich, black coffee from the French press, then added cream and sugar. One sip and she was in heaven.

"Welcome." Carson withdrew clothes from his suitcase. "Oh, and Julia? You're the most focused, detail-oriented person I've ever met, so you don't need miracles. If anything goes sideways, though, don't worry. I've got you."

Carson closed the bathroom door.

He'd *heard* her? Embarrassing. Thank goodness today's affirmation was benign. The other day she'd cooed, *I accept myself the way I am. I am gorgeous and sexy. I become more attractive every single day.*

She might've fainted if he heard her say that.

And she'd believe his *I've got you* claim when she saw it. The only person to truly look out for her, no matter what, was Dad. But he'd been three thousand miles away for half her life, and there was only so much he could do from Belize.

As for Mom... Julia understood why she wasn't available for the day-to-day stuff. LA was expensive. With a full-time job and a personal-shopper gig on the side, Mom had focused most of her energy on earning a living. Well, and dating. But that meant Julia couldn't count on anyone but herself to pack lunches, book dental appointments, or fill out FAFSA forms.

She'd been her own safety net. She didn't wait for miracles—she performed them.

After sipping her coffee, she cut into the expertly made egg-white omelet. She could murder a bacon, egg, and cheese–stuffed fry jack, but Carson was right. Showing up full to a menu tasting meant she wouldn't properly judge the flavors.

Ugh, she'd actually thought the words *Carson was right*.

Over the past few days, he'd been kind, helpful, and thoughtful. The core of him was the same confident guy dripping with charisma. But maybe…

She tilted her head.

Maybe she could trust him.

Carson tucked his nose under the neck of his T-shirt. "This is…not ideal."

He and Julia stood on the exterior esplanade with Holly, Azul Caye Resort's event coordinator. The inside space was great—dance floor, lazily spinning ceiling fans, and a view of the beach. On the website, the ocean's curling waves were crystal blue. Today, however, seaweed tinted the ocean brown and it smelled like a boiling sewage tank.

"Ugh, I can taste it." Julia held her nose. "Has there been a lot of sargassum this season?"

Holly shook her head. "This is unusual. It normally washes ashore as the water warms in the spring. We're working on it, as you can see. It will be addressed before the wedding."

Dozens of workers with rakes and pitchforks, wheelbarrows, and ATVs, stood ankle-deep in wet mounds of seaweed to comb it from the water.

"In three days? There's no way." With her fingers still pinching her nose, Julia sounded like she had a cold. "We have to move it indoors."

Her suggestion was the safe choice, but they shouldn't give up so fast.

"They have their heart set on a beach wedding," Carson pushed back.

"Not when it smells like that." She let go of her nose to gesture toward the beach and immediately winced. "We could have the ceremony at another location."

"I understand your concern," Holly said. "But you'll find

the other resorts are fully booked due to the festival, though I'm happy to help you investigate options."

"This freaking festival," Julia muttered under her breath. "What if more sargassum washes ashore? We can't risk everything happening in this stinkfest. It's better to call it now so we can plan the rest better. They'll get over it."

Carson shifted his weight. She was right, but their parents had stressed that they wanted to exchange vows in the open air, with the sand and the ocean serving as their church. Come hell or sargassum-infested high water, he'd do everything he could to fulfill his father's wishes.

How could he not at least try?

After the accident, Dad had helped him pick up the pieces of his life. Had never lectured him or made him feel like garbage while they met with lawyers. Unlike Mom, who'd basically disappeared, Dad stood with him as he grieved the future he'd thought he'd have. And when he'd accepted he'd never be Carson Miller, MLB All-Star, Dad had encouraged him to go to Cal State Fullerton anyway, take business classes, and stop beating himself up.

"Aren't you supposed to be open to miracles?" he asked.

"Yes, but I'm a realist who can't take this smell anymore." Julia delved back into the hotel's cool shelter. "You know I'm right about this, Carson."

He did, but he couldn't squelch his optimism that the ocean would cooperate.

"Can we make a game-time decision?" he asked Holly. "If more sargassum washes ashore, can we move everything indoors?"

"Absolutely." She led them toward the hotel's restaurant. "The menu is next. Three guests have a gluten intolerance, and we have a preference for seafood, correct?"

"Yes," Julia said. "Could you give us coffee beans?"

That was an odd request.

"Of course, miss." Holly paused at the maître d's stand. "James, these are the organizers for this weekend's wedding. Can you show them to table twelve?"

James stepped out from behind the stand. "This way. Your timing is fortunate. It promises to be a lovely weekend."

"Unless the sargassum returns," Julia said.

Despite his plea for a game-time decision, Carson's unhappy insides agreed.

He didn't have the stomach for rot, which he'd discovered when Phi Gamma Titan's basement freezer shorted out. He'd run downstairs to grab burgers and dogs for their Sizzle into Spring cookout, opened the warm freezer, and…

Yeah. He'd never been the same.

James led them to a table near the kitchen's double doors. "You'll find the tasting list on the table. Take notes as you sample, and enjoy!"

Carson took the seat across from Julia. "Not enough coffee this morning?"

"What?" She mindlessly circled her thumb around the diamond tattoo inked on her inner forearm. He hadn't found a way to ask about the diamond, ruby, and sapphire ink without seeming nosy. Or why she touched the diamond so frequently.

"The coffee beans. Chomping raw caffeine is impressive."

She relaxed her face as she laughed. "I'm not eating them. The beans' aroma clears the palate. I'm desperate. It's like seaweed crawled up my nose and died there."

"Appetizing." Carson filled their glasses from the table's carafe of water. "But same."

Julia sipped. "Ugh, the smell is haunting me. It's tainted everything."

The queasiness rolled his stomach again. "Can we stop talking about it?"

"Here we are." Holly laid a platter on the table.

Amuse-bouche-sized portions of fancy food that looked more

like art than appetizer covered its surface. Bright pinks, yellows, oranges, and greens reminded him of Belize's landscape as they'd driven through winding roads to the hotel yesterday.

Too bad his knotted gut wouldn't cooperate.

Holly slid a ramekin of coffee beans from the tray to Julia. "And there you are, miss."

Julia huffed the coffee beans. "Oh, *so* much better. Here. You'll thank me."

She thrust the ramekin at him.

It was worth a shot. He inhaled the robust aroma like he was meditating, and... Huh. All he smelled was coffee. Definitely better than rotting seaweed. Hopefully he'd never encounter another stench situation like this, but that was a handy trick he'd file away for the future.

"Thanks, Holly." Julia circled her gaze among the bites of food. "What do we have?"

"These are our starter options." Holly gestured toward the platter. "We're known for our catch-of-the-day ceviche, which comprises Belizean-style tiger's milk, coconut, cilantro, and cherry tomatoes and is served with corn tortilla chips. Today's catch is amberjack. Of note—we locally source our ingredients to support the Azul Caye economy."

"Love." Julia noted that on her sheet.

Should he be taking notes? Probably. She had a fetish for them.

Carson scratched *amberjack* onto his paper.

Holly hovered her hand over the next option. "Next, breaded Azul shrimps, accompanied by fried yucca, and sweet ginger-chili sauce. Finally, lobster carpaccio, which is finely sliced Caribbean lobster tail marinated in passion fruit, lemongrass, and ginger sauce, served with radish-and-sprouts salad, and complemented with Garifuna yucca bread. Any questions?"

He and Julia both shook their heads.

The descriptions perked up his appetite. Julia's, too, apparently. She licked her glossy lips, and the tiny gesture sent a jolt to his cock. A woman who savored food was unspeakably hot.

Holly backed away from the table. "Then I'll leave you to taste."

"Let's start with the ceviche." Julia shoveled the vibrant concoction onto a tortilla chip, then popped it into her mouth. "That's *good*. Try it."

"What's tiger's milk?" he asked as he scooped. "Milking a tiger sounds dangerous."

Julia snorted. "It's a marinade—lime juice, onions, salt and pepper, chilies, and fish juices. Supposed to be an energy booster and aphrodisiac that makes you feel like a tiger."

Carson did *not* need any help in that department.

He popped the chip into his mouth. Whoa, she was right. The rich, buttery flavor of the diced fish contrasted with the bright citrus, and the chilies kicked in heat. Delicious.

"Definitely a contender." He reached for a shrimp.

"Not yet." Julia tapped his hand to stop him, which shot another electric current straight below his belt. "Write notes about what you liked. We've got a dozen more things to taste. It'll get muddled if you don't have notes to jog your memory."

"Fine." He jotted what he liked. *Julia is bossy.* "Now can we try the shrimp?"

"Be my guest." She helped herself to one.

They both chewed thoughtfully, then swallowed.

As he said, "Meh," she said, "That's fantastic."

"Boo," he said. "You can get shrimp like that at home. We want local flavor, don't we?"

"This *is* local flavor. They caught these shrimp here. And did you boo me?"

"Yes," he said through a grin. "Write your review, and we'll argue later."

He couldn't wait to huddle with her, knee-to-knee, over a drink in the hotel bar and debate the menu options. Or, better yet, in their room, they'd park themselves on her bed, and he'd lobby for the ceviche because he'd give anything to watch her eat another bite of it. Maybe they'd playfully nudge each other, and then...

He'd better start thinking very unsexy thoughts or he'd never get up from this table.

"Does Michelle like seafood?" *There.* Talking about her mother was unsexy. He speared a forkful of razor-thin lobster carpaccio and braced it against a toast point. "My dad loves it."

"Oh, that explains why Mom insisted on seafood." She slipped her own bite of lobster into her mouth.

At which he was staring.

Say something. "Explains what?"

"As soon as my mom sleeps with a guy, *boom*, she likes whatever he likes. It's like a sexually transmitted palate."

He coughed. "Didn't need that image."

"Oh, sorry. Were you unaware our parents were sleeping together?"

Ballbuster. "I choose not to think about. Like the plight of the bees or the garbage island out there in the Pacific."

"Are you comparing older people having sex to environmental disasters?" She helped herself to more ceviche. "Because it's healthy and expected since they're sexagenarians. Get it?"

He groaned as he laughed. "Puns are terrible, just awful. Fine, it's healthy but still not something I want to think about."

"I hope I have an active sex life when I'm their age. It'd make up for the drought I've been in." She hid her mouth with her napkin. "Forget I said that. It must be the tiger's milk."

Of all the unjust things in this world, Julia Stone talking to him about sex while he could do nothing about it topped his list.

"Forgotten," he said with a strained voice.

"Ready to sample the mains?" Holly asked.

Twenty minutes later, they'd worked through sweet-corn

conch kissed by lime juice, rich prawn-and-chorizo risotto, pepper jelly–glazed snapper that was more like honey than heat, and pork tenderloin marinated in Belikin and black recado powder.

For that last one? The consistency was fall-apart perfect.

Belize cuisine was fucking fantastic. At home, he'd never had these foods in these combinations or with these seasonings. Everything was a more confident version of itself.

Much like Julia, actually. From the second they'd landed, she was more relaxed than she was in LA. Disappointed in her sister, yes, but at least she was showing it. In California she'd been all walls. This place was good for her, which made him like it even more.

Throughout the tasting, Julia took a bite, considered it, then jotted notes in her neat cursive. He loved that she took their parents' wedding seriously, that she was determined not to leave anything to chance.

Julia fiddled with her pencil as she reviewed her notes.

"You have the last bite," he said. "Which are the front-runners for you?"

"I'm leaning toward the snapper and the pork." As she reached for the last of the stew, he was rewarded with a glimpse of her pretty pink bra. "Loved the risotto, but if we do shrimp as an appetizer, I don't want to repeat it with the main."

"I'm good with that." Carson circled numbers on his sheet. "We timed this right. This was basically lunch."

"I could've used a few more bites." Julia pinched shreds of fried banana blossom from the nest under the conch fritters, then popped it into her mouth. "Mom'll love this because it's capital-*F* fancy, but my tastes run simpler. Like the chicken sandwich you brought me last night."

"We can't go wrong, no matter what we choose. Everything's so tasty. Why aren't there Belizean restaurants in the US?"

"There are. Little Belize is in south LA." She sipped her

water. "The restaurants there are more Maya and Kriol grub. Panades, boil cake, fry jacks, not this cordon bleu version. Which is delicious but not exactly authentic."

"Can we eat something like that for dinner?" he asked.

She raised her eyebrow. "Didn't figure you for the street-meat type."

"Let's not make assumptions." He clinked his water with hers. "Cakes are up next."

"That's all you. I don't like cake."

"You're a monster."

She laughed, then circled her gaze around the restaurant. "Ugh, the seating chart. That'll be a nightmare. We should put our parents at a sweetheart table so I don't need to sit with Mom."

"What's so bad about her?"

From what he could tell, Michelle was high energy. A little self-centered, but actively interested in her daughters. Compared to his mother, she was a saint.

"That question should be paired with wine." Julia propped her chin on her fist.

His heart thumped his ribs harder than a fastball into a catcher's mitt. She'd done that during their tutoring sessions. Usually when he was supposed to be revising something and she was absorbed in her homework. Somehow she never figured out he was too busy catching glimpses of her to get anything done.

"Stop dodging," he said. "If she's my stepmother, I want the inside scoop."

"Forget it." She wiped the air between them. "She's fine. We're all fine. Let's eat cake."

"Still dodging."

Julia twisted her lips. "It'll sound petty."

"I love petty."

"She didn't worry enough about us, okay? Like, she didn't

take us school-supply shopping or ask us for our friends' last names. She treated Alex like a bestie, and I... I was more like an exotic pet that took care of itself."

Her thumb cleared a line through her water glass's condensation.

After a few beats, she straightened her shoulders. "Yuck. Didn't mean to be a whiny downer. My childhood shaped me into the resilient, capable person you see before you today."

"Which I admire about you." *Please* let her hear his sincerity.

She waved him off. "No."

"No what?" He leaned back in his chair.

"Flirting."

He'd have laughed if her jaw wasn't clenched tight enough to make his face hurt. Christ, if she thought complimenting her was flirting, she had another think coming. And if she thought that was all the game he had...well, that was plain embarrassing.

"That wasn't flirting. You'll know when I'm flirting."

She cocked her head. "I will?"

Taking it back would be a chicken move.

But now was not the time for flirting. She'd shared something personal, so he'd return the favor and let the flirting happen another time.

"About your childhood...if it's any consolation, I had the opposite problem. My parents did everything for me, which fucked me up. It's why I leaned so hard on people for help. Becoming an adult is tough, but if you *also* need to learn basic shit like laundry, cooking, and paying bills, the learning curve is almost impossible."

She tilted her head. "I can see that. I appreciated figuring out how to be independent, even if that came later, but summers with Dad were great. He was an adulty adult with rules and curfews, but when I messed up, he helped me put everything back together again."

Julia Stone made mistakes? She was the most capable person he'd ever met.

He thumbed the divot in his chin. "I can't imagine you messing up."

As Julia lifted her water glass, the strap from her dress slid down her shoulder. He zeroed in on the spot. After a day at the beach, would she taste salty? Or sweet, like he'd imagined last night? No matter the flavor, he bet her skin was smoother than ice cream.

"I mess up. I'll neither confirm nor deny if there was a shoplifting incident when I was twelve." Julia casually returned the strap to her shoulder. "My dad waited up for me and Alex, but Mom went to bed early to get her beauty sleep, when she wasn't staying over at her latest boyfriend's place. They couldn't have been more different."

Carson's chest tightened with affection for her. That dynamic was his life, too. His dad asked him what was on his mind. His mom, however, had mostly talked to him about his future baseball career. Losing the parent who knew how to talk to you was rough.

There was a bright side, though.

"Well, the way they raised you—the end result is great. You're so accomplished."

Her laugh interrupted him. "Yeah, I'm killing it. No job, I share an apartment with two students, and I'm taking pity work from my mom."

It was unreal that she thought she was anything less than amazing.

"Hey." He playfully knocked his knee against hers to stop her spiral. "Have you ever thought maybe you're on the cusp of killing it?"

Her brown eyes were so beautiful. Warm with golden glittering flecks.

"Go on," she demanded.

"Being selective, building something takes time. Any given day feels like you've barely progressed an inch. One day, you'll make it to the mountaintop and you get to cruise downhill."

She blew out her lips. "Or another peak's in front of you."

"Even if that's true, celebrate making it up a mountain. What was your class rank when you graduated?"

She slid a palm against the back of her neck. "Third."

He knew she'd killed it in school.

"See how amazing you are? You were at the top of your program. Cheers to that." He clinked his water glass against hers. "I have zero doubts you'll find the right gig, so stop negging my future stepsister."

She drank, then held the cool glass to her cheek. After a heavy beat, she licked her full, pink lips and asked, "Do you consider me a stepsister?"

The earnestness in her gold-flecked eyes begged for the truth.

"I have to, Julia."

The atmosphere around them thickened. The ambient music, the occasional clatter from behind the kitchen doors, the low dining chatter... It all disappeared.

His whole focus was on Julia.

"Carson, we— Oh, cake."

A waiter laid a tray between them, shattering the moment. Dammit, dammit, dammit. What was she about to say?

"Here we have your cake options." Holly gestured to each flavor in the lineup. "Coconut pecan, tropical carrot, roasted banana, double chocolate, and vanilla with a lemon finish. Enjoy."

As soon as Holly left the table, Julia scooted her chair back. "Pick whatever your dad likes best and meet me outside when you're done. I'll check if the florist is open."

He started to push back, too. "Julia, wait—"

"No, I'm good." She flashed him a thumbs-up, then snagged her purse. "Please, stay and finish up here."

She didn't wait for an answer. Her orange dress lifted in the breeze as she sped away.

He sighed. She clearly didn't want his company, so he'd give her space.

Minutes later, after reviewing the selections with Holly, he headed toward the main lobby. Julia's bright dress contrasted with the bright blue sky outside the picture window.

"All set," he said as he approached her. "Is the florist open?"

She held up a finger and pointed to her phone. "That's fantastic. I'm *so* glad the best in Azul Caye happens to be available this weekend. I owe you one."

Carson tilted his head. Who was she talking to with a truckload of kiss-ass sweetness in her voice? He'd never heard her use that tone, so definitely not anyone in their families. Maybe a boss or a potential boss or—

"Okay, Roberto," she said with a smile. "Can't wait to see you! It's been *way* too long."

A jealous flare sizzled through his chest. Julia was talking to someone named Roberto who made her beam like sunshine and fidget with her sapphire stud earring. This was flirty Julia, and last night they'd been joking about torrid affairs on vacation.

At least *he'd* been joking.

He didn't like where this was going. Not one bit.

Eleven

After hanging up with Roberto, Julia uncorked her AirPods from her ears. The vacationers' low chatter in the lobby replaced the cozy calm of her photographer ex-boyfriend's deep voice. And there was Carson, who'd come after her.

Her attraction to him was an increasingly big fucking problem. Hence the call to Roberto.

She rummaged in her bag for the AirPod case to avoid meeting his striking green gaze. His big golden-retriever smile flipped her stomach. It shouldn't have, but for the past two days he'd said nice things that made her warm and tingly in places that hadn't tingled for a long, long time.

"All settled with Holly?" She looked up, and *whoa*.

Carson's golden-retriever smile was gone

"Yes. What's fantastic? And who's Roberto? Couldn't help but overhear."

He stood close enough that she caught a whiff of his cologne, something cool and crisp that evoked skinny-dipping at midnight. Argh. More stomach flippiness. She'd prefer food poisoning to this. At least food poisoning eventually passed.

"Roberto's a photographer friend. After the florist and favors, we'll head to his studio."

Carson held the door for her, and they stepped into the sunshine. The light ocean breeze should've been a relief from the dense heat, but ugh, it carried the sargassum smell with it. On their way to the parking lot, they passed a natural stone wall emblazoned with *Azul Caye Resort*. Over it rippled a gentle waterfall. Nothing compared to the real deal at Secret Sex Falls, but it was a nice decorative touch.

"Why not use the hotel's photographer?" Carson asked.

Because Julia had history with Roberto. History she could tap to satisfy her distracting horniness. The ego boost wouldn't hurt, either. Hookups with Roberto provided the same carefree bubbly boost champagne gave her...right before it made her sick.

For a brief window, though, she'd feel great.

"Roberto's really talented. I want our parents to have the best available options."

Options with whom she could also hook up.

Carson opened the driver's-side door for her. "You're the boss."

Damn straight she was.

She poked the Start button as he circled the van to his side. The breeze lifted his hair's dark waves. If possible, his profile, shaded with stubble, was hotter than his full portrait.

Julia blew a puff of air from her lips.

She needed to get this out of her system.

The car bounced a bit as he hopped in and buckled up. Jesus, sometimes she forgot how large he truly was. He might not have played baseball anymore, but Carson clearly didn't miss a gym day. This giant man-slab could probably pick her up and pin her against a wall without breaking a sweat, and then—

Get a grip, Julia.

"Where to first?" he asked.

"Everything's in the same neighborhood. We'll bop around to whichever is open. People here don't take schedules as seriously as they do in the States. Time is more of a suggestion than a social contract."

Great, so now she was babbling.

He chuckled. "That must give you heartburn."

"I deal." She lifted a shoulder. "It helps me let go a bit while I'm here. Reminds me that checklists and timely turndown service are not life-and-death."

Julia flicked on the radio. Reggae thumped through the speakers, periodically interrupted by the DJ bragging about the music festival. She tapped her fingers against the steering wheel.

He gestured toward her fidgety hands. "Should we go? You obviously love the music."

During the summers here, she'd loved going to all-ages shows, especially with Alex. The communal, ephemeral vibe was special. The scene was different in LA. A little more desperate, a lot less relaxed, so she skipped it there. Ithaca boasted a handful of live-music venues, but she'd been too immersed in grad school to make them a habit.

Now that she was back in Azul Caye, though…

"Maybe," she said.

The ride to the Fort Harold neighborhood was brief. Impossible parking, but that was standard for the city's center. The might-not-be-legal gap she squeezed into was next to one of their destinations. Luckily, the sign on the Mara's Flowers door was flipped to *Open*.

The sweet scent of fresh-cut flowers greeted them as Carson opened the door. Without air-conditioning, the potpourri was more funeral parlor than wedding.

"This one's all yours," Carson said. "I know squat about flowers."

As if who was in charge was up for debate.

"I'll be with you in a moment." The slight woman wrapping a bouquet behind the counter barely looked up.

It had been a few years, but that woman must be…

"XoJo?" Julia asked.

Short for Xiomara Junior, the nickname their summer crew

had given the daughter of Xiomara Gutierrez, owner of Mara's Flowers. It was natural that XoJo worked here. Seventy percent of Belize's businesses were family owned and operated, and most handed them down to the next generation. Like Alex had taken over Stone Adventures.

Julia clenched her jaw. Which she could help run if her sister let her.

"Jujubee? Oh my gosh, it *is* you." She bounded around the counter and caught Julia in a hug. "Alex didn't say you were coming to town."

"She probably didn't know. Our mom's getting surprise-married here this weekend."

"Another wedding?" Xio exclaimed. "Classic Michelle. And is this your boyfriend?"

"God no," Julia protested. "My future stepbrother, Carson Miller. Carson, this is Xio. She and I ran with the same crew when I spent my summers here."

Xio's curls bounced as she pumped Carson's hand. "Nice to meet you. How long are you both here?"

"Through the weekend," Julia said.

Then, back to reality, job-hunting, and upstate New York's chilly fall. Alone. Thrillsville.

Xio let go of Carson. "We should go dancing. Julia memorized the choreography to 'Oops!... I Did It Again' when we were kids. She's amazing."

He grinned. "This I've gotta see."

His attention was like a heat lamp.

"No, you do not. So, about the whole wedding thing?"

"Fine, fine, if you *must* conduct business." Xio popped her hand on her hip. "Short notice means limited options. What's your pleasure? Bouquets? Boutonnieres? Petals for flower girls? Table arrangements? Smaller bouquet for the bride to toss at the reception?"

"Yes, except for petals and the bouquet toss. Now that Alex

is engaged, I'll be the only single lady at the small reception. Mortifying."

"Alex is *engaged*? Stop it." Xio held up a hand. "I swear, eligible bachelors are snapped up faster than paletas melts in August."

She flicked her gaze toward Carson. A bolt of *back the hell off* flared in Julia's chest.

"He lives in LA, Xio."

"True," Carson said. "But I'm here for the week."

What the fuck? "And you will be *very* busy."

He held up his hands. "Sorry. She's the boss."

Julia grinned. Goddammit, she couldn't help it. She loved him calling her boss.

"Shame," Xio said. "What do we want? Bright multicolored tropical? Something with a black orchid to represent Belize?"

Julia sighed. "Roses, I'm afraid."

"Boooo." Her friend flashed a double thumbs-down. "Roses are basic."

"Agree, and if it were me traipsing down the aisle, I'd go with plumeria. But Mom loves roses. Four bouquets with a mix of colors."

"Symbolizing all the things," Xio said.

"Yep, because…" Julia imitated her mother's breathy enthusiasm. "Jim is her *everything*."

"For now." Xio caught herself. To Carson, she said, "Sorry. I'm sure your dad's great."

Ever the gentleman, Carson dismissed her concern. "He is, but don't feel bad. They'll prove everyone wrong."

"I bet you're right." She winked.

Jesus, women couldn't control themselves around Carson.

"What's plumeria?" he asked.

"There's some in the corner," Xio said. "I'll be back in a sec—I have a sample bouquet and boutonniere so you know what you're getting."

As she pushed through the swinging door to the back of the

shop, Carson ambled to the corner. He plucked up a pretty pink blossom from the bucket. "Is this plumeria?"

"Yep." Julia's phone buzzed against her hip. *Mom*.

"It looks like a star." He inhaled. "That's nice. Almost like citrus."

"Right? Hey, it's my mom. Can you handle this? Do whatever Xio recommends."

"Yeah, sure."

She shouted toward the back. "Catch you later, Xio!"

Xio would *definitely* text their old friend circle to let them know she was in town with her handsome almost-stepbrother. By tonight they'd be taking bets on whether she and Carson had hooked up. Not in a judgy way, in a small-town-entertainment way.

Her cheeks heated as she stepped out to the sidewalk. "Hi, Mom."

"How are you, sweetheart? Alex said you were depressed at dinner last night."

She pinched the bridge of her nose. "I wasn't depressed. I was…"

Surprised her sister was engaged, and bummed she was out of the loop. She couldn't say that, though, since Alex wanted to tell their mother herself. God, she hated being a secret-keeper.

Julia settled on "Jet-lagged."

"Really? Belize is only ahead by an hour."

"I was up late the night before." She yawned to prove her point. "Things are good here, but there's a slight issue at the beach you should—"

"Good, good, good." Her mother interrupted in the way that meant she was only half listening. "Don't be alarmed, Julia, but I have a slight scheduling update. The airline's changed our flight, so we'll be arriving the day of the rehearsal dinner."

Julia sucked in a breath. "That's cutting it so close."

"We'll do our best to get there earlier. Now, what's Alex's boyfriend like? He seems so nice when we video chat. What did you talk about? You can tell a lot about a man based on the way he talks about his family."

Once again, Mom prioritizing love-life discussions above all else.

"He talked about his mother and sister a bit. They seem close, even though he lives here now. And he cooked dinner."

She skipped over him making Dad's sweet-potato pone. The dessert had been Mom's favorite as well. Julia touched her fingertips to the diamond tattoo, the one that symbolized Dad and Mom. Alex was the ruby, and she was the sapphire.

"Better him than Alex. Are you and Carson getting along?"

Speak of the devil. He emerged from Xio's shop and searched the street for her. When he found her, his smile made her stomach do that inconvenient flippy thing again.

"Fine. We're on our way to pick out favors, so I should go."

"Wait, one more thing. I'd like to surprise Jim with something special after the rehearsal dinner. Can you pick up sexy lingerie for me? You have such an eye for those things."

Hell, no. This was the Rubicon.

"Mom, ew. I will *not* be doing that."

"Please? Jim might see anything I pack."

"Bye, Mom." *Shiver.*

She'd teased Carson about their parents having sex, but purchasing sexy lingerie for Mom might ruin her soul. She dropped her sunglasses from the top of her head to the tip of her nose.

"All set?" she asked Carson.

"Yep. Flowers will arrive at ten on the big day." He rocked on his heels. "Favors are next, right?"

"Yes." Her gold sandals slapped against the sidewalk as they made their way toward the chocolate shop. "Wait until you try Belize chocolate. It's life-altering."

As a kid, Azul Caye Chocolate Company's turquoise door was her destination of choice when she'd brought home a good report card. The last time she'd been here with Dad was when she'd been accepted to grad school. That was just before he'd been diagnosed and the awful six months that came afterward. She'd been avoiding this shop, this city, this whole country since.

There you go, Julesy-girl.

Her breath hitched. Dad's voice sounded clear, like he was standing next to her.

Could she do this? Carson opened the turquoise door for her, and the shop bell's chirpy tinkle snapped her into the present. With her fingers touching her diamond tattoo she decided yes, in fact, she could. Dad would want her to.

Inside the air-conditioned shop, a familiar swirl of sugar, butter, and cacao greeted them. Brightly colored treats filled jars lining the display tops. Inside the displays, all her chocolate-covered favorites were still here: sea salt caramels, raspberry jellies, haystacks, marshmallow dream bars, and the most important—pecan clusters. Emotion clogged Julia's throat. She'd been desperate for something to be the same as it was when Dad was alive. She should've known the Azul Caye Chocolate Shop would come through for her.

"Blimey!" A familiar round-cheeked woman beamed at her. "Is that Julia Stone?"

"Hi, Miss Maureen." She nervously fluttered her fingers. The last time she'd seen her was at her father's funeral.

Maureen waddled over and wrapped Julia in a hug. "Back for a visit or for good?"

Longing tugged at her insides. "For a visit."

This hug was like an emergency thermal blanket, rocketing her chilly heart back to a normal, healthy temperature.

"A long one, I hope. You're too thin." Maureen returned to her position behind the shop's display cases, then rummaged for the treat Julia always chose as a child. "Caramel-and-pecan cluster, dipped in dark chocolate. One for each of you."

Julia reached for it. "This is Carson Miller, by the way."

"You've brought a boyfriend, have you?" Maureen waved. "Don't let this one get away, young man. She's a gem."

Julia coughed.

"Something wrong, dear?"

"He's my stepbrother." Whose half-naked, fully erect body she'd drooled over this morning.

He thumped her on the back. "Our parents are getting married this weekend."

"That Michelle." Maureen shook her head. "But who am I to judge a person following their bliss? I settled here to be a windsurfing instructor with John, and now look at me, running a chocolate shop."

"Where's John today?" Julia asked.

"Placencia. The sargassum made our beaches unusable." Maureen sat on the stool by the cash register. "Isn't Alex's news wonderful? That Bo's such a nice young man. Helped me set up a website. He's been good for the Caye, and especially for your sister. Softened her up a bit."

The tips of Julia's ears burned. She and Alex and Mom *had* to do a better job of sharing their lives with each other. She couldn't do this *Surprise! I have a big life milestone announcement!* bullshit for the rest of her life. It might feel awkward as hell at first, but that was better than acquaintances like Maureen knowing more about her sister's life than she did. Unless they were shutting her out on purpose? Like she couldn't handle it?

The pecans scraped her throat as she swallowed.

"Speaking of weddings…" She had to get this out, then they could go and she could walk off her frustration. "We'd like to order favors from you. Milk chocolate with orange, and dark chocolate with chilies. Two each in a chocolate box."

"Easy enough. How many guests? And where?"

Carson answered, "Forty guests, and we're at the Azul Caye Resort."

Maureen jotted the details. "Lovely. I'll deliver them the night before, direct to the kitchen. Best of luck to your parents. Don't be a stranger, Julia. Come back any time."

Julia jerked the door open. Its happy jingle was at odds with her annoyance.

Outside, Carson caught her shoulder. "Do you want to take a break? I'm not sure what happened in there, but you seem upset."

She *was* upset, and she'd like an escape from her thoughts. There was a person right here in Azul Caye who'd excelled at helping her with that years ago.

"I'm fine." She waved him off. "Let's go."

Carson wanted to help Julia through whatever was bothering her. She'd started with her normal ray-of-light personality, but as the shopkeeper talked, a cloud wrapped around her. Seemed like her mood darkened when someone surprised her with info about her family. Like the scones in LA or the benign comments from the chocolate lady. But if Julia didn't want to talk about it, Carson wouldn't pry.

Yet.

"Here we are." She twisted the knob of a door on which an etched brass plate declared, *Roberto Hornigold Photography*.

He chuckled. "Hornigold?"

"He says he's descended from pirates." She opened the door.

"Must've gotten teased a lot as a kid. I already thought of several brutal nicknames."

"I bet you did." Julia rolled her eyes.

Ah, hell.

"Not that I'd *use* them." He took the door from her.

She rubbed her temples. "Just…don't embarrass me."

Hmph. He'd been called many things in his life. Up-and-comer. Asshole. Thirty Under Thirty. An unrepeatable nickname or five from his fraternity. But never *embarrassing*.

A young woman with a thatch of purple hair sat behind a desk. "May I help you?"

"Yes, hi." Julia approached her. "We're here to see Roberto and—"

A tan blur ran straight to Julia.

She dropped to her knees and squealed, "Ojito! You little potlicker. I can't believe you're still around, old man."

The medium-sized dog wagged his butt until he folded in half. As Julia scratched him behind the ears, a genuine smile spread across her face.

"Still frisky as ever," she said.

"Like his human." A cologne ad of a man ambled across the studio. "What's up, Jujubee?"

This tanned dude oozed sex and looked like he wanted to lick Julia like a fucking ice-cream cone. His caramel-and-blond hair skimmed his jawline, and his vibe screamed *artist*, from his untucked T-shirt to his ancient frayed jeans to his flip-flops.

"Hey, Roberto." Julia rose from the floor. "Thanks for squeezing us in."

"My pleasure. How can I help?" He drizzled his gaze along Julia's body like Carson wasn't standing there.

So he'd make his presence known.

"Hi. I'm Carson Miller." He stuck out his hand.

"Hello, Carson Miller." Roberto held out his fist for a bump. "You're the stepbrother?"

In this guy's mouth, that sounded like a taunt.

"Yeah," he clipped out.

"Lucky you. The Stone sisters are good people." He ran his hand through his hair, then shot a glance at Julia. "A lot of fun."

Carson clenched his jaw. He knew that look. Had shot it toward a few women himself.

"I take it you two have history?" he asked.

"Ancient history." Color rose in Julia's cheeks. "We dated for a summer."

"The last full summer Julia spent here. After that, she's been busy busy busy." He slipped his hands into his back pockets. "Have you learned to slow down? Breathe once in a while?"

Carson wanted to elbow this dude away from Julia. Hard.

"I…have not." She shrugged. "I'm not built that way."

"You were for a summer." Roberto winked at her.

Forget elbows. He wanted to firewall her from this guy's ooze. Hornigold was obviously horny for her. Game recognized game. Worst of all, though—Julia didn't seem to mind.

"Why don't you move back to Azul Caye?" Roberto asked. "The resorts always need staff. They're conservative, though, so you'll need to reform your wild ways."

Wild ways? Now he had questions. The wildest thing about this woman was the ungodly amount of items on her to-do list. But he'd ask those later.

Julia smiled at him. Was she actually falling for this bullshit?

"About the wedding," Carson said. "Are you free on Saturday?"

"I can be." Roberto cut his gaze to his assistant. "Can't I, Maryam?"

She clicked her mouse. "A few family portraits. Local, though, and easy to rearrange."

"What about cost?" Carson said.

"Fifteen hundred US," Maryam called.

"It's half for Belizean residents." Roberto raised an eyebrow. "Or if you intend to be? Move home, Julia. Belize misses you."

Uh, hello? In his normal day-to-day, Carson took charge of situations and conversations. He was not accustomed to being completely ignored. He couldn't blame Roberto, because look at Julia. But it was still annoying as hell.

"Just Belize?" she asked with a smile.

Carson did not like this. At all. He should ignore the caveman response Julia flirting with another man triggered in him. She'd been perfectly, painfully clear with him about their boundaries. And he *agreed* with her. Yet he wanted to drag the photographer away from her.

Behind them, a couple and a small child entered.

"Hello, Briceños," Maryam greeted them. "We'll be right with you."

"So we're on for Saturday?" Julia asked.

"Yes, please call Maryam to finalize the details. Could we catch up while you're here?"

"I'd like that," she said as they backed toward the door.

Well, he wouldn't. He'd fucking hate it. In perturbed silence, Carson held the Hornigold-leafed door open for her. Her piña-colada scent wafted over him as she passed.

Three paces from the shop, he asked, "Is that your type? An oily descendent of pirates?"

"Don't start." She waved her hand at him. "He isn't oily."

People bustled around them, pushing them closer together.

"He's *so* oily. He was undressing you with his eyes the whole time we were in there."

She hooked a left. "And?"

"I don't get what you saw in a guy like that." He almost jogged to keep up with her.

"What's to get?" she huffed. "He's hot, he made me feel sexy, and was always up for a good time, which was exactly what I wanted. Nothing deep."

"Seems like he still is." A light bulb went off in Carson's brain. "Wait, please tell me you aren't invoking Paramore for *him*?"

"Maybe? I don't know." She dragged her hands down her face. "What's your problem?"

"He's not right for you."

"Oh? And who *is* right for me?"

Me, he wanted to shout. He'd felt a lightning bolt when they met as teenagers, but it had scared him. He'd known Julia had been too good for him then, But he'd searched his soul and sought therapy to unlearn the terrible lessons his now-estranged mother had taught him. It had taken a lot of work, and he was far from perfect. But he was finally worthy.

"Not him. The Julia Stone I knew in high school would never mix it up with that guy."

"That's the thing." Julia whirled on him. "You *didn't* actually know me. You had this *idea* of me and mocked me for it. Forgive me if I don't trust your opinion."

"I'm trying to fix that." He encroached on her space.

She didn't back off. "Trusting you?"

"Yes, trusting me. And getting to know you. We've checked so much off the list already. We could go out tonight or take a day trip tomorrow. Or both?"

"No." After a beat, she stepped away from him, paused to check for traffic, then sauntered across the street. Her orange dress fluttered in the breeze behind her.

For reasons Carson didn't understand, today had been hard for her. She was pissed at something, but it wasn't him. He was just a convenient target, which he clocked because he'd done that to other people, Julia included. And that was fine—he could take it. But he'd love to take her by her sapphire wrist and go do something *fun*. Get her out of her head.

"Come on," he said. "Let's go out."

"*Why* would I do that?"

"Because we're in a beautiful place." He spread his arms wide. "And I've never been here. What is something I'd be stupid to miss?"

She paused next to the van. "I'm not a tour guide. Call Alex."

"I want to see the Belize *you* love."

Julia dragged her lower lip between her teeth. "Why?"

This was his chance to be honest. To confess he always had a thing for her and this time with her brought it roaring back to life. And along with that confession, painful and embarrassing though it might be, he'd be honest about why he'd treated her that way.

Or he could chicken out.

"Because you're right. I didn't know the real Julia Stone, and I'd like to. Very much."

She twisted her lips. After a few silent seconds, she dropped her sunglasses in front of her eyes. "Fine. We'll go out tonight."

Twelve

Julia inspected her ass in the bathroom mirror back at their hotel room. Mom apparently thought a satin spaghetti-strap dress with a plunging neckline and a thigh-high split was appropriate for a daytime beach wedding.

Groan.

"Everything okay in there?" Carson called.

Goddamn these thin walls.

"My mother is ridiculous." She marched into the room. "Does she actually expect…"

Julia swallowed. Carson wore a collared blue polo shirt that hugged his biceps, trim gray shorts, and slip-on canvas shoes. Simple, but sexy.

He sat up on his bed. "Whoa, I'm underdressed."

"No, you're fine. This is the bridesmaid's dress. I'm glad I tried it on because there's no way I'm wearing this outside. Satin shows moisture easily, and there's no wearing a bra with this thing." She pressed her fingers to the center of her forehead. "Sorry. That was an overshare."

"Don't be. You look amazing, and I like your hair down. You normally wear it up."

Because ponytails were easy and stayed out of her face if she crawled under a desk or hustled across a hotel conference center. Neither were likely tonight, so she'd left it loose and wavy against her back.

She was surprised he'd noticed.

"Give me a second and I'll change into a more appropriate dress."

One that wouldn't cause her to accidentally flash half of Azul Caye.

Julia nipped across the room to the partially open closet. Hmm. She and Carson were closet compatible. They'd both hung their clothes in the same rough order—shirts, pants, jacket for him, dresses for her. Their palette was coincidentally coordinated, too. Refreshing that he liked bright colors and wasn't afraid to wear pink.

She selected her floral midi dress.

"Back in a second," she said, then closed the bathroom door.

She whipped off the bridesmaid debacle, then slipped into the midi. She glanced at her bra hanging from the door's hook. At her size, bras were more decorative than supportive. Not like anyone saw them anyway.

Eh, she'd live on the wild side and skip it tonight.

"I am gorgeous and sexy," she whispered to her reflection. "I become more attractive every single day."

Deep breath. She was having dinner with Carson Miller.

This would be fine. She opened the door.

"That one's great, too." He grinned, then tucked his phone into his pocket. "I bought tickets for the third-stage show on the beach for local bands. It goes until midnight. Want to get dinner first?"

"Or we can do both and make it a picnic?"

"Love that idea. Should I bring a towel or something?"

Julia patted her big shoulder bag. "I've got a pocket blanket. It's a nylon blanket for camping or beaching or whatever. My dad gave them to Alex and me in our Christmas stockings one year. I've used it more times than I can count."

"Handy." He opened the door for her.

"That's me," she said. "Handy."

She'd take it as a compliment. She *loved* always being prepared. Maybe it wasn't the sexiest trait, but it topped whimsy any day, especially if whimsy meant sand up her ass.

"Any cravings?" he asked as the elevator dropped them to the lobby.

Another chicken sandwich, but that would seem weird. The fact that *he'd* found the best sandwich in her hometown was infuriating. One of her favorite sandwich places, however, was nearby. She was spoiled for choice.

"This way," she said and hurried across the checkered lobby to the city sidewalk. Above them, the setting sun's vibrant tangerine-and-passionfruit streaks would lose to the night sky's dark blues.

As they rounded the corner, the string lights above Maxi's Spot popped on and hung like fat golden fireflies over their heads while they waited in line. Maxi's popularity meant the line was tight. Carson stood close. Glued-to-her-back close. Feel-his-heat-on-her-skin close.

She rooted in her bag until she found her paper fan, then snapped it open.

Carson laughed. "Are you a *Bridgerton* character? Do you have the vapors?"

A frisson of irritation skated along her spine, and she was right back to their teenage dynamic. Carson noticed something quirky about her, pointed it out with a laugh, and she melted with self-doubt.

In LA, she might've stuck to that pattern.

Not on her home turf, where she'd bent and broken rules and expectations. Where she was planning a wedding despite its insane speed and rolled with Alex's surprise engagement announcement. Why not break more patterns and ditch insecurities, too?

"You'll be begging me for it in a minute," she snapped.

"Sorry. Didn't mean to offend you. I've just never seen one in the wild."

Hmph. A qualified apology.

"Because you've never lived in a tropical climate or been to a drag show apparently." She snapped the fan shut, then pointed it at him. "Don't you *dare* say I'm being too sensitive."

He held up his palms. "Never crossed my mind."

Smile lines crinkled at the corners of his eyes. There was a genuine kindness in his green gaze, mixed with something she'd caught in Roberto's eyes earlier today, too.

Desire? No, couldn't be.

Shouldn't be.

But it totally is.

"Good." She fluttered her fan again.

Beyond the crowd's chatter and the street noise, she picked up the quiet thump of the beach concert. The Caribbean beat was the Caye's pulse, and she swayed in time to it. Her hips could never resist Belizean reggae's strong spacious grooves.

She was *so* glad Carson suggested this.

"Any recommendations?" He inhaled deeply.

"I'll order for us." At the window, she ordered tamarind-pork sandwiches, fried plantain chips, and water. Carson insisted on paying, and she didn't argue. The restaurant readied their food quickly, and they were off to the concert.

As they headed toward the cordoned-off area, he asked, "Did you go to the beach a lot when you lived here?"

"I spent half my free time there. Alex didn't like it as much as me and my parents, but it's *so* central to life here. My dad focused his tours on the pyramids, caves, and jungles but reserved the beach for relaxation. He said he enjoyed it too much to make it his job."

"He sounds smart."

"He was," she sighed. "He told me I didn't have to push against the current all the time. That sometimes when you relax, good things come to you. There's such a grind-and-hustle culture in the States. We're told from day one we can achieve our dreams with hard work."

"That's not true for everyone." Carson's eyes took on a faraway look. Whatever he was seeing, it wasn't here. "But achieving the dream isn't enough. You have to hold on to it, too. The second I ease off the gas, some other bastard'll steal my lunch."

Well, *that* was intense for a golden boy. She recognized a hungry soul when she saw one.

"So we keep grinding away," she said.

"Or change our dreams," he said. "Are you still hell-bent on a hotelier job in the States? Because this place suits you. I can see you here."

"Should I get a job here at a competing resort to meet Alex's dumb requirement?"

He lifted a shoulder. "It's an option. You'd be here, which you clearly love."

God help her, she did. Being back in Azul Caye felt like a hug.

A huge banner arched across the concert entrance. People in matching turquoise T-shirts with *STAFF* emblazoned on them were checking tickets. Carson withdrew his cell from his pocket and held up a softly glowing QR code on the screen. After the staffer scanned it, she wrapped waterproof paper bands around their wrists.

A plastic walkway led them toward the main beach area.

"Hang on." Julia pulled a reusable tote from her shoulder bag. "Shoes."

She tossed her sandals into the bag, and Carson chucked in his shoes. *Oof.* How big were his feet? His shoes must've weighed a pound each. And if the rumors about big feet were true...

Not what she should think about.

On the white sand, she paused and breathed the salty air. This. *This* was home.

The gentle scrape and give under her feet underpinned so many memories. No other stretch of sand compared to Azul Caye. Not Venice Beach or Santa Monica or even Malibu. Certainly not the stony lakefront beaches in Ithaca, New York, picturesque though they were.

"How about there?" Carson gestured an empty pocket closer to the curling ocean.

"We'll get wet as the tide comes in." The combined noise of the surf and music would prevent conversation, too, and she could admit to herself that she liked talking to him. "Follow me. I know a good spot."

She threaded her way through the festival-goers with Carson close behind. No sargassum here, thank God. She couldn't imagine musicians choking through a set with rotten seaweed permeating the air.

"Here we are."

Snuggled next to a palm grove, this spot offered seclusion. She adored slipping away from life's demands. Pale stars shined above them in the dark sky. This was her happy place. Carson was welcome here because she wouldn't feel bad about telling him to hush, but if she didn't talk to another new person, she'd be grateful. Today had been stuffed with interactions, decisions, reminiscing.

Tonight she wanted to sit, eat, listen, and not do anything for anyone.

He tipped his head back to take in the palms. "We won't be able to see much."

"We can hear, and that's what's important." She flapped the thin nylon pocket blanket, then staked the small metal anchors into the vanilla sand. *Hmm.* This blanket was smaller than she remembered.

She parked her ass on the beach towel–sized blanket.

"Room enough for one more?" Carson asked.

"Squeeze in," she said. "Now give me my sandwich."

As he sat, his Carson's cool marine scent blended with the palm trees' pleasant sweetness, the ocean breeze's salty tang, and the richness of the food. A shiver rippled over her as she breathed deeply.

All of it made her hungry. For a meal, for love, for life.

She was starving for all of it.

His leg brushed hers as he reached into the bag, making her blood thrum. One of the things she loved about men's bodies was the subtle roughness and delicious friction as her body slid against…

No, stop.

This blanket was definitely too small.

"Here," he said.

Grateful for the dark, she unwrapped her food. The tamarind's tang combined with the tender sweet pork was heaven and contrasted with the plantain chips' salty seasoning.

Carson's appreciative moan matched hers.

"Another outstanding meal."

"You've got vacation taste buds," she said. "We studied this in school. When you're relaxed and in a good mood, food tastes better. It's science. Research *also* shows being close to the ocean's blues has a beneficial effect on social, cognitive, and emotional well-being. So, we're winning with a beach picnic."

He popped a plantain chip. "Company's not bad, either."

"Yep, I'm a delight. You on the other hand…"

"Total nightmare." After a few quiet minutes of ravenous consumption, he held out his hand for her trash. "Finished?"

She dropped the wrapper into his hand. "Yes, thanks."

He crumpled them together, then heaved himself up. The deepening twilight didn't offer much light but allowed enough for her to check him out as he ambled to a trash can at the crowd's edge.

Relaxation also triggered imagination.

Oh, the things she was imagining. This morning, she could've peeled the sheet back from where it tented around his hips. His wicked grin would've encouraged her to kneel between his thick thighs and enthusiastically swirl her tongue around his cock. Loving the feel of him, she'd take his shaft in, deep, deeper, deeper still.

With varied pressure, speed, and depth, she'd learn what he liked, where he wanted her hands. When he was close—because he *would* come for her—she'd slow, go softer, and focus on the ridges under the head until he lost his mind, clutched her hair, and shouted her name.

Carson Miller, bane of her existence, star of her fantasies, dropped onto the blanket.

She tried not to notice his thick leg against hers.

"Is that..." Carson cocked his ear toward the stage. "A reggae version of 'I'm Not in Love'? The 10cc song?"

Guess his dad wasn't the only one who loved yacht rock.

"Yeah." Julia scrunched her toes in the sand. "Thank you for making me do this."

"I knew you'd like it. It kills me that I might've met the real concert-going, foodie, beach bum you if I hadn't been an asshole in high school."

She tucked her hair behind her ear. "You met the real me."

"Not all of you. Just the study-hungry part. Back then you paid more attention to books than you did to me."

"Needy much? Also, that's not true. I paid attention to you, but I couldn't go to college without scholarships. Ergo, books."

He leaned his shoulder against hers. "Go back to the you-paying-attention-to-me part."

"*Everyone* paid attention to you." Warmth fanned over her. "Except they didn't see you working to catch up when you played travel league or your motivation crumpling when your mom texted that you should practice because the coach called to say you'd dropped a pop fly."

His shoulders stiffened.

Shit, shouldn't have said that. Texts from his mom flashed on his phone during their study sessions. As soon as he saw them, he'd shut down. Julia had wanted to ask him about it, show him she cared but instead pretended not to see them. She didn't want him to think she was nosy, and parent relationships were generally off-limits. She'd known better than to dredge up mommy issues. She had enough of her own.

Desperate to escape this uncomfortable silence, she asked, "Anything else you want to know? Now's your chance."

"No." Carson thumbed his chin. "Wait, I take it back. Did your wild Belize alter ego ever attempt sex on the beach?"

She snorted. "Nope. Too many horror stories about chafing."

An unseasonably cold breeze from the ocean cut across them, raising the gooseflesh on her arms. She hugged her knees to her chest.

"Are you cold?" he asked.

"It's fine. I—"

"I've got this." He scooted behind her, and before she knew it, he was the big spoon. Wait, no. Not spooning, since they were sitting. Ladling? Whatever this was, it set her back and arms on fire. His whole self was *right* there, surrounding her, engulfing her.

"Better?" He rubbed her biceps.

She swallowed. "Yes."

"The stars are amazing out here." He shifted behind her. "You should look."

Her read on social situations wasn't perfect, but there was only one interpretation here: Carson Miller was hitting on her.

And…she wasn't mad about it.

She tipped her head back against his shoulder. Stars winked like scattered ice chips across the inky dark sky. If she squinted, she could make out the Milky Way's mist. *These* were the skies she missed, the ones she hadn't found outside of Belize.

"See what I mean?" he asked.

The music shifted to a tempo that matched her pounding heart. With her toes buried in the sand, her younger spirit, the one that took chances, bloomed.

What a fool she'd be to deny herself a kiss with Carson Miller

Here, on the beach and under the stars, they were simply two people who reconnected after ten years. That would change when their parents married, so she'd better to do this now. She twisted from his embrace until she was kneeling in the harbor of his legs.

"Yes?" he asked with a smile.

"Sorry."

He raised an eyebrow. "For what?"

"This." She planted her mouth on his.

Oh, hell, this was better than her fantasies. His soft moan sent desire pinging through her, from her head to her heart to her hips and knocking every place in between. He caught her to him, then shifted. In one smooth move, he laid her against the cool, firm sand.

Whew, that wasn't all that was firm. Unmistakable hardness lodged against her hip.

She wanted him, all of him, and he wanted her, and that was…absolutely not possible.

What the *hell* was she doing?

"Hey, so, thanks." Julia shimmied out from under him. "I've gotta go. Away. From here."

She'd snapped under the pressure, and now she was back in her right mind. There were so many people around, people who could've seen them, who might recognize her. She grabbed her sandals from the bag.

"Julia, wait." Carson caught her knee, his hand hot and big on her body.

"No." She backed away from his grip. "Stay. Enjoy the music. Have fun."

"Not without you, I'm not."

Thirteen

With his thoughts whirling, Carson jogged to catch up to Julia.

What the fuck just happened? One second, they'd melted together, his fantasy come true. The next, she iced him out, like someone splashed cold water on them. The first Julia—she was the real one. The feel of her in his arms had been too good, too right, too much of everything he'd ever wanted. He couldn't let her disappear on him.

"Hey," he said as he fell into step beside her.

"Go away." She was as pink as the plumeria she'd shown him earlier.

"You don't have to be embarrassed." In his fist, Julia's nylon bag swung between them. He grabbed his shoes from it and hopped to put them on while keeping up with her.

She ducked around meandering concert-goers. "Can we not talk about this here? There are people everywhere."

"Nobody knows us."

"Nobody knows *you*." She twisted her hair into a bun and cinched it tight. "For all I know my primary school teacher is nearby."

Shame to discipline those lovely, wild curls.

"Did she like concerts?"

"The only personal details she shared was she grew up in Willow Bank village and was plagued by bunions. The point is she *could* be here. The walls have eyes."

As he held the hotel door open, he bit his lips to keep from laughing. "You're paranoid."

"It's *reasonable* paranoia."

"That's not a thing."

"It *is* a thing. Psych 101 taught that delusional paranoia is a false belief, but reasonable paranoia is a fear that's rooted in reality." She nudged the elevator button. "It's entirely reasonable someone might recognize me in my hometown."

"But why would anyone care?"

"Spoken like someone who grew up in the second-largest US city." She clasped her hands behind her neck. "At heart, Azul Caye is a small town. This is tough to wrap your head around, but Azul Caye's permanent population is five thousand. *Everybody's* up in each other's business. It can be good—like my dad's friends and neighbors were angels when he was sick. But it can also be a pain in the ass. Like, people notice if your car's parked outside someone's house overnight. Not only do they notice, they pass the information along and ask about it the next time you buy a cantaloupe from them."

"That's oddly specific."

"Yeah, well, that happened when I was nineteen."

Gravity tugged at his belly as the elevator rose.

He got not wanting negative attention. He'd been the center of a flood of conversations about his prospects after his accident, his potential for healing, the university rescinding its offer... His mother never protected his feelings, so every word occurred with him in the room.

This, though...

This thing between them wasn't negative. They could be *so* good together. That was as clear as the Caribbean water, and he'd wait for her to catch up to him. Something he'd gotten right when he was eighteen—Julia Stone was endgame.

One kiss and he was a goner.

"Okay, you've convinced me." He handed her the bag containing the blanket and anchors. "Here, by the way."

She clutched it to her chest. "Thank you."

He unlocked the door, then held it open for her. After flipping the security bar, he turned back to Julia. She stood behind a dinette chair, clutching it like she was a lion tamer holding a fierce creature at bay.

"Can I ask you something about the kiss?" he asked as he crossed the room to her.

"Why not?" she said. "It's not like I'll die from embarrassment."

"Why do you care if people talk?"

She clapped a hand over her mouth. Through her fingers, she asked. "Are you *kidding*?"

He peeled her fingers from her lips, wishing he could replace them with his mouth. "No, I'm not. Help me understand why other people's potential opinions on an innocent kiss made you freeze up and run away."

"That was *not* an innocent kiss." She closed her eyes. After a brief temple massage, she opened them again. "I try to live as if anything I do appeared on the *LA Times*'s front page, it wouldn't embarrass me."

He folded his arms. "Not the *Azul Caye Reporter*?"

"The *Times*'s subscription base is larger. And—" she spread her hands wide, like she was mimicking a marquee "—'Julia Stone Tongue-Kisses Her Stepbrother on a Public Beach' is a reputation killer."

He laughed. "No one's writing that headline. And it's not like we grew up together."

"Except we kind of did." She clamped her hands behind her neck. "Which is another problem. I shouldn't kiss the person who made me feel terrible in high school. That period of my life is why I try not to misstep in my personal conduct anymore. Being helpful and deflecting attention is the best way to avoid being a target."

He sat on his bed, hard. He'd been a jackass to her. That wasn't new. What he hadn't realized, though, until this moment, was he was the MVP of her origin story. That he'd superglued a cracked, warped filter onto the lens she used to view herself.

A lump rose in his throat. "I wish I could erase everything. Fix it."

"Me, too." After a beat, she waved her hands between them, like she was wiping off a whiteboard. "Ignore that. It's fine. We were kids, and I'm working on myself. It's my job to fix me, not yours."

She yanked a set of pajamas from the dresser.

"Would kicking me in the balls make you feel better?"

"That's the dumbest thing I've ever heard." She slammed the drawer. "No."

"Physical release helps with pent-up frustrations."

Julia popped her hand on her hip, then shook her clothes bundle at him like a pom-pom. "Listen, buster. I kissed you, but that doesn't mean you get to toss innuendo around like confetti."

"I was talking about kicking."

"You big gaslighter." She pointed at the bathroom. "I'll change in there and collect myself. When I come out, I'll be a better person."

The walls shook as she slammed the door.

Julia could say this was a bad idea and deny she wanted him, but she wouldn't be so easy to wind up if that were true. Big, delicate feelings were involved. She needed to be sure he cared about, liked, and respected her. He did, deeply. All that and more, actually, so he'd be patient.

As he swapped out his cargo shorts for basketball shorts, sand spilled onto the carpet. Once again, Julia was right. Anything more intimate than light fooling around on the beach would've chafed.

Nothing calmed a raging libido faster than a TBD list. At least, he hoped it would, so he flopped onto his bed to flick through their project list. On the other side of the door, the water ran, then her toothbrush clattered to the sink.

She knocked on the door. "Are you wearing a shirt?"

"Yep." He laughed.

She opened the door, and he wanted to high-five the air conditioner for chilling the room so thoroughly. Her nipples stood at attention like sweet maraschino cherries under her top.

"I owe you an apology for freaking out," she said.

Keep your attention on her eyes. "You do not. That was mild annoyance and Olympic-caliber speed-walking but not a freak-out." He sat up in bed. "Something else bothering you?"

"Besides dipping my toes into incest?" She fell back against her pillows. "That's mostly it."

Carson shook his head. "Not funny. That's not what this is. At all. If anything, this is a second-chance situation, and nothing to be embarrassed about. Don't be such a drama queen."

"How dare you," she said to the ceiling.

"You said that was *mostly* it. What else?"

She blew out a breath. "It's stupid."

"I bet it isn't."

As she dragged herself upright, the motion pulled her shirt tight and gave him an amazing view of her gravity-defying tits.

Look away, Miller.

She sat cross-legged on her bed, then dragged a pillow into her lap. He did the same, because she was the sexiest woman alive and he needed the camouflage.

"This will sound dumb. Over the top."

"Julia, out with it already."

"My mom's getting married, Alex is getting married, and you keep mentioning relationships, and…I can't have one."

He dropped his phone onto his bed. "Why exactly?"

"There's this article…"

He groaned. "Anytime someone starts with 'I had a dream' or 'my horoscope said' or 'I read an article,' there's a huge chance whatever follows is a bullshit."

"Funny, because my horoscope said I'd have a dream about this article." She twisted the pillowcase's corners. "Anyway, the article listed seven reasons a person might not be fit for a relationship, and it lives rent-free in my brain. I exhibit at least two reasons."

He scrubbed his hair. "Everyone has reasons they might not be fit for a relationship at any point in their life. You have to meet the right person to make it work. Plus, I'm not the tutor here, but two out of seven isn't a passing score."

"These two are important. For one, everything in my life is up in the air. I could get a job tomorrow in South Dakota, so what's the point of dating someone in Ithaca or here?"

"Because it's fun." He raised an eyebrow. "Are there resorts in South Dakota?"

"Yes. They involve the words *lodge* and *canyon* and *gulch*. My point is I'm on the cusp of leaving for parts unknown, so I shouldn't start a relationship with anyone."

"I agree," he said selfishly. "That doesn't mean you can't have fun, though. Stick with flirtation and sex until you figure out where you want to be. Relationships can be a lot of work."

"Not if you're in the right one. My roommates back in Ithaca are relationship goals. Healthy, supportive, casual intimacy, and…I want that. Alex has it with Bo. I'm done with hookups, and since I want a relationship and you're about to be my stepbrother…"

She shrugged.

"Fill in the blanks for me, please."

"Most romantic relationships end. If we fooled around, there are extenuating circumstances that'd make it exponentially worse when things blow up. So we can't."

Oh. Oh, oh, *oh*. He scrubbed his hair. That was what made Julia tick.

Pessimism.

On one hand, he was *very* excited Julia had imagined them fooling around. The mature side of his brain, however, caught that she wanted impossible guarantees. That must've been what her endless list-making was about—finding all the potential problems, pitfalls, and pain points and trying to plan them out of existence.

He cared about her too much not to push back.

"We have different philosophies. Everything I do—relationships, living situations, friendships, business opportunities, sex—I jump into it with the expectation it'll go *right*."

She laughed. "Reckless optimism must set you up for disappointment."

"You're not disappointed when things go wrong?"

"Yes, of course I am. I'm pleasantly surprised when the things go right, but when things live *down* to my expectations, at least I'm gratified that I predicted they would."

"But why not have a little hope? It's not like you get a cookie for correctly guessing when things go wrong."

"It'd be nice if I did. I'd have dozens."

He wanted to hug the wariness from her. "What's the second thing? From the heavily researched listicle on *Buzzfeed*."

"It wasn't *Buzzfeed*." She threw the pillow at him.

Carson caught it easily. "I need to know the second thing that's making you take an incredible person like yourself off the market."

"You don't know me well enough to call me incredible."

He nailed her with his gaze. "Yes I do."

"Agree to disagree." A sigh juddered her chest, and she broke away from his gaze. "The article said you have to understand your value. I...don't. Not in relationships."

He laughed, and she threw her second pillow at him.

"Julia, that's the most ridiculous thing I've heard today, which is saying something since I also met a person named Hornigold."

"It's *not* ridiculous. It's how I feel. I don't know what I bring to the relationship table besides anxiety and pessimism."

Her warped view of herself was partially his fault, so he'd do his best to fix it.

"Then let me help you. You've got a mind like a diamond. You intuit what people need before they do. You're thorough and efficient and—"

"Blech." She holds up a hand. "Please stop. This sounds like a performance evaluation and I'm about to get a three-percent raise."

"Stop interrupting." He threw a pillow back at her. "You're funny, you care deeply about your family, and you've always seen through my bullshit. I have no idea how a sixteen-year-old kept me on task, but you did, and I liked it."

She sighed. "Thanks for saying nice things about me, but—"

"No *but*s. And I'm not being *nice*. I'm being factual." He sucked in a breath. Maybe it was time to tell her the truth he'd kept to himself for ten years. "You fascinate me. Always have. Which is why I asked you to prom."

She held up a hand. "Whoa, buddy. Now you're reinventing history. If I recall, you said something like, 'Wanna go to this dance with me and my friends, get drunk, and maybe get laid?' I mean, obviously *The Norton Anthology of Poetry* needed to include that swoony addition, but I didn't take it seriously. I saw *Carrie*. I would've ended up soaked in pig's blood, a joke for the cool kids."

She thought he'd do that?

Carson tried to look at it through her lens. His crew had

been full of laughter, assurances they loved each other, had each other's backs. Turned out not to be true, but he didn't know that at the time. Their friendships went back to wolf dens and laser-tag parties. Hell, they'd known each other so long their parents had become friends. They'd all seemed like nice people to him. To someone on the fringes, though... They could be casually cruel. Exclusionary.

"The invitation was real, Julia. Fucked-up delivery, but it was real."

She gaped at him. "What? No. I don't... It was? But you were such a dick to me."

"And you handled it the way a smart person should." He slipped between his blankets. "So if you're wondering what you bring to the table, know this—being with you would be like hitting the fucking lottery."

Julia sat there, lotus-style. Her busy eyes scanned him, but her gaze told him nothing. He wasn't sure he liked the appraisal. Somehow it felt like she was mentally stripping him down to the bone, finding everything he'd kept locked inside.

He snapped off the light. "Good night."

"Um. I...okay, then. Good night."

Her bed linens rustled as she settled, flipped, and settled again. He'd put her on edge with the truth. *Good.* Maybe she'd start to see herself the way he always had.

Fourteen

Julia stared, unblinking, into the dark.

Of course she'd thought prom was a joke. By then, she'd learned the secret formula for being popular—be beautiful, plus a little mean. Wealth was a bonus, but not required. If you were attractive and sweetly stung the less fortunate, there was no stopping a meteoric rise in popularity.

To avoid the sting, she'd stayed in the background, kept her head down, and worked.

It was what she was still doing.

Back then, Carson made her uncomfortable because he'd *noticed* her. *Is that Blondie T-shirt your favorite? You wear it, like, every third day.* Mortification. It *had* been her favorite shirt among her limited wardrobe. Hand-me-downs and thrifting had been her main supply, and *new* new clothes were gifted on birthdays and Christmas. Back-to-school shopping? Never heard of her. She'd never worn Blondie to school again lest he make a comment.

Hilarious that she'd packed it for this trip. Like a subconscious *fuck you.*

Bet you'd be hot if you wore your hair down and got contacts. Not much she could've done about either of those. Her hair was up because her last period of the day before tutoring was Phys. Ed.

Across campus, so she was a sweaty mess on a good day. She couldn't afford contacts in high school, but her frames were stylish. Honestly, she was mad she'd ever listened to him, because pictures showed she was fucking adorable in high school.

You're good at writing essays. I'd pay you to write mine, but you'd use words no one would believe came from me. I don't know anyone who talks like you. Starting that day, she'd weeded fifty-cent words from her day-to-day conversation.

Need a ride? I see you walking after school, figured you don't have a car. She'd declined. Rumors swirled any time a girl spent time alone with Carson Miller. Hence the reason she'd scheduled their tutoring lessons in the school library.

So of *course* she'd turned down his insulting prom invitation.

That was the moment his comments shifted from backhanded compliments to downright mean. *You're saving it until marriage, aren't you? What, I didn't say anything obnoxious. You must be on your period.*

Back then, she'd soothed her hurt by hollowly celebrating being right about him.

She punched her pillow and faced the wall.

Try as she might, though, she couldn't ignore her attraction to Carson. She'd shied away from it when they were younger out of self-preservation. The popular kids *never* would have tolerated her. And with college on the horizon, she didn't see the point in entertaining the idea of him. She'd done everything she could to leave home, not drop anchors.

Carson Miller, Mr. LA, was a *Titanic*-sized anchor.

A handsome, fit anchor with a sparkling personality and a surprisingly large dick.

The flush that started in her cheeks drifted and swirled around her until she was in a giant sweaty cocoon of heat and regret about her reasoned, rational choices, past and present. Despite the blast of cold air from the air conditioner, her bed was too hot.

Julia quietly flipped back the comforter.

She had options. She could crawl into bed with him. Or murmur an invitation for him to cross the line and come to her bed.

She swallowed. God, she wanted him. Here, in the dark, she could shove away the worries about other people's opinions and their gossip. In the dark, she didn't have to be perfect or helpful or compliant. For once in her life, she'd give voice to what she wanted, let herself have no-regrets fun. Deep breath. Here goes nothing. One, two—

Carson's gentle snoring told her she was too late.

"Rise and shine!" Julia snapped open the curtain. Painfully bright sunshine bounced into the room.

A growl erupted from the pile of twisted sheets. Carson's low rumble was sexy, even if it was mostly directed into his pillow. However, he neither rose nor shone. Nope, he burrowed deeper into the blankets.

She set the large paper coffee cup she'd gotten at the Rum & Bean next on the nightstand.

"Carson?" she asked.

No response.

With uneasy hands, she reached for his shoulder. Whew, what a shoulder it was, too. Thick, tanned, and scarred. She trailed her fingers on the pale white lines radiating from his shoulder blade.

"That tickles." His voice was gravel.

"Sorry." She yanked her hand back.

"Didn't say I didn't like it." He flipped over in bed, and whew again. His neck sloped into his broad chest. His light dusting of chest hair was enough to gently scour her skin—

Stop that.

"You all right?" Carson Miller's hooded sleepy eyes resembled his sexy eyes, which she'd glimpsed last night while he ground his hard cock against her hip.

Holy shit, she was *not* all right.

"Fine."

"How'd you sleep?" he asked.

"Great." For an hour before dawn.

Then she'd woken with a brilliant idea. He wanted to see the Belize she loved? He'd have to work for it. After dressing in sturdy synthetic hiking shorts, moisture-wicking socks, and waterproof hiking boots, she'd slipped from the room to call Alex, who'd helped her plan a bespoke tour for today.

"We're making this a working tourism day and choosing a Plan B wedding spot. You should dress appropriately."

Carson sipped at the coffee. "How'd you know how like my coffee?"

"You're not the only one who pays attention." She sat on her bed with her hands shoved under her thighs. "Do you mind getting wet?"

"Almost never." He tapped the coffee cup against his head in a salute. "Especially not with you."

A thrill fluttered behind her belly.

"*Not* what I meant. Wear swim trunks, and a rash guard or a T-shirt, and thick socks."

"Thick socks?"

"You'll thank me. And bring a change of clothes. We're checking out a lagoon, caves, a jungle hike, and a waterfall. I packed a picnic, too."

"Sounds like I need this coffee. And bug spray."

She loved that he was game for this. No questions, just acceptance.

"Already packed it. Hurry—the group we're glomming onto leaves in twenty minutes."

He saluted again, this time with a wink and a devilish smile. "Ma'am, yes, ma'am."

"I'm not a *ma'am*, I'm a *miss*." She thumbed her backpack onto her shoulder. "Meet me downstairs in ten."

"Yes, miss." The smile Carson shot her sent sparkles rocketing through her.

She did not acknowledge them. She wasn't as brave in the daylight as she was in the dark. With one exception, which was why she'd saved that place for their final destination.

"You can't be serious about this as a Plan B. They're in their sixties." Carson slipped his headlamp onto his helmet. As much as he'd enjoyed staring at Julia's ass in her shorts during the forty-minute jungle hike, this would kill their parents.

"It's an aggressive stroll." Julia snapped her life vest's belts together. "And they're only fifty-eight."

"Close enough," he said. "Some guests are older, though."

"Just my aunt Mary, and she's in better shape than I am."

He doubted that. "The guide's poisonous-plant-and-pit-viper prep talk puts a dent in the romantic vibe. And the river crossings were a challenge, even with a guideline. Your sister might be into a mud-caked wedding party, but your mom won't."

"Ooh, you're right. I'll suggest this to Alex for her wedding." Julia bounced on her toes as she gestured toward the cave's hourglass-shaped mouth. "Wouldn't it make a beautiful backdrop?"

The speckled limestone gleamed in the mid-morning sunshine, contrasting with the dark mysterious entrance. Lush green trees and ferns surrounded them, and a translucent aquamarine river flowed at their feet before disappearing into the cave.

"It's gorgeous but logistically challenging."

"Atención, por favor." Pedro, the older guide, waved their group toward the wooden stairs. "Here we begin. *National Geographic* has named Actun Tunichil Muknal, also known as the ATM, the most sacred cave in the world. The Maya believed there were three layers to the cosmos. Skies were the upper world, Earth the middle world, and now we enter the underworld, Xibalba, which literally translates to *place of fright*."

Carson snorted. "Yep, real romantic vibes."

"Shut up," Julia said.

"We'll tread against the current as we enter the cave and squeeze past boulders. Once inside, I'll lead and Jorge will be the caboose. Follow our lamplight, and all will be well."

"In the place of fright," Carson muttered, and Julia elbowed him.

"Off we go." The guide waded into the water.

Carson gasped as the brisk water cupped his balls. Sunlight danced on the ripples inside the cave, but as they shimmied past the boulders, the caves dimmed until their headlamps were the loan light source.

If he were claustrophobic, this would be nightmare fuel.

Julia scrambled up a wall, leaving him behind with Jorge. He was impressed and confused. There were no obvious hand or footholds.

"Where do I put my feet?" he shouted.

"Lower right, then left," Julia called back to him.

Jorge clapped him on the back. "You've got this, man."

After a deep breath, he placed his foot on a stable hold under the water. Now straddling the rushing water, he positioned his left foot on a study surface on the other side. He shifted his weight to the left, then stretched his right leg up and across to catch the right foothold.

"That's it!" Julia cheered.

With a grunt, he grabbed the right hand hold to hoist himself up and onto the ledge.

"Didn't realize you were a professional rock climber," he said.

"There's a climbing wall at my gym. It's fun."

Her wet shirt clung to her toned arms and shoulders. She was feeling the cold, too, based on her pebbled nipples. This fucking headlamp would rat him out if he focused on anything but her eyes.

"Gather round." Pedro's voice echoed in the chamber.

The wet limestone's scent assailed them as they shuffled closer. On the group's fringe, he and Julia stood in knee-deep water as droplets plinked against their helmets.

"This is the Stila Chamber," Pedro said. "The ceiling is a wondrous stalactite collection."

Their collective lights bobbed against the alien landscape of the cave's ceiling, which was full of pointy mineral fangs erupting toward them.

"It takes a thousand years for a stalactite to grow an inch, so you can see these caves have been here since antiquity. Perhaps the beginning of time."

He caught a drop of water in the eye. Great. Better flush it out later with antibacterial eye drops. He wiped the cave juice away, then glanced at Julia.

The ceiling's glimmer couldn't hold a candle to her smile.

"You love this, don't you?" he asked.

"Yes. See, my dad got trapped in a cave once, so he was claustrophobic and avoided these places. But Alex and I really wanted to go, so he introduced us to one of his buddies who was licensed to do the tour. It was the first time Alex and I went on an adventure without Dad."

Carson was vaguely disappointed. He wanted to share a first with Julia that would live in her memory forever, too.

"Let us proceed," Pedro said.

The older guide led them through the water to a wall. Carson tipped his head back. No fucking way were they about to climb a thirty-foot boulder stack.

"It's not as bad as it looks," Julia said. "Watch me."

Oh, he'd watch. Smooth calves, taut ass, and thighs he'd love to feel squeezing his hips. Nimble as one of the black-handed spider monkeys he'd read about during his prep for this trip, she made climbing look easy. He wasn't fooled. This would be difficult, but he had a good six inches of height on her.

If she could do it...

"Your turn," she called.

...he could, too. It wasn't like they'd leave his ass behind. He took a deep breath and positioned his foot on the helpful rock bump she'd used. Once he felt steady, he swung his leg around and...immediately slipped. Pain burst in his knee.

"Are you okay?" Julia asked.

"Yeah." Aside from this fresh bloody scrape. "Be right there."

This time he made it to the top, then stretched his leg across the gap toward the ledge. It wasn't as wide as it seemed from the ground, and...he was across. With hands braced on his thighs, he breathed deep to calm his pounding heart.

"See?" Julia said. "That wasn't so bad."

Tell that to his bloody knee and aching right hand. He flexed his fingers. Ten years after the accident and the pain echoed dully in his joints anytime he worked it excessively. Probably should've told Julia about it, but he didn't want to appear less than in her eyes, in any way.

"Please, friends," Pedro called. "Remove your shoes to protect the sacred artifacts we'll encounter in the remaining chambers."

"Won't bugs crawl into them?" he asked Julia.

"Probably." She shrugged as she unlaced her boots. "Just shake them out."

Sure. Shake them out. Like spiders and beetles and scorpions were no big deal. For someone who reapplied her lip gloss routinely throughout the day, she was unexpectedly chill going Indiana Jones style. How was this the same woman who faithfully recited his Positively Productive's affirmations to boost self-confidence, encourage goal achievement, and strengthen mental resilience?

He tossed his boots onto the ground next to hers.

After scaling yet another fucking wall, they entered a chapel-sized cave. Scattered across the ground lay ancient ceramic pots, obsidian tools and…fuck, was that a skull?

"This is the ceremonial area," Pedro said. "A millennia ago, the Maya conducted rituals here—including bloodletting and sacrifices."

Carson bumped shoulders with Julia. "You *seriously* want our parents to get married in here?"

"No," she laughed. "Not in here. Outside. This tour's a bonus."

"The Maya," Pedro continued, "believed they could directly appeal to the gods through this cave. We have counted the sacrificial remains of fourteen persons, including male royals, identified by their flat foreheads and filed teeth. Blunt force trauma was the likely cause of death. Please, look around, but do not touch to preserve the artifacts' integrity."

"I want to check out the monkey pot," Julia said. "They used to keep the ceremonial hallucinogens in it."

As the tour group wandered ahead and inspected the scattered artifacts, their headlamps cast spooky shadows on the walls. Enveloped by rock, deep inside the earth, his chest hummed with…something otherworldly. If this cave was a hotline to the gods and he'd offered blood, now that he was alone he should shoot his shot and ask for what he wanted most in the world.

"If anyone's listening…" he murmured.

As much as he wanted a hot night with Julia, there was something else he wanted more.

"Help Julia embrace herself as is and stop denying how great she is. Help her go for what she wants, without apologies."

An air current brushed his skin. The hair on his nape raised. Whoa, okay. He rubbed his arms to calm the goose bumps. He wasn't sure exactly what he believed these days, but that was creepy. He legged it to Julia and the monkey pot.

"So, what were the hallucinogens?" he asked. "Frog mucus?"

"Ew, no. Probably peyote."

"Frog mucus gets an *ew*, but we're cool with human sacrifice?"

"Depends on the human," she muttered.

"The next chamber," Pedro said, "is called the Crystal Cathedral."

The group shuffled forward, and...

"Whoa," Carson breathed. "This is amazing."

The cavern's roof soared above them, easily thirty feet tall. Stalactites hung down like the pendant lights in the church his dad preferred. If the last room stirred his spirituality, this room practically yanked it from his chest.

Julia smiled up at him. "The best part's coming."

Pedro called to the group, "Gather, friends, and let's experience the caves' full darkness. Please, extinguish your head lamps."

The tourists doused their lights until Pedro's lone light remained.

"Enjoy," he said and flicked off his lamp.

Darkness swallowed them. He was in a void. Like he was floating through space. No, not space, because space had stars. The air was thick with absence...no. Presence. Whatever filled the space between him and the caves was a tangible thing, disorienting him, like when his car was upside down after the accident.

"I don't like this," Carson murmured.

"It's okay." Julia threaded her fingers with his. She was warm, reassuring, and stopped him from spinning out.

Bright star, would I were steadfast as thou art, popped into his brain.

Steadfast. He didn't remember the rest of the poem or who wrote it, but when she'd read that line to him in their first tutoring session and asked him what he thought it meant... That was when the lightning bolt had hit. Session by session, the line fit her more. Whatever turmoil was happening under his surface, Julia seemed to keep it together.

It was still true all these years later.

"I've got you," she said.

She did. She had him.

But she didn't know it yet.

"Had enough, friends?" Pedro flicked on his headlamp.

As the group laughed with relief, they followed suit.

Carson blinked. At the journey's start, their collective light seemed dim. Now his eyes could barely tolerate the headlamps' glare. As he closed his eyes and breathed deeply to clear the fear from his body, Julia squeezed his hand, then let go.

"We have one last stop on our tour." Pedro wrapped his hand around the ladder's vertical rail. "The Crystal Maiden. Experts believe a priest sacrificed this person, now thought to be a he and not a she, over a thousand years ago. Since then, the bones have calcified to produce a sparkling appearance. Only three may visit the cavern at once. I'll be one of the three. Jorge, please sort everyone into pairs."

The aluminum ladder bolted into the cave's wall wiggled as Pedro climbed fifteen feet to the cavern above.

"Looks safe," Carson said.

A rangy retiree climbed up after Pedro. As soon as he disappeared, a woman Carson assumed was his wife followed.

"Did you see ET over there?" Julia tugged on the crook of his elbow. "That's what they call the other intact skeleton."

"Can you imagine the indignity?" He chuckled. "You're a kid whose people offer you up to the gods. A thousand years later, some Spielberg-fan spelunker finds your bones and names you after a movie alien. Like, what the fuck? We can't come up with a respectful nickname?"

"You're right." Julia pinched her chin. "The other skeleton gets to be the Crystal Maiden. That's more poetic."

"But misgendered. Although we don't know what they'd prefer."

"Let's be the change we want to see. From now on, I'm referring to that skeleton as the Crystal Kid, and we'll call ET…"

"Kevin?"

Julia backhanded him. "Something in Mayan…" She paused, placing her hand under her chin in thought. "I know! Xmucane. She was the grandmother of day and night. Oh, it's our turn."

Jorge gestured to them from his sentry point. Julia disappeared upward. As Carson climbed, his thick, smooth socks slipped on the rungs. Hospital socks with grippy soles would've been nice right now.

At the top, he crawled from the ladder, then rose to his full height.

"Wow," he said. "The Crystal Kid really sparkles."

The cave's clammy chill blanketed his skin. There was a presence here, too, like human emotions had seeped into this place. Hard to explain, but he got the same feeling in empty arenas and churches. That hopes and dreams and fears had played out here, often in upsetting ways.

He jerked his thumb over his shoulder. "I'm punching out."

"Fraidy-cat." Julia teased.

"Yep, like a rational person. Those are bones."

Descending was more challenging than climbing. He had to blindly trust his feet would find the next rung. After an eternal thirty seconds, he landed on solid rock.

"This is the last stop," Jorge said. "As soon as the group is ready, we'll head to the exit."

Carson hunted for his shoes. *Ah, there.* He smacked them together, upside down, to shake out any creatures or ghosts, then slipped them on. Ugh. Wet socks and wet sneakers.

More tourists joined him, including Julia.

"You're acting weird," she said. "Twitchy."

"*I'm* acting weird? Ritually sacrificed humans surround us. Why are you blasé about it?"

"They've been dead for a thousand years. People tour the Paris catacombs, don't they? The cemeteries in New Orleans? They walk right over the tombs in Westminster Abbey. Lots of people are fascinated by and okay with being in the presence of death."

This *so* did not track with her love of pink. He loved that she embraced the darker side of Belize's culture. But he'd love it more out of these caves and in the sunshine.

"Fine. *I'm* the weird one." To Jorge, he called, "Can I climb back down the boulder?"

"Yes, but stay at the base, please."

"Like I'd wander through a tomb," he muttered. He'd already shimmied onto the ledge when Julia dangled her legs over.

"Little help?" she asked.

He wrapped his hands around her waist. "I've got you."

As she let go of the ledge, he caught her to his front and let her slide down his body. The armful of her curves was everything he dreamed it could be.

"Thanks," she said.

Once the full group gathered around them, they trawled through the subterranean river. Once again, Carson's balls threatened to climb back up inside him.

Caves could go fuck themselves.

"Is this different from the way we came?" Carson asked Julia. "Did you drag me here to seek revenge in the bowels of Belize?"

"Jesus, relax." She dipped her body low into the calm water and bobbed until just her head and helmet were above the surface. "Literally go with the flow."

Easy for her to say. Little Miss I-Grew-Up-in-Wild-Wonderful-Belize had done this before, but he was literally in the dark.

Their tour group abruptly stopped.

"Is this a dead end?" he asked as they huddled around their guide.

Pedro shook his head, then pointed his flashlight to a small hole above the waterline. "It's the way out."

Carson shook his head. "That's a solid block."

"Shh," Julia said. "He'll give you instructions."

"For what? Teleporting?"

"Listen closely," Pedro said. "We call this spot the Decapitator."

Carson sucked in his breath. "Jesus fucking Christ."

"Your helmet *will* fit through this crevice. The wall narrows below the widest part, but there is room for your neck. Most of your body will be submerged as you shimmy though the passageway. One caveat—if you're wearing a life vest, you'll have to take it off. It won't fit."

Shedding life vests seemed...not good.

"Watch me." Pedro vanished through the crevice.

The retirees followed him. Were none of them scared of decapitation? Did growing older make you that reckless?

"We're doing this, huh?" He clamped his hands behind his neck. "Seems like a bad idea."

"A worse idea is staying without guides." Julia edged forward. "Carson, come on. I wouldn't bring you into anything dangerous."

"I hate this," he said. Dark paths, blind curves. Those had cost him everything in the past. This was Mulholland Drive all over again. Risks were a part of life, but he had to *see* the risk. Not take a careless run at it and hope nothing bad happened.

"I can tell," she said. "You go first."

He stopped. "What if I get stuck?"

"You won't. Pedro's bigger than you, and he got through."

"Unless a cave monster ate him."

"Dude. Go. Now. You're holding up the line."

"If a cave monster eats me, that's on you."

Deep breath, and he angled his head to fit through the narrow channel. The cave wall brushed his throat. Fuck, fuck, fuck. This was terrifying. The crazy part was some explorer went through this system and was like, *Huh, I wonder what's over there*, and shuffled forward, hoping they didn't get stuck, and—

Oh. He was through. Shaking, but through.

"Congratulations," Pedro said.

Once Julia popped through, Carson hauled her to him. "That is the dumbest thing anyone's ever made me do."

"I didn't *make* you do anything. You said you wanted to see things you'd regret missing. You can't beat glittery skeletons."

"I'd regret dying in a cave."

"Kids do this." She pushed away from him. "There was a sign at the trailhead that said you have to be at least four feet tall."

"It should also say tourists should be *less* than six-two." He jerked his thumb over his shoulder. "That felt like the trash compactor scene from *Star Wars*."

"Excuse me?" Jorge interrupted. "Could you proceed so we don't lose the group?"

"Sorry, yes," Julia said.

Around the bend, relief flooded through Carson. Glorious natural light glinted against the river. They were nearly free of the dark. Outside, the vibrant greenery seemed to glow after spending an hour in the dark. It might take a minute for his eyes to adjust.

"Ready for our next thing?" Julia asked.

"Anything that gets me away from the cave."

"Great," she said. "There are changing stations at the park entrance. Once we're in our dry gear, we'll be on our way."

Fifteen

Butterflies erupted in Julia's stomach.

After they'd changed into dry clothes at the caves, they'd hopped into the minivan to check out their next Plan B destination—Maya ruins. As far as Carson knew, that was all that was on the agenda. Julia, however, planned to tack on a hike he'd never forget.

"Jules, I'm dying." His stomach protested louder than a howler monkey. "How are you still in a good mood?"

"The parking lot's right there." She flicked on the blinker and eased into a parking spot adjacent to a rustic cabin. "Want a snack?"

"Nah, I'll wait for lunch."

"Suit yourself." Julia grabbed a rucksack from the back. She'd eaten an extra big breakfast today to pregame this trip. She wanted to show him her personal secret entrance to paradise, and hangry sniping would kill the vibe.

"Can I carry that?" he offered.

"Sure." As she handed the bag to him, their hands brushed. If his casual touch on her hand sent shivers running through her, she might faint when he touched more intimate places.

Outside the van, he asked. "Ready?"

"Almost. Bug spray." She hosed herself down, then tossed the can to him. "Your ankles will thank me later."

As he sprayed, Julia locked up the van and zipped the keys into her shorts. Once he finished, they marched toward the ticket booth.

"Hi," Julia said. "There should be tickets waiting for us? I'm Julia Stone. My sister, Alex Stone, said she'd call ahead."

"Nice to meet you!" The gray-haired woman beamed. "Alex is here often with so many tour groups. Xavier would be proud of you both."

The enthusiasm for this hike that had expanded over the course of the morning fizzled. For once, she hadn't been reminiscing about Dad and the universe still surprised her with him.

"I take it you knew him?" she asked.

"Yes, and he talked about you nonstop, so I already felt like I knew both of you. We miss him around here. Bright smile, and an even brighter soul." The woman slipped wristbands across the counter. "Wear these while you're on the grounds, and enjoy."

"Will do. Thank you."

With the bracelets clutched in her hand, she entered the park area. Bringing Carson here…where Dad brought her…

This was a mistake.

Julia gestured toward the ruins peeping above the tree line. "That's it. Ready to go?"

"You're nuts if you think I'm skipping the ruins." He stuck out his wrist. "I'll do yours if you do mine?"

Guess they were staying.

"Okay." She fixed the adhesive ends together.

He ran his finger around the inside of the bracelet. "Ouch. You got some hair in there."

"Sorry." She thrust her wrist toward him. "Want to seek vengeance?"

"Nope." He peeled the paper tabs from the ends, then carefully fitted the band around her wrist. His touch was gentle, intimate in a way she couldn't explain, and lingered on her tattoos.

Julia cleared her throat, then eased from his grasp.

"Shall we?" she asked.

They marched along the trail, protected from the sun by the thick tree canopy. The day's heat barely made its way through, but the humidity was thick on their skin.

"This is easier than the caves—so far," Carson said. "Will we need to swim across a raging river? Walk a tightrope across a crevasse? Limbo under a two-ton boulder?"

"No." She laughed. "Stop complaining. The caves weren't that bad."

"They were great, unless you're an undiagnosed claustrophobic like I apparently am." As the path opened up to the ruins' bright green plaza, Carson whistled. "This is outstanding. Picturesque and easy to get to. Nice find."

Normally, she deflected praise, but...she might have actually preened.

"It's available at the perfect time, too. They only allow events after the park closes at five. They'll still get sunset vows."

He rotated on his heel. "Dad would love this. More than the beach, actually. He'd appreciate construction that lasted for a millennium as the backdrop. It's a nice metaphor."

"Great." She clapped. "This is officially Plan B."

His stomach rumbled again. "Agreed. Can we please eat now?"

"Yes. This way to the perfect picnic spot." Julia veered left, away from the park's tidy trail and onto the secret overgrown path. "My friends and I came here a lot. When you grow up in a small town, you find secret spots to get away from everyone's eyes."

"Best we could do in LA were the lookouts on Mulholland Drive."

"I wouldn't know," she said.

"You could've." He winked. "But, uh, considering that's where I lost it on road debris, it's better you didn't come with. Ever bring the horny pirate here?"

"You are *obsessed* with Roberto," she said. "Why?"

She suspected why, but she needed him to say it.

When she tackled him on the beach last night, he was more than happy to kiss her back. The minute her lips touched his, she wanted more than a hookup. If he admitted he wanted something more, too, she'd feel safe to confess that her thoughts had turned that corner. Brave? Nope. But, given their history, she'd allow herself to be a little bit of a chickenshit.

"Easy. I'm jealous. He knows you in a way I don't."

Her stomach fluttered. He'd *said* it. "I'm sure you've slept with people."

They crashed through bramble and were greeted by a dull roar of rushing water.

"Several, but that's not what I meant." Carson kicked a rock. "At least, not *just* that. I'm jealous he's seen another side to you—he said you were wild. What does *wild* mean?"

"It means I was a kid and I did stupid things. Then I got older and my prefrontal cortex matured." She huffed as the path steepened. "I understand consequences so I'm not—" she scratched air quotes "—wild."

"You can still have fun, though."

"I have fun! Reasonable, not-wild fun. Because headlines."

"No one's writing headlines about us, Julia. You can't live your whole life based on nameless, faceless people's opinions. Never take criticism from someone whose advice you wouldn't take, either."

Her shoulders stiffened. Philosophically, she agreed with that last part. But the hard pivot into toxic-Positively-Productive-affirmation mode bothered her. Especially considering the image he pushed. He cared just as much about his public persona as she did.

"Oh, like you don't care what people think?" Her turn to kick a rock. "I've seen your socials. Showy parties, bottle service, mid-tier ex-child celebrities at Chateau Marmont. Very bold, very carefree, very LA."

"And very curated. That's my brand for my business, Julia. At this stage potential clients want to feel like they know me before they agree to work together. That's all that is. The only people whose opinions truly matter to me are my dad's, my friends, and yours. And I promise you know who I actually am."

A brilliant red trio of macaws shrieked as they flew overhead.

Julia dragged her lower lip through her teeth. She…she could buy that explanation. The photo galleries and Insta feeds for the places she'd interned were different from the day-to-day reality. Same with Stone Adventures—pics of Alex carefully teaching people to kayak, but never the ones where she'd tumbled into the Mopan River.

Over these last few days, she'd rediscovered Carson. And this guy? The one who'd accompany her into the wilds of Belize, notice when she seemed down, and kiss her senseless under the stars? If this was who he was now, he might have been worth the wait.

"I do, actually. Feel like I know the real you, I mean," she admitted. "Since the party, I've had a lot of big feelings. You've been really understanding. A little too 'Rah-rah everything will be great!' sometimes. But overall, I'm glad you're here with me."

Carson stopped in his tracks.

She turned. "What—did you see a scorpion?"

He beamed an extremely goofy, very Carson smile at her. "You are? That's the nicest thing you've ever said to me."

"The thing about the scorpion?"

"No, the other thing. About being glad I'm here with you. It just jumped past, 'Wow, you really get Byron.'"

Julia scratched at her neck. Well, shit. She'd *thought* nice things about him.

"Sorry," she said.

"Don't be." He caught up to her. "Are there really scorpions out here?"

"Never say *never*, but they're usually on the beach or in piles of wood. And they're nocturnal, so I think we're safe."

The rushing water sound competed with the blood whooshing in her ears.

"Carson Miller, I present to you…" She stopped at the pink plumeria tree that marked their destination, then held the branches aside. "The world's most perfect picnic spot."

Please let him love this view as much as she did.

"We climbed a fucking mountain?" he asked. "How? We weren't hiking for long."

She joined him in the mountainside meadow. Spread out in the distance were sharp peaks with steep, tree-covered slopes that faded into the blue horizon.

"The parking area's close to the top. Minimal effort, maximum view."

Carson whistled. "Your sister should add this to her tour list."

"Bite your tongue. We have a pact to keep this private. Can I have the backpack?"

He shrugged it off, then handed it to her.

"Here." She tossed him the pocket blanket. "Spread this out?"

He shook out the blanket. "Did this thing grow?"

"I brought the bigger one. It *is* a picnic."

Julia extracted containers from the backpack, then handed him a bottle of wine and a corkscrew. "Open this, please?"

"Sure." He uncorked the pinot grigio faster than she tied her own shoes. "Here you go."

"Thank you." She poured wine into plastic tumblers. "To climbing mountains."

They clinked. The white wine was cool on her lips.

"Now lunch." She peeled the lid from a container, then handed it to him with a fork. "Bollos. They're like tamales—cornmeal dough filled with seasoned chicken, then steamed in plantain leaf. They're tasty hot or cold. I've also got cheese dip with tortillas, and sea grapes. Oh, and I packed hot sauce if you're into that."

"I'll give it a shot." He shook a generous amount onto the bollo. After a bite, he coughed, then guzzled the liter of water she'd set out for him.

"The cheese dip helps if the sauce is too hot," she said. "Dairy breaks down the spice."

"Thanks." He used a tortilla chip to scoop up a generous portion of the creamy, tangy cheese blend. "That's better."

Julia popped a sea grape, the sweetness bright against her tongue. Everything about this moment felt right. The place, the meal, the company.

"I can't believe I avoided coming back here after my dad's… Anyway, I shouldn't have stayed away. Being here, in Belize… The good outweighs the sad."

"Don't take this the wrong way, but you're less twitchy than when we were in LA. Every day, you seem more yourself. Less worried about other people." Carson hurled a grape off the side of the mountain. "Why don't you live here?"

"Because it would be weird not to work with Alex." Julia popped another grape. "From a distance, I can ignore the weirdness. Pretend like us working in similar fields isn't a big deal. But I might resent her if I'm here. I don't want to feel like I'm not enough."

Then again, she might not feel that way.

No way to know unless she actually lived here. Something to consider. As the mountain breeze cooled the sweat that slicked her, she sipped her wine. The rest of the meal passed in comfortable chitchat, the kind two people enjoyed when they knew each other well.

She rubbed her calf along her shin. They could head back to the car. Or... As long as they were here, she might do something wild.

Julia swung her gaze toward Carson. He leaned back onto his elbows, with his face tilted toward the sun, wavy hair brushing the collar of his T-shirt.

She licked her lips.

Hell. Yes. She was definitely doing something wild.

"Do you have a short hike in you?" She stood and dusted her hands together. "There's a special place up the hill. After forcing you through the Decapitator, I feel like I owe you."

"I'll follow you anywhere." He folded the pocket blanket, then slung the backpack on his shoulders.

"It's this way." She hiked a few yards, then eased between trees camouflaging the path.

The green swallowed her up. "Julia? Where'd you go?"

"I'm here." She stepped back through the trees and caught his hand, like when they'd been underground. "There's a tight squeeze up ahead, but it's nothing like the Decapitator."

He grunted as he followed her through the rocks. "Disagree. This is exactly like the Decapitator, except it's scraping my junk."

"It's worth it," she said.

The rushing water intensified, and the path opened to a turquoise mountain lake. This was her favorite place on the planet. As gorgeous as the swimming hole was, the star of the show was the twenty-foot high waterfall coursing through the lush green forest.

Carson whistled. "What's this place called?"

"It's not on any map, but we call it Secret Falls."

He pulled out his phone to take pictures.

"There's no cell service," she said. "So you can't post it."

"It's for the memory, not the clout. Take one with me?" He slung his arm around her neck and held the phone out. Their grinning faces smiled back from his phone with the waterfall in the background. She could swear his gaze fixed on her lips.

"There." He squeezed her shoulder. "Perfect."

His low voice rumbled into her ear, and heat crept up her body. An excellent way to cool off was right there.

So she tugged the elastic from her ponytail. "Let's swim."

Carson's heart stoppered his throat as Julia whipped off her top.

Their day in the sun yesterday had turned up the gold in her skin, a rich contrast to the cream-colored barely-there string bikini under her clothes. He swallowed, hard. The gentle slope of her breasts, her slightly rounded belly flaring to her hips, and, oh, her perfect peach of an ass stole his ability to think.

Julia was such a surprise. Among the ways he'd imagined undressing her, this scenario had never come up. His fingers buzzed with anticipation, ready to tweak her stiff nipples, to tug at the strings at her hips and explore her ripe flesh. His cock stirred under his trunks.

He could almost cry that he wasn't already with her, on her, in her.

At the pool's edge, with her hands on her hips, she dipped her toes to gauge the temperature. Against the water's intense turquoise and the dark slate of the rock formations, Julia stood out like an angel.

An angel he'd like to devour.

She jumped into the water.

He shucked his shirt and slipped into the pool. Unlike the cold cave river, this water was cool, refreshing. Julia broke through the surface, circling until she found him and graced him with an inviting smile. He sliced through it toward her.

This far in the lagoon, his feet found no rocks on which to stand.

"You came here when you were a teenager?" he asked.

The water lapped at her chin. "And in college."

"What did you do here?"

Her mischievous grin was kissable. "Lots of things. Watch."

Wherever this was going, he was a hundred percent along for the ride. She swam closer to the falls' churn. At its base, she hoisted herself from the pool.

The water's downspout licked her the way he'd like to.

In nature, she was a different person—carefree, wild, hair loose, clothes tight. Her water-darkened curls were squiggles against her back, and her muscles shifted as she climbed the rocks next to the falls.

Um... Wait.

She might stop at the ledge, but... Nope, she kept climbing. Surely not all the way... Shit. His suspicions were right. She climbed to the top of the falls.

Fear gripped his throat. "Julia, don't—"

She disappeared into the lush ferns. *Please* let her return via a safe path. As he searched the brink, a whooping blur hurtled from the green.

His heart plummeted with Julia as she cannonballed.

Her splash was swallowed by the frothing water. He didn't breathe. Where was she? He swiveled his head, searching, searching, searching as he swam to where she disappeared.

"Julia!" Her name was raw in his throat.

The image of her bashed and broken stole his breath. *Focus.* Panic wouldn't help. He might have to perform CPR, carry her on his back. What were emergency services in Belize? 911, like in the States? Or 112, like in England and France?

"Julia!" he shouted again.

She popped up two feet away. "Hi."

He tipped his head skyward. Thank God she was safe.

"Your *face*." She giggled.

Anger shoved the fear aside. "Why the hell did you do that? That was so dangerous."

"Jumping from the falls?" She raised an eyebrow. "I've been doing it for years. The waterfall's carved out a deep plunge pool. You should try it. It's exhilarating."

Exhilarating? *Risky* was more like it.

He wanted to hug and yell at her, which meant he should take a breath and swim away.

"Carson," she shouted after him. "Wait."

He should. Even if he didn't get lost on his way back to the minivan, she'd zipped the keys into her cargo shorts. But he was too angry to stay still. She casually dangled herself in harm's way, tempted fate to break her beautiful self. For what? A three-second thrill?

He scrambled up the rocks.

"Carson." She grabbed his biceps. "Why are you pissed?"

His chest burned, like someone scrubbed a fistful of jagged rocks inside his ribcage. The bright Belize sun caught the golden flecks in her big brown eyes, eyes that could have been extinguished by one misstep as she leapt from the cliff.

"The last fucking thing I want to do is explain to our parents that you broke your neck."

As she closed the distance, the water dripping off of them formed a single puddle.

"I'm okay, Carson." She rested her hand against his chest. "This is me—wild. I've done that a thousand times."

"It only takes once." Every cell in his body paid attention to her simple, calming, intimate touch. "I lost you for a second, and it terrified me. I like you, Julia, so much, and in ways I shouldn't since we're family."

"We're not." A deep breath expanded her chest. "Family. Not yet."

Liquid heat pooled between his hips. But she'd drawn this

line. As much as he wanted to clutch her to him, he couldn't cross it for her. The next move had to be hers.

He clenched his fists at his sides. "What do you want, Julia?"

"You." She bit her bottom lip. He'd like to, too. "These last few days with you... I feel like myself again. Lighter. A person you seem to like. Here, we're isolated, and I..."

"You what?" His body vibrated with tension.

She caught his hand, then traced the network of fine white lines, a memento from the accident. "I was wrong in California. People can change, me included. I'm done denying how I feel, Carson. I want you, in all the ways I shouldn't."

The combination of her gentle touch and words lit a fire in him.

"You do?" He tipped her chin up to meet his gaze.

"Yes." She slipped her hands behind his neck, then tugged his head toward hers.

The waterfall, the cool rocks under his feet, the chirping birds...it all faded until all he knew was her velvet mouth's heat, her inquisitive tongue, her strong grip on his head, and her breasts against his chest. The dance they'd done since their parents' engagement party—gentle collisions, stolen kisses, baring their soft spots to each other—there was only one place in his mind it was headed.

As she took a surprisingly firm grasp of his ass, he cupped her face.

"Are you sure about this?" he breathed.

Her lips quirked into a smile. "I've never been more sure in my life."

Sixteen

Carson's neck, cooled by the water, was salty under Julia's tongue.

"Promise me something?" she asked.

"Anything," he rumbled.

She tunneled her hands into his hair, then turned his head so he was staring into her eyes. The dark spread of his pupils, his flushed face, and his heavier breathing… For the first time in their history, she was the person with leverage.

In control. She liked it.

"We can only happen here. Whatever happens here, stays here."

"Like Vegas?" His dimple popped as he grinned. "I promise."

She caught his hand, then scooped up her bag. "Follow me."

The familiar path led to a carve-out behind the falls. The curtain of water would provide privacy in case anyone hiked here today. A small possibility. Still, this place was less risky than the hotel with its paper-thin walls.

Behind the falls, she faced him.

She couldn't be happier Carson Miller was looking at her like he wanted to consume her. After the fantasy she'd indulged in last night at the concert, she might eat him first.

She tiptoed her fingers up his chest.

"I've always wanted to do this here." Now that she'd admitted she wanted him, her hesitation melted away. "I never found the right guy."

"I'm glad it's me." He caught her wandering hand, brought it to his mouth, and kissed it. "I have potentially bad news, however. I don't have a condom. I have a clean bill of health, though, and it's ah…been a while."

She tugged him to her. "The great Carson Miller hit a dry spell?"

"Keep calling me great." The light scrape of his nails under her top's strings sent pleasure waving through her. "Start-ups don't leave much time for anything else. But we can still have fun without sex."

"Hold that thought." She dipped into her bag for the pocket blanket and shook it out, then placed it on the hip-high sloping ledge nearby.

"Always careful. I plan to change that." He turned her to him, hooked his hands under her ass, then hoisted her onto the ledge.

"I can't wait." She caught his hand and kissed his fingertips. "Also, I have an IUD, so…"

"Those might be the sexiest words I've ever heard."

Her pliant mouth eagerly greeted his as he fiddled with the bikini's knot at her nape. She could help him, but no. She enjoyed his eagerness. Soon the skimpy triangles fell forward. The rushing water's breeze perked her nipples.

"Rose," he murmured before bending to lick them.

The sensations made her gasp. Too many to absorb. Warm, tingling delight as he sucked and lightly pinched her nipples… His stubbled chin's rough scrape against her flesh… The cliff's coolness at her back… His big, hot hands roaming her body.

She tipped her head back, basking in his guttural moans. Carson Fucking Miller made her feel like the most beautiful, desirable person on the planet.

"I want to taste all of you," he growled.

Sounded like an amazing idea to her.

His tongue swept her lips, and she opened for him. As he devoured her, he braced himself against the cliff, his arms bracketing her head. Julia loved the feel of the taut boulders of his biceps under her fingers. She hooked her ankles around his thighs, running her calf along his leg.

If this simple slide of their skin made her insides sparkle, imagine what—

"Yes," she gasped as he slid his thumb into her bikini thong.

He dragged his thick thumb along her seam. *Yes.* Her hips kicked forward, urging him to go further.

"What do you want, Julia?" His voice was raspy, low. "Help me make you happy."

With other lovers, she'd been hesitant to be direct. Because the fucking filter on her mouth got in the way of saying what she wanted. With Carson... The filter was already gone. Plus, she loved bossing him around and had ample proof he took direction well.

"Feel how wet I am," she said. "Play with my clit, and then slip your fingers inside me."

"Like this?" he asked.

As he caressed the sensitive nub between her legs, electricity jolted through her. The slow wheeling gesture bowed her back. The bridesmaid's dress wouldn't hide the scrapes on her back, but she couldn't give a fuck. Not when it felt this good.

"Faster," she breathed.

He picked up the pace.

"Yes, like that." She crossed her wrists behind his head, then rested her forehead against his. Tension coiled between her hips, low and tight and glittering. "But more."

Julia's core greedily clenched the finger he slipped inside her. The animal sounds between them rivaled the rush of the falls.

"More," she moaned into his ear.

Unhesitatingly, he obliged with another thick finger, gently coaxing her from the inside. She bloomed for him, like a flor de pato in direct sun.

"Keep going," she said. "Don't stop, or I'll scream."

"I won't." He licked the shell of her ear. "Scream my name while you come."

The added pressure, thickness, and steady rhythm broke the dam inside her, faster than expected. All she could do was whimper as she pulsed against him, hips bucking with the pleasure rippling through her.

He kissed her temple. "You owe me a scream."

She'd give him that and more. Her orgasm hadn't quenched anything. No, it ignited a need that demanded satisfaction. Without breaking eye contact, she undid the ties at her hips.

"I don't go back on my promises. We're not finished."

"Agreed." He shucked his shorts. "We're just getting started."

Water droplets coursed his body. His broad shoulders, trim waist, and ready cock jutting from his hips were a landscape she wanted to explore. Julia caught his wrist and lifted his hand to her lips. She kissed the knotty bumps of his scars, licked her way up his arm, until she'd pulled him back to her and his iron length pressed between her legs.

"Is this for me?" she asked as she stroked his shaft. "I can be greedy."

"I'm a giver, so that works out." Carson palmed her cheek, then ran his thumb along her jawline. "I might die if we don't do this."

"That would ruin the wedding."

His hands worked more magic as he stroked her flesh, and his mouth was at her neck, making her gasp.

Yes to all of this.

"What do you want, Julia?"

Her name on his lips caused something hot and urgent rise up inside her.

"You." His heart raced under her palm. "Hard and fast, and I want you to come inside me."

"Are you comfortable?" he asked, his voice raw.

She laid back against the rocks. "I won't be 'til you're inside me."

Dark spread over his eyes. "I want you so much."

"Then what are you waiting for?"

"I want to burn this into my memory." He slid his cock against her slick folds. "Once I'm inside you, I'll lose myself."

"Good." She shifted her hips under his slide. "Now, Carson. *Please*."

As he eased himself into her, her breath caught. He stretched her, filled her to the brim, and her body hummed with pleasure. She reached between her legs, fingers parted, to feel his shaft slide against her skin.

This moment was years in the making.

The water's constant rush competed with his groans. Carson draped her legs over his shoulders, kissing the inside of her knee. Bliss shone on his face. *She* was doing this to him. Turning him on, making him forget himself.

Carson Miller wanted her.

He was in her to the hilt, hips flush against hers. It felt like they were the only two people in the world.

"Have you ever—" he thrust "—done this here?"

"No." She gasped as he thumbed her clit.

"This place is for you and me. No one else. Promise."

"Yes." She arched her back as he switched his attention to her nipples. "Only you."

His steady pumping, his masterful manipulation of her sensitive spots, the rock under her back, and the cool mist from the waterfall overloaded her senses. The intensity was building inside her, pressing against her seams, until the glorious moment when they burst.

He pumped his hips faster. "I'm about to come."

"Me, too," she moaned in surprise.

A sound she'd never heard herself make tore from her throat.

Carson sped up between her legs, groaning, his orgasm chasing hers. As they drifted back to themselves, he released her legs, then folded himself onto her.

He brushed her damp hair from her face. "That was…"

Mind-blowing? Special? Unexpected?

"Perfect," he finished. "Like you."

Ah, so they were back to lying. She closed her eyes.

"Hey, hey, hey," he said. "Look at me."

Reluctantly, she fluttered her eyes open.

A tender smile played on his lips. "You know you are."

"Nobody's perfect." She brushed his bangs to the side.

"You come closer than others." He kissed her forehead. "I like your birthmark."

"The one above my—"

"That's the one." He withdrew from her, then licked the strawberry mark between her legs. "Not everyone gets to see that."

She swirled her fingers through his hair. "Because I don't prance around naked."

"If you want to, I support it. I may even demand it." He settled next to her on the blanket.

"That'll make Christmas awkward," she said.

"Let's not think about Christmas yet." He kissed her shoulder, then nipped her ear. "I can't believe we waited so long to do that."

"We waited five days. That's a land-speed record for me."

A fleeting kiss on her mouth. "I've been waiting ten years."

"If you'd been *you* back then, you wouldn't have waited at all."

"I'll regret that every day." He tucked her hair behind her ear. "Please tell me we live here now and can skip the hike back."

"I regret to inform you…"

"Damn." He trailed his fingers down her sternum, between her breasts. Goose bumps fanned across her skin, and her nipples perked to attention. "But we don't need to go back right away, do we?"

"No, we—" She gasped as he flicked his tongue over her nipple, then caught it gently between his teeth. "Have time."

"Excellent. I have ideas I'd like to run past you." He delved his hand between her legs.

"About?"

"The way I'd like to spend today."

During the drive home Carson found tiny ways to touch Julia. A light caress on her knee, brushing hair from her shoulder, slinging his arm against her headrest. He'd left the hotel this morning expecting a field trip into the beautiful Belize landscape.

He was coming back a changed man.

Julia finally showed him who she was in the wild, without deadlines or tasks or demands… She was *not* a buttoned up taskmistress. No, his Julia was a melting pool of desire, one he wanted to drink from for the rest of his life.

"What's next on the agenda?" he asked.

"A hot shower," she said. "For two. Because efficiency."

He drifted his fingers to her thigh. "Unless we get distracted."

"I'm never distracted. Everything I do is intentional."

"Like leading me to Secret Falls so you could ravage me and steal my innocence?"

"Please." She winked. "You gave away your innocence ages ago."

"You've got me there, but I've been judicious since then."

"Why do I find that difficult to believe?" She cut a gaze his way. "What's your body count, Mr. Judicious?"

The light up ahead changed to red.

"Including today, seven."

She hit the brakes hard. "Stop it. You're twenty-eight. And hot."

"Why, thank you."

"So how…why…" Julia scrunched her face.

"Don't I have a higher number?" He lifted a shoulder. "Hooking up isn't for me. I prefer buildup and meaning behind physical intimacy. The light's green."

"Sorry. Just a little shocked over here." She eased on the accelerator. "What was all that talk the other night—about relationships being a lot of work?"

"Because they are, but I bet they're worth it."

Her knuckles blanched. She'd leave dents in the steering wheel.

"Twelve," she said.

"Twelve what?"

"Including today, mine's twelve."

"Congrats." He didn't care about who came before as long as no one came after.

Julia glanced at him. "Do you care that I've slept with more people?"

"No," he answered honestly. "I hope it means you know what you like and will generously share that information so I can make you come a thousand times."

A blush pinked her cheeks. "Oh."

Oh indeed.

She parked, and they slipped from the minivan. Inside the hotel, the crisp air felt like a slap after a day in Belize's heat and humidity.

"After showers and dinner," she said, "I want to take you on the coolest tour in Belize."

He shifted his backpack. "Nothing can top Secret Falls."

"Obviously. Tonight's the new moon, though, which is perfect for—"

"Julia!" a familiar voice trilled.

Carson had never seen color drain from someone's face before, but Julia went from sun-kissed gold to white in an instant. She eased away from him as Michelle catapulted herself from the lobby's lounge chair. Dad followed, and Alex twisted around in her seat.

As Julia hugged her mother, she said, "I didn't expect you until tomorrow!"

Her voice was as artificially bright as Michelle's diamond-patterned *Golden Girls* caftan.

"We boarded an earlier flight after all. When you didn't answer your phones we decided to come here and surprise you with a dinner invitation." Her mother gestured to the coffee table laden with frozen fruit–skewered drinks. "And decided to grab a cocktail while we waited."

Dad, dressed in a pale green company polo and khaki shorts, slung an arm over his shoulder. "Hope you've been squeezing in some fun."

His bulky phone holster pressed into Carson's hip.

"We have." He avoided eye contact with Julia. "We toured a cave system this morning and ruins this afternoon."

"Did I hear you say you went to Secret Falls?" Alex asked.

"Yep." Julia flopped her hand out. "It's close to the ruins, so I figured why not?"

Her feigned nonchalance impressed and scared him.

"Where's Bo?" Julia asked.

"Parking Betty," Alex said.

She gasped. "You let him drive Betty?"

"Who's Betty?" he asked.

"Her Jeep." Julia crossed her arms. "She doesn't even let *me* drive Betty."

"Because you hate driving stick," Alex said.

"You two go tidy up," Michelle said. "We'll go to dinner when you're ready."

"Great idea." Carson tugged Julia's elbow. "We'll be back in a few."

As the elevator doors closed, Julia dropped her face into her hands. "Oh my God, they know."

"They don't know." He rubbed the spot between her shoulder blades. He'd been startled to see their parents, but this was not worthy of a freak-out. He wished they'd been kissing as they entered the hotel. Ripped that bandage right off. But that wasn't how Julia operated, and she'd snap at him if he tried to find a silver lining.

"Alex knows. There's one reason anyone takes someone to Secret Falls."

"To bask in the nature's glorious splendor?"

"To bone." Her reddened cheeks were adorable. "I only ever went there to swim, but Alex and most of our friends snuck dates up there for privacy. I can't believe our parents showed up early. I had our whole night planned. A full-moon beach walk, nudity, and room service."

"I like those plans." He kissed her forehead. "We'll swap out room service for a family dinner, then come back here and pick up where we left off."

"Okay, but keep your distance," she said. "Alex can read me like a book."

The elevator doors opened.

Minute by minute, the carefree Julia who'd taken him to the falls disappeared behind this shuttered version of herself. He'd be patient. The more she could be herself freely with him, the less tempted she'd be to dim her light around everyone else.

Even if that meant being honest and inviting scandal.

At their door, he kissed her soft nape as she held the key to the reader.

"That tickles." She giggled.

The nearby elevator dinged. Julia sprang away and practically fell into their room.

"Jules?" Alex said.

She swiped her hair from her face. "What's up?"

Alex dug into her handbag. "Mom forgot to give you this. She wants us to wear matching hair pins to dinner."

"Ew, why?" She took the pin from her sister.

A nickel-sized starfish, studded with pearls and blue-and-green crystals was fixed to the end of the hair pin. Cute, actually, and a fun nod to their island setting. But the *matchy-matchy, we're all one happy family* symbolism felt so forced.

"Continued tattoo jealousy. She doesn't believe the diamond is for both her and dad."

Aha. So *that* was what the gems represented. He'd take a closer look later.

Maybe with his tongue.

Alex surveyed him. Slowly. "So, Carson. How'd you like the falls?"

Tread carefully.

"They were beautiful. Best waterfalls I've ever seen."

She raised an eyebrow. "Any plans to go back?"

"I'd like to. Once wasn't enough."

It was killing him not to look at Julia.

"I bet," Alex said. "Your shirt's on inside out."

"You shower first, Carson," Julia interrupted. To Alex, she said, "We'll meet you downstairs soon."

Julia closed the door, then leaned her forehead against it.

He massaged her shoulders.

"She definitely knows," Julia moaned. "She's insufferable when she knows something I'm keeping from Mom."

Her muscles were bunching faster than quick-set concrete.

"We could tell her. Not the details, but tell her we're—"

"What? No." She slipped from his touch. "Saying anything is premature by, like, a million years. We need to keep this quiet."

He, on the other hand, wanted to shout it from the rooftops.

"Especially this week. Let's not distract from their wedding. Okay?"

The earnestness in her gold-flecked eyes meant there was one possible response.

"Okay," he said.

Relief relaxed her pinched features. "Good."

Seventeen

Mom raised her wineglass. "A toast to our blended family."

Reluctantly, Julia raised her glass and clinked with Alex, then Carson. Yep, these were the faces she'd see around the dining room table at Thanksgiving, the tree on Christmas morning, the picnic table on the Fourth of July.

Jesus, she was *so* screwed.

Carson's white shirt sleeves complemented his emerging tan. His resort clothes hung loosely on his big frame. She could attest to his underlying casual strength. He'd heaved and held her in multiple positions this afternoon without wobbling once.

"Are you okay, Julia?" Alex asked. "You're redder than a macaw."

She gulped her rum punch. "Fine."

If it weren't for the breeze cutting through the restaurant's open windows, her face might explode into flames.

"So, Bo," Mom said, "are you planning to sell your home in Baltimore?"

He dipped his chin. "Yes. My sister, Delilah, is buying it."

"That's wonderful. How much profit will you clear?"

"Mom," Alex interrupted, "we don't talk about money at the dinner table, remember?"

The childhood rule made Julia smile. For once, she wasn't the one enforcing it to keep the peace.

"Fine, fine." Mom brushed Alex's admonishment aside. "Delilah's your twin sister, isn't she? Do twins run in your family? You two will make such beautiful babies, but you're not getting any younger. The clock's ticking."

Julia held her breath and a giggle as she widened her eyes at Alex.

Mom was unhinged. As kids, she and Alex didn't know their mother's tactless questions were considered rude. When their friends pointed it out, the sisters had convinced Mom to soft-pedal her thoughts. But with family, she dropped the pretense. Silver lining—she must've already considered Bo and Carson family.

"Great questions," Alex said. "We've decided to have seventy-three children. Also, I *am* getting younger. The doctors are baffled."

Julia blew out her lips as Bo and Carson chuckled.

"Oh, you." Her mother placed her elbows on the table and rested her chin on her latticed hands. "I know you think I'm too blunt, but I'm trying to get a sense of you as a couple."

"We're good," Alex said and grabbed Bo's hand.

"Very," he said.

The shiny adoration on her sister's face was reflected in Bo's. Her heart was happy for them. That was how an engaged couple should behave. But a shard of jealousy wedged itself in that happy heart, because they could be open in their affection.

Julia poked her food and surreptitiously eyeballed Carson's hand. He circled his thumb around his wineglass's rim, just like he'd circled her nipples under the waterfall.

"Yoohoo, Julia," her mother singsonged. "How's the job search?"

She stabbed the fish. "In the same spot it was when I left LA. I'll send out fresh applications when I'm back in Ithaca."

"How do you live there?" Alex shivered. "I can't stand the cold."

"This time of year's nice. Fifties, and the fall leaves are beautiful."

"Exactly. Frigid."

Julia sipped her rum punch. "I'd like to move back to warmer weather someday."

"Are you dating anyone?" Mom asked. "What about that Roberto fellow you ran around with here? High school crushes burn bright. I think we always carry a torch for them."

Julia choked on her cocktail. Carson patted her back until her coughing fit subsided.

"'S'cuse me," she wheezed. "I need to powder my nose."

"I'll come with," Alex said.

Groan. Perfect. When she wanted advice, Alex was a ghost. Today, when she wanted to be left alone, Alex's sandals *flop-slap flop-slapped* after the clicks of her own fussy heels.

Inside the ladies' room, Julia locked herself in a stall.

She closed her eyes and massaged the anxiety-reducing pressure point between her thumb and index finger. She needed to regroup. If she sat here quietly, maybe Alex would get bored.

"Juuules. I can talk to you through the door."

Dammit.

With a sigh, she slid the latch and opened the stall. Her big sister was a lunatic if she thought they were having this conversation, out loud, in a public restroom. She found her trusty tube of lipstick in her purse. A creamy swipe of bold pink always made her feel invincible.

Alex parked her hip against the sink. "Anything to share?"

"Nope." Julia popped her lips on the *p*.

"So, taking our stepbrother to Secret Falls *doesn't* warrant a sisterly conversation?"

Double dammit. She *knew* Alex caught that.

"Did you suffer from sunstroke again, Alex? You should wear hats on your tours."

"We both know Secret Falls is actually Secret *Sex* Falls."

"I don't know what to tell you." She dabbed her shiny nose with powder.

Alex slapped a dramatic hand to her chest. "I can't believe my sister, my flesh and blood, is lying to my face."

Julia crossed her arms. *Best defense is a good offense.*

"Why do you think I'm lying?"

"Because you're terrible at it. Do you remember Lydia?"

Julia's stomach dropped. Ugh, she shouldn't have eaten so much fish.

"Your friend from Bronson?"

"That's right. She messaged me to tell me Carson Miller is in Belize. She had a huge crush on him in high school, which I convinced her to squash because you said he was an asshole. He posted a picture of himself and hashtagged it #BelizeDreams."

"So what?"

"The picture was him standing at Secret Sex Falls with a huge smile."

Her breath came fast. "He...he posted a photo?"

"Hey, hey, hey." Alex clutched her shoulders, grounding her. "*Him* at the falls. That's it. Not you, and nothing incriminating. I'm the only person who can put two and two together."

Alex's calming grip and tone snuffed out Julia's brewing anxiety.

"I've been meaning to talk to you for ages," Alex said. "As nuts as Mom is, I'm glad the wedding's here. I haven't been a big sister to you since I returned to Belize."

"You've been fine," she lied. "Dad and everything after... it's been rough for both of us."

Even if her sister was about to tell her something she wanted to hear, Julia wanted this to end fast. Other people's discomfort made her cringe more than her own. So the quicker she could absolve Alex, the better.

"Let me own this," Alex said. "I didn't have answers or advice, so I avoided talking about Dad, and Mom's relationship-o-ramas, how much I struggled with the business, and how challenging school was for you. If I could do it over, I'd stand shoulder to shoulder with you and we'd talk through it all. The best I can do today is promise to do better."

Something eased in Julia's chest.

"I'd like that," she said.

"You might not. I practice tough love, so let me offer you some recently acquired pearls of wisdom."

"Oh, so we're starting this now?"

"Yes, hush." She locked eyes with Julia. "Sometimes the bad, illogical, impossible ideas are the best ones. I resented Mom for leaving Dad, but I get it now. At a certain point, you need to live your life for *you*. I'm not saying go full hedonism, but don't put yourself last on your unending task list, okay?"

Tears welled up in Julia's eyes.

No one had ever told her to prioritize herself. Sure, there were the #SelfCare threads on social media, but they always seemed like a sales tactic for wineries and yoga retreats. But Alex had been there with her. She understood the burdens they'd had to bear. So, despite their different life paths, Alex understood Julia on a bone-deep level.

If Alex was telling her to prioritize herself, consequences be damned, she must've meant it.

"That's not easy," Julia said.

"Why?" Alex said. "Julesy-girl, go for what you want, no apologies."

"What if it hurts someone, though?"

"The only person I'm worried about is you. If he's who you want, it's okay to make that choice. Except…" Alex chewed her lip.

"What?" Julia said.

"I'm not retracting anything, but maybe keep this Carson thing under wraps until after the wedding? Otherwise Mom will make it about her."

Julia knew what Alex meant all too well.

At her eighth grade science fair, Mom met Julia's Biology teacher, Mr. Z. Instead of celebrating Julia's first-place win, Mom complained the whole ride home that Julia hadn't told her she had an attractive eligible bachelor for a teacher. They dated for the six most awkward weeks of Julia's life.

Then there was the summer she'd worked as a spa attendant at the Waldorf Astoria, and she mentioned that Mom's favorite Bollywood actor was staying there and got a facial. She'd thought it was a fun piece of celebrity gossip, but guess who'd shown up three nights in a row to hang out at the Rooftop?

And oh, *cringe*, that Thanksgiving that she'd stayed in Ithaca and couldn't pick up Mom's call. So Mom called the hotel's main number, asked for Julia's boss, and asked him to find her. Why? So Mom could brag about how well dinner had turned out.

"That's good advice," Julia said.

"Told you I've turned a corner. See you back at the table."

Alex understood she needed a minute to process her thoughts. Her exaggerated people-pleaser tendencies meant she was so tuned into other people's emotions that she paused her personal feelings until she was alone.

She scrolled on her phone until she read today's affirmation on the Positively Productive app. Hmph. It was like it was written for her. Fuck, it probably *was* written for her. She could totally see Carson texting his friend to do him a solid.

"I'm unafraid of what might go wrong," she read aloud. "I'm excited about what can go right."

Untrue, but she was getting there.

Carson's social media post still raised her hackles. She shouldn't have cared what people say on the internet, but she did. More than she should've, which was why she wasn't on social media. But she couldn't ask Carson to delete the photo without seeming like a weirdo. Best to let it go.

One more pink swipe, and she left the bathroom.

As she returned to the table, Mom said, "*There* you are. I was about to send in the rescue squad."

Sweat beaded at Julia's nape. Could her mother not notice her for *once*? She slipped into her chair next to Carson. His fleeting touch on her knee under the table promised they'd fall into each other's arms as soon as they were on the other side of their hotel room door.

Quietly, of course. Because thin walls.

"Julia," Michelle said, "I understand Carson's hosted you these last few days. I hope you've behaved."

Jesus Christ. If she could hide her face in her napkin, she would.

"I was happy to help," Carson said.

"We can take her off your hands." To Julia, she said. "We have a lovely large honeymoon suite with a sleeper sofa. You can stay with us."

Every fiber of her being screamed *no*. There were not enough earplugs in the world. She'd lived through enough of Mom's previous boyfriends and husbands to know she was *loud* in bed. And on an almost-honeymoon? Goodbye to her peace of mind.

"That's kind, Mom, but I'll be on the phone a lot, coordinating, confirming, finalizing."

"We don't mind, do we?" Mom placed a bejeweled hand on Jim's.

"Not at all," he said.

Dammit. The problem with providing logistical excuses was people removed them to be helpful. If she were honest and said she preferred rooming with Carson, they couldn't argue. They could, however, harbor suspicions about her preference. Suspicions Alex advised her to keep under wraps, which meant she had no choice but to say...

"Great. It'll take me few minutes to pack my stuff." *Please* let Carson read the apology in her eyes. "Isn't this great? No more fighting over who gets the bathroom first."

"Yeah. So great."

No one else seemed to catch the hollowness in his voice. After Jim picked up the check, the parents and Carson piled into the minivan to return to the hotel to collect Julia's things.

Next to the driver's door, Alex said, "Bo and I are taking off. See you tomorrow."

Julia caught her in a hug and whispered, "This is a nightmare."

"Hope you packed earplugs." Alex giggled.

The drive back was brief, and Julia managed to find a space close to the entrance. As they headed inside, Mom threaded her arm with Julia's. "I'll help you pack. Boys, have a cocktail and we'll meet you back here."

Oh, hell. Had she been bamboozled into a mother-daughter chat?

Julia closed her eyes as she held the keycard to the sensor.

Inside the room, her mother said, "It's so small. You must be relieved to have an escape."

"Yeah," Julia said. "Relieved."

"I apologize for the subterfuge, but there *was* a reason I wanted to get you alone. I couldn't ask in front of Jim..."

Julia's heart hammered in her chest. This was it. This was the moment her mother found out about Carson and berated her with scandalized *how could yous*.

"Did you have a chance to visit the lingerie shop?"

Carson slid onto the stool next to his dad. They were father and son, but Dad was his buddy. Knew his frat brothers, called a few of them to bust their balls when their hometown baseball teams lost to the Dodgers. He couldn't get a read on Dad tonight, though. He fidgeted with his phone, checking texts, moving too fast to actually read anything.

"Everything okay?" Carson asked.

"Yeah. Work thing." He put his phone face down. "Wish I could toss this into the sun."

"I hear that."

Ugh. Had he actually said that? But he was struggling for a conversation topic. He was amped about Julia, but that was a no-go. Per her wishes, mostly, but a fraction of him didn't know how Dad would react, either. No need to stress him out for the big day.

"How are you and Julia getting along?" Dad asked. "Michelle was worried you'd be like oil and water. Says she can be demanding."

He pursed his lips. Demanding? No, *exacting* was the better, more accurate description. She knew what she wanted and had excellent taste.

"We get along great, actually."

The bartender laid cocktail napkins in front of them. "Apologies for the wait, sirs. What can I get for you?"

"Bourbon," Dad said.

"And a Belikin," Carson said. "Could you charge it to room 612?"

The bartender nodded. "Back in a moment."

"What's a Belikin?" Dad asked.

"Belizean beer."

Dad flipped his phone over, then dropped it back onto the bar. What was his deal? He'd been his normal self at dinner. Gregarious, chatty, energetic. As soon as Michelle left his side, though, he'd fallen into this twitchy funk.

"Michelle says Julia's desperate for a job. Your company's tripled in size this past year—maybe you could hire her?"

He wished.

"I would, but she got her master's in hospitality management, so she's looking for hotel jobs. She likes front-office stuff best."

The bartender delivered their drinks. After thanking him,

Dad clinked his glass to Carson's beer and downed half the bourbon in one gulp.

Okay, then.

"You know people, don't you? Michelle says Julia's worried about making ends meet."

She was?

"I'll put her in touch with my contacts." The golden lager chilled his throat. "I wanted to see how she operates so I didn't embarrass myself if she wasn't a professional."

"Son, we help family unconditionally. Like your aunt Charlotte did for you, and like you're trying to do for Danny. If they don't keep up their end of the bargain, that's on them."

Carson jumped as Michelle placed an unexpected hand on his shoulder.

"There are my men," she said. "Are you ready, Jim?"

"As I'll ever be." Dad slid from his barstool.

Carson left colorful Belizean dollars on the bar for the bartender, then grabbed Julia's suitcase handle. She didn't protest, which he took as a good sign. As they marched out to the parking lot, her bag's wheels click-clacked against the lobby's tile seams.

Every cell in his body protested this situation.

Julia should stay here, with him. It killed him that he couldn't say so. Today was, hands down, the number one sexual encounter in his history. But he wanted her to stay because he liked being with Julia more than he liked being alone. Life was more fun, more interesting with her nearby. She was the first woman to enter his life where he couldn't see the upside of her leaving.

"If we had more room at the resort," Michelle said, "I would've invited you to stay with us, too. This inn is lovely, but the resort is a level up, luxury-wise."

He could give a fuck about luxury. Nothing would be more awkward than sharing a suite with the woman he wanted to strip naked, plus her mother and his father. That was some *Game of Thrones* shit.

"How about a round of golf tomorrow?" Dad asked.

"Oh, you." Michelle waved him away. "You can golf anytime. There must be something we can do together."

The minivan's taillights flared as Julia hit the Unlock button on her key fob. "Alex wants us to visit her at the office tomorrow."

"Yes, but that won't take long." Michelle slid into the rear passenger seat. "Oh, I know! Alex can take us on a tour. What do you think, Jim?"

His dad joined her in the van. "That could be fun."

Once their parents shut their doors, he had a few seconds of privacy with Julia. After he placed her suitcase into its back, she shut the rear lift gate.

"Jules, a question." He caught her hand.

A quiet, gentle touch, but it sent his heart racing.

"Let me guess—you're wondering how my mother can be complimentary and condescending in one sentence?" She blew her hair from her eyes. "It's her gift."

God, he wanted her. He had the sneaking suspicion he'd never drink his fill.

Hell was their parents sitting three feet away.

"When can I see you again?" he asked.

"Soon?" She cut her gaze toward the car. "But it can't happen when I'm within a hundred yards of my mother. I can't keep my volume down around you."

A smile tugged at his lips. "I guess I'll have to accept that."

"Don't get cocky." She punched him in the shoulder.

"I'm always cocky. Especially around you."

She clutched her forehead. "I'd love to banter all night, but I'm driving our parents to their resort so I can couch-surf in their honeymoon suite."

"Have fun with that." He risked touching her hip.

"I won't," she said and backed away.

He stayed in the lot until their taillights disappeared.

Eighteen

Julia wasn't hungry for luxury, but it was nice to dip her toes into it. After room service delivered a bottle of merlot to the palatial honeymoon suite, she dug out her tablet to review the list of things she and Carson had accomplished.

Miraculously, Mom listened attentively. This was new. Maybe she really was excited to marry Jim? She'd asked questions and requested reasonable tweaks.

Jim, on the other hand, was distracted by his phone. He periodically paced the room. Like now, as she mentioned the Plan B for sargassum, he wandered to the kitchenette.

"Can I top you off?" he called.

"Yes, please," Mom answered.

"No, thanks," Julia said. Two rum punches at dinner was enough, and she had plenty to do...mostly to distract herself from playing the afternoon on repeat in her mind.

Warmth fanned over her chest.

Carson, the man whose touch put her fully in her skin. Made her feel sexy, desired, enjoyed...instead of just *useful*. Made her relax, too. At first she'd been all prickly nerves around him, made worse by her attempts to hide twitchiness. He picked up on her feelings and didn't try to invalidate them.

Nope.

He gave her a sandwich, apologized, and joked with her. The fiery glitter that exploded inside her when they were naked together didn't hurt, either, but they'd never have gotten there if he hadn't been gentle with her old hurt feelings.

Jim refilled Mom's glass. "That's the last of it. Shall I order another?"

She shook her head. "Not if you want me to function tomorrow."

"If you'll excuse me, then." Jim rested a hand on her shoulder. "I'll unpack and shower."

"Be there soon." Mom squeezed his hand.

As he closed the bedroom double doors, Mom relaxed into her gossip pose. Legs tucked under her body, elbow perched against the back of the couch, body fully turned toward Julia.

"It's not the penthouse," Mom said. "But it's nice."

This couch probably cost more than every stick of her furniture in Ithaca combined.

"*Very* nice." Julia scrolled her list. "What do you want to do after we visit Alex's office tomorrow?"

"We can figure that out later." Her mother took the tablet from her and laid it on the table.

An act of treason.

"Alex seems happy," Mom said. "Are she and Bo living together? Are they serious?"

The people pleaser in her wanted to provide answers. But this was Alex's story to tell. She'd been in the middle of her mother and sister's relationship for way too long.

"You should ask Alex, Mom."

"You're no fun. And she'd never tell me, but I'll leave you alone."

That was different, too. Mom would normally keep going until it started an argument.

Mom swirled her merlot. "You know, ever since I had the audacity to put my wants and needs in life on equal footing with yours, you two stopped confiding in me. You punished me for centering my happiness."

Julia's insides burned. "At the cost of ours."

"Yes, sweetheart, at the cost of *some* of yours, versus *all* of mine. What should I have done? Stayed married to a man who was more of a coworker than a husband? I loved your father dearly, but if I hadn't left, our marriage would've toxified while I lost myself. Terrible examples to give the independent girls I was raising."

The air left Julia's lungs. Mom…was right. The way she'd phrased that made perfect sense. No one should sacrifice their shot at total happiness. Julia took a deep breath.

Definitely did *not* have boulder-sized personal revelations on the to-do list this evening.

"Mom." She mirrored her mother's tucked-legs position. "Why didn't you tell me this before?"

"When?" Mom ran her index finger around the lip of her glass. "When you were ten? A teenager flying here at every opportunity? Barely keeping your head above water in college while you worked two jobs and refused financial help? Or when your father passed, God rest his soul? I couldn't speak ill of a man beloved and mourned by all who knew him. It wasn't really ill, either. He was lovely. We just grew apart."

Cold trickled down Julia's spine. She wished she could dispute anything her mother was saying, but… Fuck. Her mother was absolutely, one hundred percent correct.

"The truth is, honey, the greatest sin I've ever committed is not sacrificing myself at the altar of motherhood. If I don't care for myself, who will?"

"I…" Julia gestured to the closed bedroom door. "Isn't that why you're getting married? For someone to take care of you?"

Her mother dropped her head back and laughed. "No. I have my own financial security, Julia. Statistically speaking, I'll be the one taking care of him. Between generous settlements and my last promotion, I'd be fine if we parted ways. I'm with him because I *love* him. The sex was great from the first date—"

"Ugh, Mom, please." Julia pinched the bridge of her nose.

Mom laughed again. "Fine. But a month into the most delightful relationship of my life, I suggested couples' therapy. Most men would run screaming, but he agreed that with four previous marriages among us, we might need help to keep us in tune."

Julia pursed her lips. For once, her mother was making emotionally stable sense.

She had to call Alex.

"Oh, stop looking like I've shaken your worldview. Let's talk about something fun, like a bachelorette party."

Julia's stomach flattened. "What bachelorette party?"

Her mother touched her knee. "More like a bachelor-and-bachelorette party. Having everyone together at dinner was fun, wasn't it? So let's do it again. A group activity."

"What do you have in mind? I'll just jot it down." Julia picked up her tablet, added a task to the project in the Positively Productive app, then assigned it to Carson. *Joint bachelor & bachelorette party, God help us all.*

"You'll figure it out. Whatever you decide will be perfect." Mom finished her wine. "There's one more thing."

"Please don't tell me you want a martini luge."

"I have no idea what that is." Mom propped her head on her fist. "What do *you* think of Bo, now that you've met him?"

Ah, this she could answer. "He makes Alex happy. And he's a good cook."

A Carson text buzzed her phone. **WTF? A bachelor party?**

Sheesh, was he staring at the project, waiting for tasks?

Something low-key, she texted. **Maybe two birds with one stone. Adventure with Alex = a bachelor and bachelorette party?**

"I like him." Her mother fiddled with an earring. "He grounds her. Like a firm foundation. Since he entered the picture, her ideas for what you two can do with your father's estate have blossomed. She found the right person to dream with."

Ouch. Stab to her heart.

She was supposed to be Alex's idea partner, not Bo.

Her phone buzzed again. **Call me or I'm booking erotic dancers.**

Can't, she wrote back.

"My only hesitation…" Julia set her phone down. "Is they've only known each other for six months. Don't you need longer to know if you're right for each other?"

"Nonsense." Mom waved her hand. "Sometimes you know in ten minutes, other times it takes ten years. Don't hesitate when you feel the *yes*ness of someone."

"What does that mean? *Yes*ness?"

She had a sneaking suspicion she knew. No, that was ridiculous. Their hormones had raged out of control, but that didn't mean Carson was her *yes*.

"Let me see if I can put it into words." Her mother touched her fingertips to her lips. "It's more solid than attraction tingles. It's… It's like you find their eyes across a crowded room, and everything that's churning inside you relaxes because you know your person is there."

Fuck. She *did* know that feeling.

"I want that for all of you." Mom squeezed her knee. "Maybe Alex and Bo could be a good influence on Carson. Jim says he never has the same pretty young thing hanging from his arm twice. He's in his prime, and he should find someone who makes him happy."

Oh, he was in his prime all right.

The heat rose in her cheeks. She made up tasks to add to the project to keep her eyes focused on her tablet because her mother had an uncanny ability to read her thoughts.

Shower. Buy earplugs. Punch out of this conversation.

Mom squeezed her knee once more. "Good night, sweetheart. Sleep tight. I'm sure Jim and I won't."

Her mother winked at her, then slid off the couch.

Ew.

Julia flicked on the TV. *Please* let the sound drown out any bedroom noise. Commercial, commercial, *Jane the Virgin* rerun, news, and—bingo. A reality show where people got married three months after meeting and were shocked they had disagreements.

Her phone buzzed against the coffee table.

Another text from Carson. Why are you blowing up the project?

She texted back, Stalker.

I'm not stalking. The app has an alert—every time you add a task, it sends me a text.

She widened her eyes. I didn't know! That's an amazing feature.

Thank you. I called your sister to set something up tomorrow. She's on it. We'll meet at her office as planned, then go from there.

Her heart thumped an extra beat. Had she not already been attracted to him, his lightning-quick ability to handle business would've sealed the deal.

Another text balloon popped up. Why do you need ear plugs?

She glanced at the bedroom door and texted three eggplant and water splash emojis. Because our parents are frisky.

That's awesome. Good for them.

I'd like to never talk about our parents' sex life again, thanks.

Pulsing dots… Can we talk about our sex lives? I can't stop thinking about you.

Before she could respond, another text came, fast and furious. Or your bikini, and how easy it was to untie.

That was it. She couldn't have this evidence on her phone.

She stepped out to the patio and called him.

"Hey," he said after one ring.

God, she loved his voice. A thrill zipped up her spine every time she heard his deep smoky rumble. She flashed back to earlier today, when his chest vibrated with his groans.

"Hi," she whispered. "Please stop sending me flirty texts."

"I'm not flirting. That's just how I am with you." The smile was audible in his voice. "Can we meet up somewhere?"

"Someone might see. And we won't have time for…anything…tomorrow. We'll be with them day and night, and then guests start to arrive, and then the wedding's the next day."

"I see alone-time opportunities."

Shards of moonlight rippled on the waves in the distance. If they bumped a few things around, and… Wait, no. This was ridiculous. The real world was settling back on her shoulders. Julia Stone, as always, reined in the flights of fancy.

"Wow, long pause," Carson said. "Don't second-guess us, Jules. I mean it when I say I can't get enough of you. I want you a hundred ways, in dozens of different places. You don't have to admit you want that, too, but I'll be here waiting for you when you can, okay?"

"Okay," she said. "Good night, Carson."

"'Night."

She clutched the dark phone. No one had said anything like that to her in her entire life. Plain, honest, and hot. Energy frizzled under her skin. If Carson was here, her reserves would melt like chocolate under his gaze.

She blew out her lips.

Unfortunately, she was alone and the television did nothing

to drown out the noises emanating from the bedroom. Nope, nope, nope. She grabbed the pillow and blankets stacked on the sofa and took them outside to the patio's chaise longue.

Tonight would be lovely under the stars.

As Carson rose from the lobby couch, he grinned at his phone like a dope.

We're here, Julia wrote.

They'd been apart for twelve hours, and he hated it. He missed her jokes, her teasing, her firm opinions, her scent. The golden flecks in her eyes that glittered when she was amused.

Her touch.

So even though their family would cockblock him all day, he'd be with her. That was all that mattered. He shoved his phone into his pocket, then collected a small bag from the couch. Julia left behind a few things in their room. Scrunchie, lip balm, toothbrush. He'd picked up a bag of the cookies she'd devoured on the plane, too.

Outside, the thick, muggy air swallowed him. Early-morning LA was humid like this, but it burned off by nine. Belize's damp dome, however, lingered. He didn't mind it the way he had that first day. Must've been getting used to it.

Julia waved as he approached the minivan. Her simple greeting boosted his mood to the stratosphere.

He opened the passenger door and slipped inside. "How'd the paperwork pit stop go?"

"Great." Julia jerked her thumb toward their parents. "We officially have everything they need to get hitched in Belize."

"Congrats!" He twisted toward the rear seats.

Michelle seemed fine, but Dad's color was off. He clasped his phone, his thumbs worrying the rough bumps on its case. This was the same expression that had blipped on his face during the engagement party—the one he'd blamed on a renovation project. Carson bought that explanation, but Dad never brought project drama on a vacation.

"Everyone sleep okay?" he asked.

"No, but for the best reasons," Michelle said.

Julia pinched the bridge of her nose. *"Mom."*

"Don't be such a prude, Julia." To Carson, Michelle stage-whispered, "She's cranky because she slept on the patio last night. Trying to be like her sister, I suppose."

"It wasn't to be like Alex," Julia merged onto the road.

The city's candy-colored buildings were different from LA's reflective skyscrapers. Same with the people out and about on foot and bikes, heartily greeting each other on the street. Running errands with Julia had been like that—the florist, the chocolate-shop lady, the horny pirate—they'd all greeted her with hugs and warmth.

So different from the fake-nice air kisses to which he was accustomed.

Julia flicked her gaze to the rearview mirror. "I slept outside to give you privacy."

Aha. That was a perfectly organic opportunity.

"If you want..." Carson swiped his fingertip along the window frame, doing his best to feign nonchalance. "I still have a spare bed at my place."

There, that was subtle.

"Oh, she couldn't possibly stay there," Michelle said. "Our friends start to arrive this evening. When do you relocate to our hotel, Carson?"

Damn. "Tomorrow."

"Danny arrives tomorrow, too." Dad squeezed his shoulder. "Aunt Charlotte's grateful you've taken your cousin under your wing."

Danny was the only passenger who didn't sue him after the accident. He'd felt protective of the guy ever since. So when Aunt Charlotte asked if Carson could hire and mentor him, he'd agreed because he owed her one. He'd started Danny on back-of-house event work. Nothing client-facing, because they needed to work on the way he presented himself.

"Is this the Danny who went to Bronson with us?" Julia's tone was light, but her plastic smile and stiff grip on the wheel ratted her out.

She was pissed.

Fail. Carson's stomach clenched. How had he not thought to prep her for Danny's arrival? While his own bad behavior in high school had been rooted in immature complicated feelings, Danny's had been an inferiority complex swizzled with booze and wanting to impress Carson.

Too much to say in front of their parents, though.

"That's right," he said. "He's changed a lot in ten years, too."

"I hope so," she said under her breath.

Crushed oyster shells crunched under their tires as they pulled under a freshly painted Stone Adventures sign. A+ marketing. They'd used a classic adventure-themed font from old-timey movies.

Julia parked next to Alex's red Jeep. Three newish minivans and an older golf cart served as Stone Adventures' fleet.

"Oh, she still has Jasper." Michelle sighed.

"Jasper?" Jim asked.

"The golf cart," Julia explained. "My dad named his cars. Alex continued the tradition."

They unbuckled and marched into the small colonial-style turquoise building. As Alex glanced up from the laptop behind the counter, a smile spread across her face.

"Hey, family," she said.

"You've spruced this place up, Alex." Michelle surveyed the space. "Love the color choices and the new signage."

Carson and Dad read the framed articles on the wall: Tripadvisor Best of the Caribbean, *Condé Nast* Honorable Mention, and a human-interest piece in *Amandala*.

He whistled. "This is great press."

That was how his company had taken off—Thirty Under Thirty and Best Of articles. Great press led to bookings, which translated to sustainable business growth. If Stone Adventures was on that same trajectory, Alex might be able to hire Julia sooner rather than later.

Then Julia would move here.

He rubbed at the twinge in his chest.

"Thanks. I'm excited we're catching on," Alex said. "Business has been great these past six months. Bo's revamped the website and our social media accounts, and reservations are booking weeks in advance. I even hired Espy as a full-time assistant to help me keep up."

Julia's shoulders stiffened. "So you *are* hiring, then?"

Oh, *that* bothered her. He shoved his hands into his pockets to stop himself from massaging the tension from her neck.

"For clerical work. Part-time." Alex turned to Michelle. "You remember Espy, Mom?"

"She's tough to forget. I assume she's no fan of mine?"

"Not even a little." Alex laughed. "She's made herself scarce. Before we head out on our adventure, I need you to sign waivers."

Alex twisted a mounted tablet toward them.

"I wouldn't sue my own daughter." Michelle scrawled her signature on the display.

"Bo likes adhering to insurance requirements."

Jim signed his next. "This whole building is yours?"

"Yep, and the beach adjacent to it. We have big plans for the plot if we can secure funding. Julia—come check this out."

Alex opened a slide deck on her laptop.

"What is—oh!" Julia's eyes lit up when Alex paged to an illustration of a mid-sized hotel.

Her enthusiasm was palpable, the kind she'd need to sustain her through their start-up years if she joined the family business. That was how he was five years ago, how anyone creating a new business *had* to be to have a shot in hell at success.

These sisters? They had that energy.

"Is that what I think it is?" Julia bounced on her toes.

Alex nodded. "If revenues keep pace, we'll be able to break ground in a year. We have room for eight beachfront cabanas."

"The business is doing *that* well?" Michelle asked. "It was a dead-end fifteen years ago."

"Belize is more popular than ever." As Alex advanced through the deck, Julia widened her smile. "I shook up the business model to provide a variety of tour options."

"Wait," Julia said. "Go back to the overhead shot."

Alex clicked back three slides. "Here?"

"Yes. Eight cabanas is great, but…" Julia hovered her finger over the screen. "If we build two piers, we get twice the cabanas. We have riparian rights extending a hundred meters, right?"

"Hell *yes*." Alex slung an arm around her sister's shoulders. "You're a genius, Julia. We double the cabanas without acquiring more land."

"We could qualify for unique-stay status if we embed clear panes in the floor to see the marine life."

With the enthusiasm lighting up their faces and their curly heads nearly touching as they pointed to various places on the screen, the sisters resembled each other more than Carson realized. Alex might've been more brash, but Julia could be just as adventurous.

Julia lifted her gaze from the screen, and the smile she gave him stole his breath.

This was what she was meant to do.

She was an excellent event planner because she was great at everything she set her mind to, but this planning, ideating, building… It would be a crime if she didn't move here and work with Alex at this crucial initial phase.

The contradiction hollowed out his chest. He couldn't convince Julia to move to LA to explore this thing between them *and* encourage her to move here, where she was happiest.

Where she was home.

"It's nice to see you two getting along," their mother said.

"We've never *not* been getting along," Alex said. "Just busy."

"Another idea," Julia said. "This might sound bonkers, but hear me out. The resort I interned with in the Finger Lakes leaned into catering to introverted travelers. Smart tech allowed guests to basically never talk to someone. Mobile check-in, check-out, concierge, lobby grab-and-go for the basics, in-room cocktail station. Room service left on tables by the door."

"Isn't that, like, the *opposite* of hospitality?" Carson laughed.

"Nope. Silent salons and spas are totally a thing. Another trend is curating vacations for guests. People are so plugged in they hit decision fatigue by 9:00 a.m. These boutique hotels survey your likes, dislikes, health concerns, etcetera and cruise direct your vacation. No planning or decisions required. Total passenger princess."

Carson bumped his shoulder against his dad's, then tilted his head toward the conversation. "Are you hearing this?"

"Sounds like the only thing holding them back is capital," Dad murmured.

"You could help with that."

Julia twisted her hair into a bun. "We could accommodate anything guests might want. Alex can take them on adventures, then they head back to their oceanfront cabana and avoid people if that's their choice. We'll provide touches that teach them about Belize—interesting history printed on artisanal paper, maybe with handcrafted souvenirs. We'll use local vendors, too. Bed pillow chocolates by Mo, flowers by Xio."

"I can see that." Alex tapped her chin. "Rodrigo could hook up the cocktail carts, too."

"Are the Marandons still running their bakery?" Julia asked.

"Guests would be *beside* themselves to wake up to a carafe of local dark roast, the Marandons' authentic French fresh-baked pastries, and local fruit."

"Shut up, because you're making me hungry," Alex said.

She laughed. "Sorry. Now I'm dying for a jambon-beurre from Lamberts, too."

"We'll get one before you leave," Alex promised.

"You know your stuff," Carson said.

Julia lifted a shoulder. "It's *almost* like I have a degree in hotel and hospitality management."

"Do you two have any investors?" Dad asked.

Alex shook her head. "No. My family has bad luck with financial partnerships. I don't trust them."

Carson scratched the back of his neck. That was strange. Taking a business from a corner stop to a global shop required investment. It didn't sound like they wanted to stay small. Julia was touchy about anything to do with Stone Adventures, but he'd try to ask her about it later.

"Been there," Dad said. "But what if the investment is coming from within the family?"

Michelle beamed. "Oh, Jim, that's *so* generous."

Alex's and Julia's gazes swung toward Dad, unblinking. He could've predicted his father would do this. He'd done the same thing for Carson five years ago.

"I like to invest in the next generation," his father said. "Before coming here, I read up on Belize, and development's exploded. It could be the next Punta Cana."

"I know you've had bad luck." Carson draped his arm around his dad's shoulders. "But my dad's the best. Silent partner, unless you ask for advice. Seriously, five stars."

"You're not exactly unbiased," Alex said with a laugh. "Can we think about it?"

"Of course," Jim said.

Julia wrinkled her nose like a mountain of sargassum just washed ashore. "Who's we?"

Alex bumped shoulders with her sister. "You and me."

Carson breathed deeply. That would make Julia happy. And Julia being happy? Made him fucking ecstatic.

Bo entered through the back door. "Hi, everybody. Ready?"

"Paperwork's in order, sir," Alex said. "Prepare to douse yourself in bug spray, everyone. Today, we're zip-lining."

The carabiners attached to Carson's harness jingled as he hiked up to the platform. They'd already done a few short hops, and they were about to tackle the longest line. Prehistoric-sized ferns and trees and other plants he couldn't name surrounded them, a gorgeous green sea.

Every breath was filled with rich, deep energy. The cave had felt like this, too—like something watched them. Actual spectators were more likely in the rainforest, though. Howler monkeys had grumbled at the last launch point, and a toucan had taken a dive at Bo as he zipped to this stop. A brief shower passed overhead, making everything feel fresh.

"You'll love this, Mom," Alex said. "It's Belize's longest zip line."

Michelle shook her helmeted head. "The things I do for my daughters."

"Ready, señora?" Harrison, the zip-line company's guide, clipped her onto the line. "Don't forget—use the glove to slow down."

Harrison beckoned to Alex, who shoved her mother from the platform.

Next to him, Bo laughed. "I bet she promised him a big tip if he let her do that."

"Do they...not get along?" Carson asked.

"They do, in their way. They've been talking more, which helps."

Alex gestured for him to go next.

"That's my cue." After clipping in, Bo sailed off into the green.

"Do you not love him?" Julia asked Alex. "He'll be alone with her for three minutes."

"He'll be fine. He's unflappable."

Julia crossed her arms. "Mom can make people flap."

"Not me. At least, not anymore. See you on the other side!" Alex stepped up for Harrison to clip her in, then jumped and disappeared into the lush rainforest.

"I'd never do that to you," Julia said to Carson. "Alone time with my mother is cruel-and-unusual punishment."

"I've *been* alone with your mother, Julia. She asks inappropriate questions, but I've dealt with way worse. Her heart's in the right place even when her filter isn't."

"Oh," Julia said. "Right. I keep forgetting you've known her for longer than I've known your dad. What if you'd known she was *my* mother?"

"Yeah." He rubbed at his chest. The secret he duct-taped to his heart chafed. "What if?"

Harrison clipped Julia in. "Your turn, señorita."

"Here I go." Her low blond ponytail flapped in the wind as the trees swallowed her.

"Who's next?" Harrison asked.

"Dad?" Carson prompted.

"Actually, can we talk?" Dad asked him.

His ass puckered. Dad had started conversations with him this way when he was in high school. It meant Carson was in some shit. Did he and Michelle know about Julia?

"Take your time." Harrison invited another tour guide to bring her group to the line.

"What's up?" Carson said to his father. "You seem off. Nervous?"

"Not about the zip line." Dad leaned against the railing. "About Michelle."

Dad's admission felt like a thud to the chest. "Do you have cold feet?"

"Not cold," he said. "But I'll be honest, they're a little chilly. I don't get it, because things between us are great. She suggested couples' therapy early because of our track records, and that's been eye-opening. Helped me see patterns about myself. But it's all happened so fast."

Carson's gut twinged. This wasn't good. If the wedding took a nosedive, he'd take Dad's side and Julia would take her mom's, making anything between them messier than it already was.

"Fast isn't necessarily bad, Dad. You've both been around the block and know what you want. She seems good for you."

"All true." His father folded his hands.

Carson leaned his elbows on the railing. "What's the problem, then?"

"The first time I did this, my heart was the only one I risked." He glanced at Carson. "Now there's yours to look after, too. The way your mother hurt you... I should've seen it coming. Shielded you from it."

He wouldn't lie—his mother's disinterest in him post-baseball still stung. But that was her failing, not his. Definitely not Dad's. And he'd be damned if Dad carried guilt about it.

"Dad, no." Carson clapped a hand on his dad's shoulder. "You came through for me. And there's no way Michelle could hurt me as much as Mom. But if you're having doubts, postpone—after you talk to her. You two should figure things out together."

"You're right." His dad released his grip on the railing, then slid a palm against his neck. "I got hit with nerves...that's all. I love Michelle, and I'm pretty sure she loves me. Thanks, Cars. And I'd like to keep this between us, okay?"

He approached Harrison. "I'm ready."

Harrison clipped him onto the cable. "Enjoy the ride."

As Dad slipped away into the forest, cold flushed through Carson. *Pretty sure?* Growing up, he watched his dad bend over backward to keep the peace with Mom while she built her business. The only time they seemed like a solid unit is when they watched him play ball.

Carson snorted. No pressure for him to succeed, right?

After his accident, his parents fell apart. Dad gave his mom an ultimatum—if she couldn't get it together and be supportive to Carson, she needed to get out. She chose out, and the shifting moods and uncertainty in their home left with her.

He'd catch Dad alone later and encourage him to talk to Michelle again. He was sure they'd come through a tough conversation fine, but if they didn't…

Where did that leave him and Julia?

"Ready?" Harrison asked.

He stepped toward the precipice of the steepest drop of the day. "Yes."

As Harrison secured him with a comforting metallic clunk, he'd made a decision. Despite his dad's wishes, he'd talk to Julia about Dad's chilly feet.

Their parents might've been rocky, but that didn't mean *they* had to be.

Just like he was about to plummet toward the zip line's next stop, he was falling for Julia. Scratch that. *Had* fallen for her, years ago. The problem was they'd met *way* too early in life. As a teenager he couldn't handle his big, intense feelings.

He hadn't been ready for her.

He'd needed to go through some shit, like…losing his career; being sued by his friends; shedding his mother's toxic love; and feeling the weight of people depending on him for their livelihoods…to truly become a man who, finally, was good enough for her.

"Have fun." Harrison pushed him from the platform.

Above him, the pulley's whir sounded like a tiny screaming jet engine. As gentle forces tugged on his insides, the dark green tunnel of trees opened and revealed a forest spreading in all directions under his feet. Golden sunlight dappled the canopy, and hazy purple mountains lay in the distance.

Beautiful.

The destination platform waited for him up ahead. He was too far away to see faces, but that person, that one right there, watching the arrivals—that was Julia. From the way she held herself, the angle of her body. She was the person he searched for in a crowd, the eyes he wanted to connect with when he entered a room.

Tonight. He'd talk to her tonight.

Nineteen

After zip-lining, Alex and Bo went back to work and Julia and Carson split up to take their parents on errands. One of which, for Julia—*ugh*—included the lingerie boutique. Then another group dinner which lasted an hour longer than Julia planned but involved three hundred percent more under-the-table action with Carson.

He was *very* good at inching his hand up her thigh and accompanied her to the valet as everyone else finished their after-dinner desserts and drinks.

After she'd handed the valet her ticket, Carson had tugged her into the ferns near the entrance. Shrouded in dark green cover, she'd sealed herself to him and he'd snuck his hands up her dress. His lips had almost made her forget herself. Almost.

"We can't tonight," she'd breathed. "It's too complicated."

He'd reluctantly agreed, and she'd driven their parents back to the resort, where she'd showered and was about to check in on the wedding TBDs. She tightened the belt on the resort's robe. Under it, she wore a skimpy pajama romper. Perfect for warm nights, but awkward around her mother and almost-stepfather.

"Today was such fun, Julia." Mom covered her mouth as she

yawned. "Thank you for organizing it. Jim fell asleep as soon as his head touched his pillow."

Julia braced herself for *but we also should've* and *I would've preferred* and *I didn't care for* comments. But for once, none came.

"You're welcome." Julia scrolled through her task list.

For every two items she crossed off, she added something new. Still, progress had been made. The list had pleasantly thinned.

"Tomorrow's schedule is light," she said. "I'm stuffing welcome bags in the morning. Carson's running loops to the airport to pick up guests. Then we've got the rehearsal dinner."

"Jim's got a few calls he can't miss, so he and I can't play tourist. I'll be at loose ends."

"There's always the beach." When they were kids, her mother basked in the salty waves. "But wear sunblock. We don't want a lobster-red bride."

"Actually, I'd like to go to Alex's. You and I were together for the holidays, but it's been two years since I've spent any meaningful time with her."

A knot in Julia's heart loosened. "Good idea, Mom."

Life would be so much easier if the people she loved most in the world had a solid relationship. Sometimes keeping everyone glued together, serving as the connective tissue of her family of origin made her feel good. But other times they tugged so hard she felt like she'd snap. She loved them, but they drained her energy. Many people did.

But not Carson.

No, he filled her well. She snorted. Literally and figuratively. He made her feel like the sexiest, most interesting woman in any room. She really, *really* liked him. Maybe even…

She widened her eyes.

"Something wrong, sweetheart?" Mom asked.

"Nope. Everything's fine."

If *fine* meant *I had a shocking epiphany*, then yeah. She was fine.

Mom tapped her on the knee. "I'll head to bed, too. Love you."

"'Night." She offered her mother a small wave. "Love you, too."

Julia chewed her lip. The moments after everyone went to bed were her most cherished part of the day. She could switch off the people-pleaser part of her brain. With no one around, there was no one to please but herself.

Speaking of pleasing herself…what was Carson up to?

She withdrew her phone from the deep pocket of her robe and texted, Hi.

A return text popped up. Hi back. I like your smile.

That made her smile wider, enough to strain her cheeks.

And that's a nice robe.

Wait, what? She scrunched her forehead.

Look up, he texted.

Her heart skipped a beat. Standing in the patio door's frame was Carson, with his hooded gaze and smirky smile and damned Dodgers T-shirt. She dropped her tablet on the couch and hurried to the door.

Her nervous fingers fumbled the lock, but she got it eventually.

"What are you doing here?" she whispered.

"I missed you," he said.

Those words made her dizzy. *I missed you* conveyed longing, craving, yearning. It showed he thought about her when she wasn't there, and *that* was delicious.

"We were together all day." She joined him on the shadowed patio.

"With other people around." He slid the door shut, then tugged her to a hidden corner. "So I couldn't do this."

He caught her against him, his lips an electric homecoming.

She slipped her arms around his neck, desperate to pull him into her. He kinked his knees, curving and melting with her.

Desire, thick and hot, blossomed between her hips.

No. Not happening here on the patio. Too risky.

But it *was* happening.

She grabbed his hand. "I have an idea."

"You always do."

Julia led him through the courtyard and past the pool. They snuck past the thatched-roof bar with a dozen café tables where laughing strangers drank big fruity cocktails. Thank God the wedding guests hadn't arrived yet. None of these people knew who they were.

"This way," she said.

As they hit the sand, the ocean's crash and boom matched her heart.

"You said no sex on the beach." Carson squeezed her hand.

"I stand by that." She scanned the numbers on the cabanas dotting the beach. "One of the perks of a honeymoon suite is a beach cabana. Ah, there. Number four."

She tugged him inside. "You get the shutters, I'll get the curtains."

"Yes, ma'am." Carson slapped them shut.

She shook out a few enormous beach towels on the double lounger, then tackled the curtains. As she tied the sash tight, Carson hugged her from behind. Encased in his strong arms, she felt like a treasure. She wanted to give into it, to trust it, but good things in her life had been snatched from her before. If she expected this to fall apart, she might save herself a broken heart.

On the other hand, she could try Carson's optimism.

His lips brushing her throat was an excellent argument for optimism.

"You smell so good," he murmured against the nape of her neck.

"The resort has excellent taste in toiletries."

The tips of her ears burned. *Why* did she say that? She couldn't take a compliment to save her life. Always deflecting attention to someone, something, *anything* else.

"Nope." He licked the spot behind her ear. "It's all you."

She loved that he refused to be put off by her awkwardness. He might've been the only person in the world whose attention she craved.

The thick terry-cloth robe pooled at her feet.

"Being so close today but not able to touch you…" He dragged his fingertips up her arms. "It was torture. I couldn't stay away tonight."

The carefree part of her bubbled to the surface. Over the years, she'd constrained herself, buckled down, presented as flawless a veneer as possible. Stress had broken through her mask, though, and Carson saw, touched, tasted her whole self and still came back for more.

"I'm glad you're here." She nudged him onto the double chaise longue, then straddled his lap. "Because I couldn't look at your fingers without wishing they were inside me."

Yep, that actually came out of her mouth.

Based on his groan and the rigid length of his dick prodding her, he liked what he heard.

"Always tell me what you want. Understand?" In the dim light, his eyes were dark pools, like the caves they'd explored yesterday. Endless, ancient, but where those caves were cold, his eyes were full of heat.

For her.

The power she felt was delicious. Animal. With him between her legs, hot and hard and desperate, she could make him do or promise anything.

"Yes, I'll always tell you what I want," she said.

"Good." He slid a hand up her romper to caress her ass. "Because tonight we're both going to learn new things about you."

She rolled against him. "Sure you're up for it? After all, I was a straight-A student, whereas you..."

He clutched her hips. "Mastered a thing or two I can teach you."

The heat from yesterday was back in Julia's eyes, but it didn't overwhelm the sparkle. He loved that about her. While she was here, everything was suffused with this irrepressible joy.

"You're beautiful, you know that?" he asked.

Carson hadn't come to the resort for this. He'd wanted to talk to her about his dad and figure out what their plans C, D, and E should be if Dad went full cold feet. Then Julia smiled like he was the exact person she wanted to see most in the world, they kissed, and anything to do with their parents became a distant memory.

"No, I don't." She planed her hands on his chest. "So say more."

A lifetime listing delightful things about her wouldn't make up for the confidence he'd stolen from her in high school, but he could try.

"The way you carry yourself through the world—efficient, elegant, like a dancer."

"Like when I stubbed my toe against the bed frame?" Her lips tipped into a smile.

He pressed a finger to her smile. "Don't interrupt. You look like you're always *this* close to bursting into laughter. Your hair curls stubbornly, even when it's wet from the shower. Then there's this unexpected glimmer of jewelry."

He touched her ear, just below the double sapphire stud.

She caught his hand and kissed his palm. "Thank you."

"Not done yet." He twisted her forearm toward him, then kissed her soft skin. "These tattoos, and the way you rub your thumb over them when you're feeling anxious."

"Do I?" she asked.

"All the time." He ran his finger down her wrinkled nose. "I love the way you scrunch this when you're confused, like right now."

"Okay, you've said more." She smiled, but doubt lingered in her eyes. "Mission accomplished."

He'd change it up. Show her how beautiful she was, too.

"I beg to differ." Carson slid her pajama straps from her shoulders. "You have perfect breasts. I came in my sleep dreaming about them. Haven't done that since I was a kid."

He swirled his tongue around her rosy nipples. She gasped and wiggled in his lap, which, *fuck*, made him want to cut to the chase. But she needed to hear the next part loud and clear.

"I love watching your face when you come, and I plan to see it many times tonight."

She raised an eyebrow. "You've got that much stamina?"

"With you? No doubt." With his hands clamped around her, he swiveled and placed her on her back. "But I said *you're* coming many times tonight."

"What about you?"

"It makes me happy to make you happy," he said, shimmying her pajama-onesie thing from her body, then shedding his clothes. He tugged her hips toward the double lounger's edge, then coaxed her legs apart. "You have such a pretty—"

Julia laughed and covered her face. "Don't say it."

"Why not? It's true." He lapped at her delicate flesh with languorous strokes, like licking the sweetest ice cream on Earth. He alternated with fluttery swirls around her clit.

"*Yes.*" She wriggled under his mouth. "There. Keep... going."

Heaven was between Julia Stone's legs.

She gently bucked her hips, begging for more, and he was happy to oblige. He loved the eager way she responded to him. She'd been wet to start, but now she was ripe as an August peach.

His physical advantage as a ballplayer had been his big hands and long fingers. Good for snatching baseballs from the air. Also good for coaxing orgasms. He eased two fingers inside Julia. Her core squeezed as he adventured forward, his tongue never letting up. He curled his fingers up slightly, feeling around for the—

Aha. There was the ridged patch.

Carson rubbed it gently. "How's that?"

She raised her head. "What are you—oh." She dropped back to the lounger. *"Oh."*

With his other hand, he pressed the gentle hill above her vulva. Inside, he kept massaging her spot, picking up speed. Above them, lightning flashed, followed by a thunder crack. Rain pounded the cabana's canvas roof.

"What do you want?" he asked.

"This," she gasped. "But harder."

He followed her orders. God, she was beautiful as she chased her pleasure. The muscles in his forearm were starting to burn, but he'd rather get carpal tunnel than stop.

"Oh, fuck... I'm about to—"

Her inner muscles squeezed his fingers as she raised her hips. Carson waited until the echoes faded before withdrawing. He laid next to her.

Catching her breath, she laughed. This was the secret Julia, the utterly unfettered version no one else got to see. He didn't take the privilege for granted.

After her giggles died down, she asked, "What was that?"

"An orgasm, I believe."

"I've *had* orgasms. That was... I've never—I don't...how?"

She was incoherent. A sign of a job well done.

"That was a g-spot orgasm. Or so I'm told." He feathered his fingers along her smooth skin. "Figuring out how to deliver one takes practice."

"My gratitude to your former lovers." She threw her arm

over her eyes, then heaved a deep breath. "Could you get me a water?"

He kissed her elbow. "I don't want to get arrested for indecent exposure."

"Not from the resort bar." She gestured vaguely toward the corner. "Mini fridge."

"That makes more sense." He flipped open the mini fridge door. The tiny freezer stocked with ice cube trays gave him an idea. "Here you go."

Julia took the bottle. After guzzling, she offered it to him. "Want some?"

"Nope. Turn over."

She set the bottle on the side table, then flipped to her stomach. The speed of her compliance was beyond hot.

"Like this?" she asked.

"Yes." He knelt next to her. "Guess the letters I draw on your back."

She peered at him. "What do I get if I'm right?"

"I'll make you come again." He plucked a cube from the tray. "If you're wrong, I'll still make you come again. This is a win-win for you."

As he drew the first letter, she shivered. *"F."*

"Correct." He traced another letter.

"U."

Another letter. She giggled. *"C.* Carson, are you trying to make me say *fuck*?"

"Yes." He licked the water glistening on her back. "You never swear. Curse words coming from your mouth in bed is my kryptonite."

"If you like dirty talk, you don't need to play games. This whole tell-me-what-you-like thing is a two-way street." She batted her eyes. "Could you fuck me senseless, please? Oh, unless you want me to suck you dry?"

Carson groaned. Her mouth on him would be glorious, but that wasn't what he had in mind.

"Maybe later." He positioned himself behind her, straddling her legs, then tugged her hips upright. He palmed her ass, circling the flesh before skating his hands up the column of her back.

He glided his cock against her opening, teasing her, drunk on her inviting slickness.

She backed against him, encouraging.

He slapped her bottom gently. "Impatient."

"Carson, please."

The *please* was sweet in his ears.

"I'll give you anything, everything you ask for."

On a groan, he sank into her until his hips met her ass. As they moved together, a wave of affection overwhelmed him. No, not a wave—a tsunami that swept him off his feet and whirled him into the deep.

This wasn't plain affection. He *adored* Julia.

She reached back for him, and he locked his grip around her forearms. He held her steady as he entered her, again and again and again. Julia was wild in his grasp, enthusiastically meeting each thrust. They stayed locked together like this for an eternity and no time at all. Thank God for the rain and thunder drowning out their moans.

Soon, tingling tension coiled around his balls.

"What do you want?" He ground out. "I won't last much longer."

"I want you to come for me."

He let go of her arms, and she planted her hands on the lounger. After three strokes, the base of his cock contracted, and he was gone. With each throb, the pressure inside him was eased. He rested his face against Julia's back.

"How do you feel?" she asked.

"Empty," he said into her sweat-slicked skin. After a few

deep breaths, he kissed her shoulder blade, then eased himself from her and fell back against the chaise.

Julia laid her head on his chest. Her hair smelled amazing. Coconut and citrus. Shoot it into his veins, whatever it was, because he was already high on her.

He traced lazy circles on her shoulder. For several minutes, they lay in the dark, nothing in the air but the sound of their breathing and the rain pelting the cabana.

This was peaceful.

Ten years ago Julia met the worst version of himself. Today she was in his arms. Proof he'd become the man he'd aspired to be—a person worthy of her.

"I did not have this on the itinerary today," she said.

"Glad I could tempt you away from the almighty list." He kissed her head. "What else is on there? Time travel? World peace?"

"Mostly getting a job."

That he could help with. "You'll get snapped up in a day by someone in my network."

"Sleeping my way right to the top." Julia lightly tugged at his chest hair.

"You shouldn't apply to entry-level gigs. You should be running shit."

She snuggled into him. "Who'd take orders from me?"

"Anyone with a brain. I've been taking orders from you for a week, haven't I? You learned about this wedding less than a week ago, and it's *done*. Planned. Boom. You make it look easy because you just...handle things."

"Okay, now I'm full stoplight blushing." Julia covered her eyes with her hand.

He peeled it free, then threaded his fingers with hers.

"You're great at this, Julia. Own it."

"Okay, okay. Owned."

Carson loved their casual conversation with her in his arms.

Some people enjoyed this every night of their lives, which blew his mind. He wanted that, and he wanted it with her.

"Have you reconsidered LA?" he asked. "You and your sister have the drive to start something big. My dad can infuse the development with cash. LA could be a soft place to land while you figure it out. And I can help you."

Her deep swallow gently rocked his chest. A moment passed, then two, then three. Yep, he'd pushed, and now she was spinning, figuring out how to say no without disappointing him. He wished she'd answered with an enthusiastic yes, but that was about him, not her.

He kissed the top of her head.

"I can hear the lists you're drafting, Jules. Don't answer now, okay?"

"Okay," she said. "Can we lie here and listen to the rain?"

"You've got it." He closed his eyes and tried to ignore the itchy sensation in his heart.

Twenty

Above Julia, bright canvas came into focus.

Oh, fuck. Fuck fuck fuck.

They'd fallen asleep and stayed in the cabana until morning.

"Carson." She shook his shoulder. "Wake up. We fell asleep."

After Carson dropped that LA question on her last night, she'd frozen. If Jim was serious about investing in the "and Resort" part of Stone Adventures and Resort—which she hadn't even had a chance to discuss with Alex—she'd be crazy to prioritize LA. She loved the city, but sacrificing her dreams for a shot at love was a recipe for disaster.

Which she'd never say out loud, because her mother and sister would be offended. Mom moved to Belize after a holiday hookup with Dad, which she'd never say was a disaster because they'd produced two lovely daughters. But still—heartbreak. Bo had moved here, too, for one of those daughters, and Julia hoped that worked out, but who knew?

The heart could want what it wanted, but hearts changed.

She'd lain there, unable to articulate any of her worries, and been lulled to sleep by the soporific cocktail of rain; Carson's broad, comfortable chest; and the ocean's rhythmic crash.

He stretched. "Yeah, I know. I set an alarm for seven."

"You set an *alarm*? You should've woken me up last night." She found her romper. "We left the patio door open. Mom might think I've been kidnapped, or—" She clapped a hand over her mouth. "Someone could've murdered them."

As he sat up, the plush resort robe they'd used as a blanket fell to his waist. "Murder rates at five-star resorts are pretty low."

She whipped the robe from him to slip it on. *Oh, hello.* No. Back to reality. His morning wood was not her problem to solve at the moment.

"Julia, calm down. Everything's fine."

"For *you*. For me?" She knotted the robe's belt. "Anyone who's on their way to morning yoga will know I'm doing a walk of shame."

"Who's ashamed?" He jumped into his shorts.

"Poor word choice." She scrubbed her forehead. "I hate people knowing my business."

"No one knows." Carson kissed her forehead. "Even if they did, who cares?"

"Me." His cozy arms soothed her. "Maybe I shouldn't, but I do. I care what people think, even strangers. 'There go the almost-stepsiblings,' they'll say."

"No one's saying that. Caring that much is a tough way to live."

"It can be." She extracted herself from him. "I've gotta go."

"I'll walk you."

"You will not." She swigged the water from last night. "Stay here and throw everything in the hamper or the trash and wait at least ten minutes before leaving."

Delicious tingles flowed from her nape as he played with her hair. His eyes twinkled in the morning sunshine that set the cabana aglow.

"I love it when you tell me what to do," he said.

"And I love *telling* you what to do. It's why we make a good team."

"A great team."

He covered her mouth with his. This was no *good morning* kiss or *have a nice day* kiss. This was a persuasive *let me jump your bones right now* kiss, and he was fumbling at her belt.

No, no, no. She had to leave right now, or they'd end up having sex in broad daylight surrounded by vacationers.

"You don't play fair." She clutched the curtain, ready to whip it open.

"Never said I would. Can you do me a favor, Jules?"

"What, you monster? I have *got* to go."

An alert sounded on her phone. He'd added a new task in their project.

Stay with me at the resort tonight.

Desire twirled between her hips.

"If it's on the list, consider it done." She disappeared through the curtain with his chuckle chasing her.

The tangerine sun was unforgivably bright. She blinked at her phone and called up today's affirmation. *The only force that can stop me is me.*

She paused to let three women with yoga mats cross her path.

"Morning," she said. "Coffeemaker in my room's broken."

What was *wrong* with her? It wasn't necessary to spin up a plausible non-sex reason to explain why she was running around in a bathrobe.

The only force that can stop me is me.

Her paralyzing fear at getting caught was overwhelming. Anxiety spirals about being judged. Contorting herself to meet every demand, even those detrimental to her mental or physical health.

The only force that can stop me is me.

She could try *not* doing those things. The worst that would happen is someone might dislike her, be disappointed in her, or complain she did a bad job. There was a time when she thought she'd combust if that happened. Now…not so much.

She grabbed the patio door's handle.

The only force that can stop me is me.

Oof. And apparently a locked door, since it didn't budge. She shaded her eyes and found her mother sitting at the dinette table, watching her phone and drinking coffee.

Tentatively, she knocked.

Mom looked up, then ventured toward the door. It clicked as she unlocked it.

"You're an early bird today. Did you catch Jim? He went for a jog a few minutes ago."

"No." She left off the *thank God*. What if he'd caught her at the cabana? *Oh, hi Jim. Please excuse me while I go tame my spent-all-night-tangled-up-with-your-son hair.*

"Why don't you get dressed and we'll head to breakfast? We've got a big day, and I don't want you melting down about a nonissue because you skipped the day's most important meal."

Julia sighed. "Okay."

No matter how capable she showed herself to be, her mother and sister pigeonholed her as the sensitive one. The emotional one. The fragile one who sprang apart at the slightest flick.

Wait. What was she doing? This was not okay.

"When's the last time I had a meltdown?" she asked.

Mom lifted a shoulder. "Don't be so dramatic."

"This isn't drama." Julia crossed her arms. "It's clarification. When was it?"

After the longest sip of coffee in human history, her mother answered. "When you missed the deadline for National Honor Society applications."

She laughed. "You had to go back to *eleventh* grade?"

"I'm sure there are others I'm not remembering."

Julia shook her head. She'd spent so much effort evolving herself into a resilient self-starter, and her mother hadn't even noticed. Carson was right—people thought whatever they wanted, irrespective of truth, so worrying about it was a waste of energy.

"There aren't, Mom. I haven't had an anxiety attack in six years. That's what those were, by the way. Not 'meltdowns.'"

"Be nice to me," Mom pouted. "It's my wedding weekend."

"I know!" Julia threw her hands in the air. "I planned it!"

Her mother cocked her head. "What's gotten into you?"

Carson. She snorted.

"Did you get enough sleep last night?" Mom asked.

"I'm annoyed, that's what's gotten into me. You're treating me like a child. I'm not sleep-deprived or hungry or hormonal. This is plain and simple irritation."

Her mom flipped her palms toward the ceiling. "All I did was ask you to breakfast. Where's this coming from?"

"From here." Julia glanced her hand against her heart. "I never told you it bothers me when you treat me like that, and now I am. So, could you stop?"

"I suppose I can't say *anything* without sending you into a tizzy." Her mother sighed.

"Now who's being dramatic?" Julia laughed. "I'll be ready in ten."

Her heart was lighter than it had been for a long time. A week ago she would've tried to get Mom to admit she was right to be annoyed. But now? She'd let it go. Mom wouldn't change, but she didn't need her to. She could enjoy her mother's extraness and choose to laugh instead.

"Julia?" Carson carried a crate of Belizean rum into the resort's meeting room. Somewhere behind the mound of sturdy canvas beach totes and tissue paper was the person he wanted to see first in the morning and last at night.

"Hi!" She popped up from behind the table, clutching a spool of ribbon. "What's that?"

"My dad's contribution to the welcome bags. Want help?"

When he'd tried to corner his father for a heart-to-heart, Dad had thrust this crate at him, then shooed him away as he took a business call. Another reason to be concerned, actually. Dad channeled anxiety into work.

She twisted her toe against the carpet. "If you're not busy?"

"Nothing pressing." He set the rum on the table, then withdrew a chicken sandwich from the box. "I thought you might not have eaten."

"You're a god." Julia unwrapped the foil and chomped an enormous bite. After she swallowed, she glanced at him, then back to the sandwich. "Want to split this?"

Insincerity dripped from her words.

He laughed. "It's all yours. How many bags do you have left to put together?"

"A dozen." She winced. "Breakfast took forever, and then Alex was late picking my mom up for their outing, so I'm behind."

Carson inspected a completed bag. "These are nice."

"Mom calls them the essentials. Sunblock, sunglasses, bug spray, water bottles, a rattan fan, a copy of *Destination Belize* magazine, Mama Belize potato chips, and cashews." She swigged water. "Plus the rum. Oh, and monogrammed beach blankets."

"Swanky." He crushed the tissue paper to create a base, then carefully arranged the goods in the bag. He shook out a blanket, then folded it so their initials peeped above the bag's lip at a jaunty angle. "What do you think?"

"You're better at this than me."

Julia smiled at him, and it made his shoulders tense. He should tell her about his dad's confession, but it might be nothing. Why stress her out, too?

Instead, he said, "I have many hidden talents. Wait 'til you need a foot rub from your wedding heels. No shot they stay on all night."

"They'll stay on. The bridesmaid's dress, however…" She quirked an eyebrow.

"Happy to help with that, too." He rearranged another bag. "Want to check out the view from room 228? And while you're there, I want to check out a view."

He winked, and she rolled her eyes.

"That's an empty offer, sir. You're supposed to pick up my aunt Mary while I'm doing the final checks with the vendors. Once that's handled, I'll head to the restaurant for the rehearsal dinner and set out the place cards."

Damn, she was right. This day was getting away from them.

"When did your mom settle on seating arrangements?"

"This morning, finally. She had many opinions for someone who's 'easy breezy.'" Julia tossed the balled-up wrapper into the garbage. "You're with your family, Alex is with my mom's college roommates, and I'm Aunt Mary's date for the evening. She's more like a buddy since she's Alex's and my godmother."

Calm wafted off her. This was an outrageous turn of the tables. Julia Stone was efficiently working while he was a combustive mess on the inside.

"Both of you?" When she bent to gather more items from under the table, he straightened her bag's monogrammed blanket corner.

"Yep," she said from under the table. "She didn't have kids, so she spoiled Alex and me. You met Mary at the engagement party, didn't you? She's a retired teacher, but she still lives in LA. My mom must have had her over before."

The bottle of rum he'd been holding thumped against the bag as he let it go.

Nerves of the shit-I-might-get-caught-in-a-lie variety erupted in his stomach. He had met her aunt Mary before, but he'd forgotten about their conversation. Until now.

"Is she tall with short blond hair? Wears scarves?"

"That's her."

Fuck. He'd been in the kitchen at his dad's Labor Day barbecue when she'd asked him to uncork a bottle of sparkling wine. As he'd obliged and poured her bubbles, they'd chatted. She'd said she was a happily retired teacher and asked where he'd gone to high school.

"Bronson Alcott," he'd answered.

"Oh!" Mary widened her mouth in a smile. "Then you might know Michelle's daughters—Alex and Julia Stone."

He'd squeezed his tumbler tight. Over the years he'd casually surfed for Julia's social media, but she kept her shit locked down tight. Either that or she'd preemptively blocked him out of spite, which he couldn't blame her for.

"Michelle's their mom? But her last name is Doll."

"That's her fourth last name. I take it you do know them?"

His dad had rescued him by calling to him to help with the sound system. Later, snooping around the photos Michelle had stuck on the fridge since she'd moved in, his heart had squeezed when he saw a grown-up Julia Stone.

Chances were slim that Mary would remember or reveal he'd known who Julia was months ago. But if Julia found out, she'd lose her mind, and she'd be right to do it. At the time, he'd thought it'd be better to tell her in person...but then he took one look at her, and all of his logic had fallen away.

He had to tell her. If it came from him, he could salvage things. Should he tell her before or after mentioning that his dad was having doubts?

Christ, this was messy.

He riffled his hair. The best way to rip off a bandage was fast.

"Carson?" she prompted. "Everything okay?"

He turned to face her. "There's something I've—"

She held up her finger. "Whoops. Hold that thought. It's my mom."

Dammit.

"Hey, what's up?" She nodded at whatever Michelle said

on the phone. "Oh, okay, I'll let him know. No, it's fine. He's right here. Yep, see you soon."

She clicked off the phone, then sighed. "Aunt Mary got in early, so you're off to the airport. But what were you about to say?"

He couldn't confess now. This information required a big cushion of time afterward so he could answer her questions, absorb her anger, explain why he'd lied in a way that didn't make him seem like a manipulative asshole.

"Just that I can't wait to see you tonight." He caught her to him, then dropped a sweet, gentle kiss onto her lips. "Call or text if you need anything."

"I'll take you up on that," she said. "Now scoot. Aunt Mary's mean if she's kept waiting."

Twenty-One

At the rehearsal-dinner venue, Julia glanced at her slim silver watch. "Where are they? They're twenty minutes late."

She huddled with Carson, Alex, and Bo near the bar, sampling the specialty cocktail Carson requested for tonight. Alex approved of the chili-passion martini, a sweet and spicy blend of local passionfruit, chilies, and vodka.

"Probably having sex," Alex said. "Mom could *not* stop talking about Jim's beautiful penis when we were hanging out earlier today."

Julia coughed as a red-pepper flake stung her throat.

"No more locker-room talk about our parents." Carson rubbed the spot between her shoulder blades. "You almost killed Julia."

"I'm fine," she wheezed.

Alex bumped shoulders with her. "I nearly tossed myself from the golf cart when she said it. Mom said she tried to bring it up with you but you shut her down. Well done."

Much as Julia enjoyed Carson's touch, she stepped out of his reach. "So you're besties again?"

"Yes." Alex sighed. "God bless Aunt Mary, because she'll take the brunt of it this weekend. They were giggling so much during the rehearsal. Good job with that, by the way. A fifteen-minute rehearsal is wedding-prep goals."

"Seconded," Carson said.

"Thanks." Happy warmth flooded through her. She was a sucker for her sister's praise. "It helped that they didn't want to reveal their vows yet. I hope they've written them."

"They have," Carson said. "At least, my dad has."

"Mom will probably extemporize a haiku." Julia sighed as she tilted her wrist. Now they were twenty-*five* minutes late. "How do you do this for a living, Carson? Making sure a large group is having a good time is stressful."

"Don't look at it that way," he said. "Most people will have a good time if we provide a fun atmosphere. A few won't, but you can't please everyone."

Alex slipped her arm around Bo's waist. "What do you think for us? Fancy resort wedding?"

Bo adjusted his glasses. "Nah. Exchange vows while parasailing?"

"You know me so well." She kissed him lightly on the lips. "Oh, Jules—our houseguest left today. The spare room's all yours."

"Oh." *Do not look at Carson.* "Thanks, but the couch in Mom's suite is surprisingly comfortable."

Was what a person might say if they'd actually slept on it.

"Suit yourself." Alex lifted a shoulder. "Guests are finally arriving. Time to mingle as blended-family ambassadors."

She and Bo ventured toward the people picking up their table assignments.

"When will you come to my room?" Carson murmured as he trailed sneaky fingers up the back of her arm. "Immediately after dessert, or should we sneak away now for a quickie?"

Goose bumps fanned across her body.

"Stop that," Julia said.

"This?" He tickled the diamond inked on the delicate skin of her wrist.

No one's attention was on them.

"Yes." She shifted in front of him and brushed her ass against his pelvis. "Stop it some more."

He chuckled and grazed her exposed back. She'd selected this bright pink sundress because it stood out against the ocean's bright aquamarine. Tonight, though, she wanted to be seen by one person in particular.

"This dress is something else," he said. "During the rehearsal I wanted to lick your back."

"You weren't riveted by the readings? Love leaping like a gazelle and all that?"

"Frankly, I'm surprised my dad didn't go with Jimmy Buffett lyrics." His fingers skated dangerously close to her waistline. "Some people say that there's a woman to blame."

She might be able to orgasm from this alone.

"I'll come to your room as soon as I can." Julia forced herself to leave Carson's wandering touch. "Don't forget to make a list of everything you want to do later."

"Already did." He tapped his temple.

She pressed the chilled glass to her face. It might've been the red-pepper flakes, but it might've also been the heat in Carson's green eyes.

"Okay, then," she said as she crossed the room to greet guests.

Damn, she had to work on her sexy goodbyes.

"Julia!" Aunt Mary swaddled her in a hug. "It's been ages since I laid eyes on you."

She breathed in Mary's classic jasmine-and-lily fragrance. "You saw me at the engagement party."

"But before that it was last Thanksgiving. Ten *months* ago. I get lonely for you. Come stay with me in LA. We can have sleepovers like when you were a little girl. Though I suppose you'll be the one working and I'll be the one on a permanent vacation."

The universe was not subtle. Aunt Mary was the second person in twenty-four hours to urge her toward LA.

She guided her aunt to their table. "That's generous, but..."

"You've always done better in the sunshine."

Mary was right about that. Pretty as upstate New York's autumn was, the harsh winters weren't it for her sun-kissed soul. But it wasn't about the weather. Not really. In the handful of days she'd been back in Belize, friends she hadn't spoken to in years had done her favors without hesitation. She missed that kind of community—people looking out for each other.

"Promise me you'll consider it." Mary took her seat. "You've always been stubborn about accepting other people's generosity."

More people arrived. By her estimates, half the guests were here, but still no Mom or Jim.

"Not stubborn," she said. "Wary."

"Of your fairy godmother?" Her aunt hung her purse on her chair's back.

Of everybody, usually. Carson, though, was making a case for giving people a chance.

"Okay, I'll consider it. Can we stop talking about this?"

"Yes." Mary rested her chin on her hands, then followed Julia's gaze to the corner, where Carson huddled with Jim's business partner. "Jim's son is certainly handsome. Successful, too, from what Michelle tells me."

A thrill fluttered in Julia's belly. She liked that her mother and aunt thought well of him.

Before she could share what she knew about his company, applause erupted around them.

The guests of honor had arrived.

"Finally." Julia sighed. Their table started to fill with Mom's cousins, and the remaining empty seats would be claimed by Mom's work bestie and Jim's scuba buddy.

"It's nice to see your mother happy again," Mary said. "She lost herself after you and Alex left the nest. Then your father passed, and she didn't know what to do with her grief."

Julia finished her martini before asking her aunt, "What do you mean?"

Mom had been sad for her and Alex when Dad had died, had chipped in for the funeral and burial costs, but she didn't seem to mourn him herself.

"She didn't feel entitled to it. Xavier was a good man, and she loved him. But since she'd left him, and you girls were bereft, she didn't burden you with it. Too complicated and messy to explain."

Julia's breath shuddered in her chest.

That was an echo of what Mom said the other night. If she'd walled her daughters off from her sorrow because theirs was deeper—what else had she protected them from? Family should make space for messy feelings and situations, not force you to shove them in a closet.

Aunt Mary plucked a martini from a passing waiter.

"Since I've retired, giving unsolicited advice is my new hobby. You and your sister would be happier if you accepted Michelle for who she is and stopped resenting her for not being who you wanted her to be. Oh, and while I'm on a roll..." She tipped her head and cut her gaze in *check it out* gesture. "You're twenty-six, not sixty-six. Cut loose and have fun. As the lone single woman here, you're a bit spoiled for choice."

Julia turned in the direction Aunt Mary indicated, and her stomach squeezed.

On his way into the room, Danny Cox's sharky smile gleamed like the Cheshire cat. Ugh, the only difference between Danny's vibe now and high school was a pair of overly distressed skinny jeans. She knew he'd be here, but it was surreal to be in a room with *two* former nemeses.

Thank goodness she'd seated him across the—wait. Why was he heading this way?

Danny plopped into the lone empty chair at their table, be right next to her.

"Mind if I sit here?" he asked as the waitstaff delivered field greens salads to the table. "I swapped 'cause I thought it'd be fun to catch up."

Oh, she minded. If Aunt Mary and the rest of their tablemates weren't here, she might stab him in the hand. Instead, she nibbled on a crouton.

"I take it you two know each other?" Mary asked.

"Yes, ma'am." Danny leaned forward, all smiles and kiss-ass earnestness. "Julia, Alex, Carson, and I went to high school together."

Ick. Objectively, he was an attractive man, but his ooze negated the handsome. This was exactly his vibe at Bronson Alcott. Friendly with the adults, snarky and obnoxious with peers. Julia jabbed her fork into the lettuce.

"A veritable reunion." With a wink, Mary scooched back from the table. "If you'll excuse me, that cocktail ran straight through me."

Julia was alone-ish with Danny. Fantastic. Super. Everything she never wanted.

"Julia Stone." Danny draped an arm along the back of her chair. "It *is* still Stone, yes?"

She'd never had better motivation to sit up straight.

"Yes." She didn't owe him politeness, but she didn't want to make things weird for their dinner companions.

"Good, good, good." He twirled his fork but didn't eat a speck of the salad. Annoying, considering she'd sampled three to select this one. "Carson said you run hotels these days?"

This guy made her feel like botfly larvae were crawling out of her skin. He'd been the other half of the Sad Puppy conversation, about which she'd like to never think again.

"I don't run hotels yet. I'm looking for the right fit, job-wise."

"Oh, *I* could provide the right fit." Danny raised an eyebrow.

Ew. Time for more salad. The resort's citrus vinaigrette was amazing, and she'd hate to see it go to waste.

"You seem way more interested in that lettuce than me." He crunched his ice cube. "Nice earrings, by the way. My mom has a pair like that."

Yep, same old Danny. Backhanded compliments for days. She got that Carson was grateful Danny hadn't sued him, but come *on.* He'd lose clients daily if this was how he interacted with people.

"Clearly my game's off, but I'm stunned that goody-two-shoes—" he leaned in "—stick-up-her-ass Julia Stone became a total smoke show."

"Could you not," she said.

Family or not, she'd kick him in the balls if he crossed the line.

"Carson called it back in high school. Said you were cute. Was a little obsessed. Now that you've filled out, though? I get it." He raked his gaze over her. "It's like those movies where the nerd was secretly a supermodel, but she's all insecure and shit. It's a hot combination."

Okay, enough.

Before she could push back from the table, he said, "We even had a bet about it."

What. The. Actual. Fuck.

"A bet about what?" she asked.

"That he could get you to bang on the first date. General consensus was you were frigid, but look at my boy. He can always get it."

Across the room, Carson animatedly chatted with Holly.

"But then he bailed on the bet. Said you looked at him with sad puppy eyes and it'd be too easy, so there was no point."

She snapped her butter knife through the cold butter ball on the table. "Say *sad puppy* again and I'll stab your thigh."

The woman on the other side of Danny glanced her way. Good, let her see what a prick he was. Not like it was her job to help him hide it.

"Whoa, spicy." Danny held up his hands. "I couldn't fucking believe it when he said Uncle Jim was dating Sad, uh, Julia Stone's mom."

The word *dating* snagged her attention like a fish hook.

"Don't you mean *marrying* my mom?"

"That, too." Danny nodded. "But this was right around Labor Day, I think? It was kind of a getting-to-know you 'cause Michelle had just moved in. Carson snapped a pic of a family portrait and was like, *Is this Julia Stone?*"

Julia went cold.

She could give a fuck about Bronson Alcott. She hadn't peaked at sixteen and didn't plan to for at least another forty years. She rubbed her index finger along the top of the knife.

No, this was about Carson's dishonesty.

She'd *explicitly* asked him if he'd known Michelle was her mother, and he'd lied. She *refused* to cause a scene at this perfectly planned rehearsal dinner. No, she'd find him later tonight, as planned, and demand an explanation.

An explanations that might ruin this thing between them before it had a chance to fly.

"Oh, good," Aunt Mary said. "I haven't missed the salad course."

Julia pinned on a smile, inched away from Danny, and opened up her task list to distract herself. A new task that Carson added popped up on her project.

Final run of show meeting, room 228 @ 10 p.m.

She glanced at her watch. Two hours until their reckoning. *Please* let him have a good explanation. She'd give him the benefit of the doubt, but not at the cost of her dignity. She'd never compromised that and never would.

A knock sounded at Carson's door. "Just a second."
Please don't let that be Julia. Not yet. She was an hour early, an hour he desperately needed her to be somewhere else. When dinner ended, she'd gone to the suite with her mom, sister, and aunt, and he was supposed to hang out with his dad and the boys in the bar.

He glanced through the peephole. Julia was in the hall with her enormous suitcase.
Dammit.
He opened the door. "Uh, hi. You're early."
Her smile faltered at the lack of warmth in his voice. Double dammit. He couldn't let her into his room right now, and he couldn't tell her why.

"Expecting someone else?" she asked.
"Room service." He slipped into the hallway, then closed the door. "Sorry—I'm in the middle of something. Can I text you later?"

She scrunched her nose. "But I need to talk to you."
"About what?" His guts knotted. He couldn't tell her the truth without causing problems and couldn't conjure a plausible lie that'd send her away happy.

The scrunch turned into a furrow. "Why can't I come inside?"

A terrible, awful solution popped into his brain. But honesty would take too long, and he had faith in his ability to grovel and explain it later.

"Because… Paramore."
Her face crumpled. No, no, no. In his desperation, he'd gone nuclear. He couldn't do this to her. Before he could take it back, she backed away.

"Good for you, stud." She circled her hand between them.

"Smart. This was fun, but it's too serious, too fast. Which is what I was coming here to say, but you beat me to the punch."

She jabbed the elevator button, which was right there waiting for her.

"Jules, wait," he called.

"No." As the elevator swallowed her, she said, "Don't stay up too late. We have an early day."

He scrubbed his hands through his hair. *Shit, shit, shit.* But he only had bandwidth for one crisis at a time. Carson entered his room, closed the door, and briefly considered banging his head against it.

"Who was that?" Dad asked.

"Julia, but she's gone." He parked himself on the bed. "Talk to me."

Lying was terrible, but Julia would understand. She had to. If he'd said Dad was calling things off, Julia would've looped in Michelle, who dialed emotions up to a million. His father was a great guy, but he ran for the hills in the face of intense relationship drama.

No, this—talking him down, man-to-man, was the best choice from a bad menu.

In the guest chair, Dad sat with his hands folded between his knees. "I don't know what else there is to say. I love her, but I've been ignoring the four failed marriages between us."

"That means you know a lot about what *not* to do," Carson offered. "What I said yesterday is true—you're great together."

Dad palmed his neck. "She'd be great with anyone. I don't know what she sees in me."

"Are you kidding? Dad, you're the best."

The people he loved sure had trouble understanding how incredible they were. Dad, Julia... He widened his eyes. *Hold the fucking door.* People he *loved*? Julia came back into his life seven days ago. A week was way too soon for words like *love* to enter the equation.

Then again, he'd actually known her for ten years.

Stop. Dad needs you right now. This isn't about you.

"Not kidding, son." He jiggled his knees. "I have a mirror. I'm four inches shorter than her, pudgy, and bald. She looks like Elisabeth Shue."

Carson had no idea who that was.

"That was true when you met. Michelle doesn't seem to get hung up on appearance."

Dad raised an eyebrow. "You haven't seen her morning routine."

"No, I mean she doesn't judge a book by its cover. Where's this coming from?"

"It started at the engagement party. All those people, cheering us on, and a voice in my head told me it would be a disaster. I thought it'd pass, but as we get closer to the day, there's this ball of worry." He tapped his sternum. "I'm not sure I can bounce back from heartbreak again."

As Dad paced, understanding clicked into place for Carson.

Unflappable Jim Miller, who offered a wise word about every facet of life—business, houses, taxes, politics, parking tickets—didn't know shit about how to handle a different future sneaking up on him.

The good news was he could help.

Carson had way more experience with literal and figurative curveballs. His planning the wedding was to pay Dad back for everything he'd done in the wake of his baseball-ending accident. Maybe talking Dad through his own rough patch was the *real* payback. And if he couldn't do it, based on what his dad just said, he knew who could.

Carson sent an SOS text, then tossed his phone onto the bed.

"You've seen the men your mom's dated since we divorced."

They were ex–Major Leaguers with endorsement deals for car-rental companies, shoes, and underwear. Man candy, because Mom preferred handsome guys who thought little, which meant she could direct them more easily.

"None of her relationships last more than a year, Dad. And Michelle isn't Mom."

"How do you know?"

"Because I've met her daughters." He crossed his arms. "You can't raise grounded, kind, smart people without possessing those qualities yourself. Especially Julia. She's amazing."

Dad paused and gave him a look he couldn't decipher. After a beat, he scratched his jawline. "You're all those things, and your mother raised you."

There went his hero, once again not taking enough credit.

"*You* raised me, Dad. Mom managed me. Until the accident, and then she stopped doing that. You and Michelle are the real deal. Nobody can guarantee what happens next, but you love each other now. You'd rather be with her than without her, right?"

Dad hiked up his lips in a half smile. "That's right."

"Then don't hold Michelle to account for Mom's jackassery. That's not fair."

The knock on the door startled him. She'd gotten here fast.

Please let this have been the right person to text.

Carson opened up. "Hi."

"Hello." Michelle eased around him. "And hello to you, too, honeybun."

Dad was on his feet. "How'd you find me?"

"A little bird told me." Michelle glanced at him. "Well, more like a six-foot bird."

Better make a break for it. "I'll give you two privacy."

"Stop. I want you to hear this, too." She clasped Dad's hand. "You're nervous. Me, too, and that's good because it means we're risking our hearts. If you don't want to get married, we won't. We'll have a nice party, and I'll be happy. I love our life, with or without the paperwork."

Tension evaporated from Dad's shoulders. "Do you mean that?"

"With my whole heart. You must have been so stressed, trying to hide your feelings."

Dad reached for her hand. "I got in my own head. You're right."

"I usually am. On this occasion, though, credit goes to my daughters." She winked at Carson. "They prize honesty. Even hyperbole falls into the arena of 'lying' to them. Every time I embellish the truth, they hold it against me. They rarely forgive bald-faced lies."

Carson narrowed his gaze. "Are you trying to tell me something?"

"Me?" Michelle pressed her fingers to her chest. "Not a thing. I'm dispensing advice since we'll be in each other's lives for a long time if things go according to my plans."

He had to call Julia, run to her, tell her everything right the fuck now.

"Thanks for the advice."

"You're welcome." She tugged Dad's hand. "Let's get out of Carson's hair, honeybun."

Twenty-Two

Julia wrapped herself in the blanket she and Alex snuggled under as kids. Her big sister rubbed a soothing circle on her back, and Julia dabbed at her eyes with a tissue.

"Anything I can do?" Bo asked from the archway.

"Snacks," Alex said. "Savory. Then leave us in this time of sisterly need."

"On it." He pivoted toward the kitchen.

"Okay," her sister said. "Why did I have to speed to the resort to pick you up?"

"I slept with Carson."

"Obviously. What else?"

Julia chose to ignore the *obviously*. "I like and maybe love him, but he's been lying to me this whole time, and he has another woman in his room, and I've been a goddamn fool."

Alex slid off the couch. "This calls for a drink or five."

After ice clinked into glassware, followed by glugging liquid sounds, she returned from the kitchen with a charcuterie board and two pink drinks.

"I sent Bo to bed." She placed a glass in Julia's hand. "Here."

She sniffed at it. "What's this?"

"Cranbarrel. Cranberry juice and One Barrel Rum." Alex

clinked her glass to Julia's. "Good for heartbreak and fighting UTIs."

She gulped the potent cocktail.

"Who's the other woman?" Alex asked.

"I don't know. He said *Paramore*."

Alex pinched her lip. "I'm not following."

"It's a code-word thing my friends and I did in college to avoid awkward situations with overnight guests. I thought it'd be prudent." Julia's breath shuddered. "Being around Carson twenty-four seven was…doing things to me. So I thought I'd scratch an itch with someone safe, like Roberto. But then Carson used it."

Paramore. Carson's pained expression as he said it burned in her brain.

Like it stung his lips.

"Well, he's a dick." Alex collected her empty glass and disappeared to mix more.

A minute later, after shoving another Cranbarrel into Julia's hands, Alex plopped onto the couch. "Who did Carson have in the room?"

"I don't know." She lifted a shoulder. "It might've been the hotel's event coordinator. They talked at the rehearsal dinner tonight."

Alex nudged her knee with her toes. "Call her."

"It's ten p.m."

"The night before an event. She'll pick up." More toe nudges, like when they were kids. If she didn't comply, Alex would literally keep poking her until Julia pounced in frustration.

Also just like then, she'd lose any wrestling match with Alex.

Julia flipped over her phone. She'd missed calls and texts from Carson. She'd read those later. Right now she was Detective Stone.

With a wobbly finger, she poked Holly's number.

After half a ring, she answered, "Julia! I was checking the

weather reports. We'll have clear skies during the ceremony. Sorry about the background noise. I'm at my friend's show."

Relief flooded her.

"Oh, good. I was calling to...uh...um..." She glanced at their drinks. "Can you make sure we have cranberry juice at the reception tomorrow? My sister's getting a UTI."

Alex flipped her palms to the ceiling and mouthed *What the fuck?*

"Absolutely," Holly said.

"Thanks. Have a good night." She tossed her phone onto the couch. "Not her."

"I gathered," Alex drawled. "Are you *sure* someone was in there?"

"I told you, he wouldn't let me in." She scrubbed her hands through her hair. "There's still the gigantic problem of him lying to me this whole time. At Mom and Jim's engagement party I asked him point blank if he knew Mom was *our* mom, and he said no. Tonight his smarmy cousin said he'd known for months."

Alex pulled her knee to her chest. "That's not great. But he seems protective of Jim."

"He is." Julia twisted the glass against her palm.

"So if he came clean to his dad, and then Jim told Mom—both big ifs—then what? Mom might've dumped Jim, which Carson wouldn't have wanted. He might've been hoping you were over it and it wouldn't be an issue."

It would be very Carson to try to smooth things over, but Alex was wrong. He hadn't hoped she was over it. Grudgingly, she gave him credit for approaching her at the party and sincerely acknowledging and apologizing for what he'd done.

Except he'd been lying to her this whole time, so did that apology even count?

Fresh anger sizzled through her.

"Are you defending him?" she asked.

"Nope. I'm Team Julia. This sucks mega-bananas, but there's a silver lining." She threw her arms around Julia. "Finding this out today is better than three years from now when he runs away with all your money."

A giggle escaped Julia as she swiped away another tear. If Alex could poke fun at that emotionally tender spot from her own romantic past, maybe Julia could, too.

Someday.

"Let's stop talking about me. I'm sick of me. What about you?" Julia shut off her phone. The only people who might call her tonight were her mother, Carson, and wedding vendors. Mom could call Alex, and the vendors had Carson's number.

Let him handle any wedding emergencies, the jerk.

"What about me?" Alex asked.

"Tell me the love story between you and Bo. The details, not just the highlights."

"That could be a novel," she said.

"Good." Julia settled against her sister's shoulder. "I've got nowhere else to be."

Carson thumbed the Caribbean-blue shirt's last button through the buttonhole. Uncle Bill and Danny would wear matching outfits—untucked Oxford, khaki pants, and leather flip-flops.

Ideal for a beach wedding, not so much for running errands.

Especially when he hadn't slept. He'd tried texting and calling Julia until Alex texted to say Julia was staying there but to please leave Julia alone so she could rest.

Once he knew she was safe, he laid down to sleep.

Never actually conked out, though. He was too busy berating himself. *When* would he learn he couldn't control reality by controlling information? Honesty might not get him everything—or the one person—he wanted, but at least he'd have integrity.

Instead, all night he'd felt like a childish ass.

Before the sun split the horizon, he'd been up, distracting himself with wedding prep. On the beach, he'd checked the wedding arch placement and chairs tied with turquoise bows. There, he'd also run into Xio, who'd artfully arranged bright green palm fronds weighted with coral conch shells next to each row. As he helped her unload the table decorations, bouquets, and boutonnieres from her truck, she'd asked about his wedding date.

"Julia's my plus-one," he'd said.

Bold claim, since she hadn't responded to his messages or the task he'd added to the project for her to call him.

"Oh really?" Xio raised an eyebrow as they loaded the flowers into the resort restaurant's walk-in refrigerator.

"Yes," he said. "Why?"

"Roberto. She has a weakness for him. I figured he'd be *her* plus-one."

Carson raised a shoulder. "I'm not worried about him."

He was, however, worried that he'd screwed up so royally last night that Julia wouldn't talk to him since she *still* hadn't returned his calls. Now here he was, knocking on his father's door to meet up with the groomsmen.

The women had a separate prep room nearer to the beach. He could go there, take Julia aside to clear the air, and apologize for the subterfuge. Before he could turn on his flip-flop, though, the door opened.

Dad pulled him in for a hug. "There's the man of the hour."

"Isn't that you?"

"We'll share the honor. We wouldn't be having a wedding if you hadn't talked me off a ledge last night." He gestured toward the boutonnieres. "Do you know how to attach these?"

"I do, actually." He pinned the bright orange flowers to the lapel of Dad's tan suit. After finishing, he gestured to Danny. "You're up next."

"Cool." He set his Belikin down and approached. "Dude, I can't believe Julia Stone's your sister now."

"Stepsister." He lifted the blue shirt away from Danny's undershirt. He didn't like her name in Danny's mouth. "And she isn't yet."

"She will be, though, which is *crazy*."

Carson worked the straight pin through a pinch of Danny's shirt, then poked it through the boutonniere's taped stem. Last thing to do was to poke it through to the shirt's other side.

"She was *upset* when I told her about our bet."

The pin slipped and lightly stabbed Danny in the chest.

"Fuck, that hurt." He rubbed the injury.

"Uh, I'll do my own." Uncle Bill headed toward the bathroom.

"Here." Carson yanked a tissue from the box. "Don't get blood on your shirt. What bet?"

Danny slipped the tissue under his shirt. "How about 'Sorry I stuck you with a pin'?"

"It slipped. What bet?" Vague, dread-inducing memories tried to present themselves, but nothing took shape.

"Come on. Ms. Goody Two Shoes'll let Carson rail her on the first date. *That* bet."

Carson wobbled on his feet. "We had no such bet."

"How can you not remember this? We were at Jeannie Sinclair's party, the Jäger was flowing, and I asked you who you thought was hot. You said Julia Stone, and after I stopped laughing, you bet me a hundy you could get her into bed on the first date."

Hazy memories came back to him. He didn't remember making that bet, but it sounded like something he'd do back then. If he made the mistake of letting something personal slip and a buddy pounced on it, he'd backpedal or double down.

The bet would've been a classic backpedal for admitting he'd thought Julia was hot.

Fuck his past self sideways, seriously.

"What's the big deal?" Danny asked. "I let you out of the bet when you said it was too sad and pathetic to go through with it. I thought you were a good guy for that."

"I wasn't a good guy." Carson ran his thumb and index finger along his eyebrows. "I was an asshole. And I really liked her."

Between this and her thinking he'd fucked around last night, he didn't blame her for shunning him. He checked his phone. He'd texted Julia updates throughout the morning about the setups and the flowers but gotten nothing back.

He couldn't take it anymore.

"I've gotta go." He pivoted away from Danny and toward the sliding glass door.

Text me back or I'm coming to the bridal room.

Three dots. Don't you dare.
Those three dots represented hope.

Jules, I need to talk to you.

She thumbs-downed his text, then wrote, You don't get to call me Jules.

Because *Jules* was reserved for family.

Nothing else in the chat. No dots. He'd take an emoji or a salty string of curse words, but the nothing was killing him.

"Everything okay, son? You're attached to your phone."

"Julia's…" He stopped himself. Dad shouldn't worry about cleaning up his son's mess on his wedding day. He slapped on his event-CEO smile. "I screwed something up, so she's upset with me. I want to go apologize, but she wants me to keep my distance."

Dad placed his hands on Carson's shoulders, the way he did every time he was about to drop wisdom on him.

"Everyone makes mistakes, but you can't force forgiveness. Give her space, and you'll be fine." Dad let go of his shoulders, then winked. "Unless you screwed up dinner. Then you're on my shit list, too."

Carson fake chuckled.

Dad didn't know the whole story, but his advice might've been right anyway. He'd give Julia the space she requested, and they'd get through today. Once she knew the truth, all of it, she might forgive him.

He ruffled his hair.

She had to.

Twenty-Three

Julia bit her freshly glossed lips. Okay, Carson *must* have asked his friend to push this daily affirmation out to the Positively Productive app.

I release worry and choose forgiveness and trust.

She'd never released worry in her life.

"Jules." Alex thumped on the door. "I appreciate that you're having a crisis, but I need to pee and Roberto's on his way."

"Be there in a second."

She pulled the shallow zipper of her bridesmaid's dress up to her waist. Hmm. Much as she hated to admit Carson was right…this dress was fire. The midnight blue deepened the brown of her eyes as it tastefully bared her body.

Julia tilted her head.

She'd never pick this for herself, but it worked. After flicking her loose blond curls over her shoulders, she opened the door.

"Just gorgeous, honey," her mother said. The simple column of Mom's pale blue wedding dress showed off her figure. "I *knew* that would suit you. Can you believe the next time we do this, it'll be Alex at the altar?"

Alex's snort contrasted with the elegant picture she made. She wore her hair in an intricate network of braids that faded into curls. Their mother had chosen the same midnight-blue shade for Alex's dress, but the shape was more fitted, like she could hop into a kayak and paddle to Azul Caye if circumstances demanded it.

"Our wedding won't be a fancy shindig." Alex bit into a croissant that Julia had had delivered from Marandons' Café this morning. "We're not traditional."

Julia couldn't bring herself to eat.

"I'm aware," their mother said. "Tradition isn't always handed down. It can be something you make for yourself. When did you know Bo was the one for you?"

Alex's eyes gleamed like smoky quartz. "It might have been the first time I saw him."

"That's the flechazo." Mom peered in the standing mirror as she applied lipstick. "The women in our family fall fast and hard. It will find Julia someday, too, if it hasn't already."

Julia locked gazes with Alex.

Tell her, her sister mouthed.

She closed her eyes. Tell Mom? Mom loved to dissect every juicy detail about relationships, to languish, to wallow. Julia, however, preferred to make quick decisions on her own.

But this was too big.

If she didn't confide in Mom, she'd be keeping her at arm's length about a huge chunk of her life. They'd managed to bridge so much over the last two weeks. Like the dress, maybe this sharing style suited her more than she knew.

Quietly, Julia said, "It has."

"What was that, sweetheart?" Mom fluffed her shoulder-length curls. "I didn't hear you."

Dammit. Julia cleared her throat. "I said it has. Found me. The flechazo."

"Oh?" Mom pivoted from the mirror. "Who's the lucky person?"

Oh God. Deep breath. There was no taking it back if she

said it out loud, but she had to tell her. Her mother wanted to know what was happening in her life.

I release worry and choose to trust.

"Carson." Julia braced herself.

Her mother blinked. "Carson?"

"I tried to stop it because we're stepsiblings, but I couldn't, and Christmas will be hella awkward every year, but don't worry because it's already over, and I'm sorry if this makes your wedding day super weird."

Mom slid an arm around her shoulders. "Julia, dear, take a breath."

She did as ordered, then took another one. "Sorry."

"Don't be silly." Mom squeezed her shoulder. "I thought this might happen."

"You—" She clutched her phone. "What?"

"Carson went to your high school, didn't he? I recognized his name as soon as I met him. You covered him *extensively* in your diaries."

Alex snickered. "I told you journaling was trouble."

"Mom." Julia's cheeks heated. She'd written *everything* in those journals. Roberto…edibles…how much she hated coming back to LA… Her mother must have been devastated. "Those were private. And hidden in my closet."

"Oh, *privacy*." Her mother shooed away the concept. "If you wanted to hide them you wouldn't have stored them in a box marked *Journals*. It was obvious that you adored Carson. Even if the words are unkind, no one spills that much ink on a young man unless they have a crush. When I found your yearbook and found his photo, I could see why."

Julia worried the tattoos of her forearm. Huh, Carson was right—she did that when she was anxious. "Setting aside your disregard for boundaries, did *he* know you knew who he was?"

"It didn't come up, but I spent time with him as Jim and I

got more serious. I couldn't bring him back into your orbit unless he'd changed. I'm happy to report he has."

That was Julia's opinion, too. At least, it had been.

"Why didn't you warn me before the party?"

Her mother released her. "If I told you he'd be there and Jim was his father, would you have come?"

"*Mom.* You've got to stop manipulating me!" Julia put distance between she and her mother. "Adults don't do this to each other."

Her mother shrugged. "Am I so terrible? You two obviously hit it off."

"Ms. Stone?" Holly called as she rapped against their door. "I have unfortunate news. I tried calling."

Julia flung the door open. "Is everything okay?"

"No, I'm afraid not." Holly's eyes were wide and shining.

This must've been serious. *Please, please, please not Carson.*

With a pounding heart, Julia opened the door. "What is it?"

"Sargassum. It's back. This is *so* unusual. We may be able to clear it, but the odor…"

Oh thank God. It wasn't anything serious.

Holly froze, waiting for her reaction.

What, like she'd rain hell on her for not controlling nature and stopping rotten seaweed from beaching itself? A small giggle bubbled from her, became a river, then an ocean of laughter. She might've a week ago, when she was wound tighter than a fishing line that hooked a marlin. But now? After a week in the most beautiful home on Earth?

She doubled over, bracing her hands on her knees as she quaked.

"Julia?" Alex palmed her shoulder. "Are you okay?"

"Never better." She rose and thumbed tears from her eyes. "The benefit of dealing with lifelong anxiety is I'm weirdly calm when a legitimate crisis hits. How's my makeup?"

"Intact," Holly said.

"Hooray for waterproof mascara." She hesitated, then fired off a text to Carson.

Sargassum has landed. Activate Plan B. I'll arrange transportation and text Roberto. Holly's handling flowers. You inform the string trio and the groom's side, I'll do the bride's.

Immediate response. Got it. Thanks for forcing us to have a Plan B ready to go.

"What'll we do?" her mother moaned. "Our wedding can't smell like rotten eggs."

Julia texted Esperanza, who'd agreed, after some choice words, to be on standby with Stone Adventures' vans to provide transportation if they needed to go with Plan B.

"Already handled, Mom. Instead of the beach, you'll exchange vows on a pyramid."

"Just like that?" Mom dropped her shoulders.

Alex grinned. "That's impressive."

"Thank you." She savored the moment.

For her mother and sister to recognize she knew what she was doing was a rare treat. But she couldn't dawdle. Too much to convey before they decamped to the ruins.

Julia invited the events manager inside. "Holly, let's huddle."

Three dozen people gathered on these ancient ruins for the bride to make her appearance, but Carson's eyes were hungry for Julia. He, Uncle Bill, and Danny lined up behind Dad as the string trio kicked off the song Michelle picked for their entrance—Fleetwood Mac's "You Make Loving Fun."

"Thanks for making me see sense," Dad said.

Carson clapped a hand to his shoulder. "No problem."

Sweat prickled his back. They'd busted their asses to help park staff set up chairs and the wedding arch he'd swiped from the stinking beach. Luckily, he'd had enough forethought to order the groomsmen to strip off their blue Oxfords to prevent sweat stains and wrinkles.

Bedraggled was not the best aesthetic for the wedding photos.

A giant smile split Dad's face. "There they are."

The bridesmaids emerged from the ancient pyramid's tunnel to the platform. Carson sucked in a breath. Julia was stunning. The setting sun's golden beams loaned her an angelic glow, and the dress—the one she'd said was not her style—caressed her curves the way he'd like to every day for the rest of his life.

He had to fix this.

Whatever it took, whatever she demanded, he'd do it. The past eighteen hours of radio silence were miserable. He'd finally learned the lesson life had been trying to teach him for years: It didn't matter how well-intentioned his half-truths and lies were or how scared he was that someone he loved might abandon him. Honesty was the only way.

People didn't always love the truth, but they fucking *hated* lies.

Julia most of all.

"This is better than the beach," Dad said.

Mary led the way down the makeshift aisle. Julia and Alex flanked their mother and escorted her toward his dad. The simple smile Dad and Michelle shared was deep with meaning.

"Shall we?" Dad offered her his hand.

"Yes, please," Michelle said.

Carson paid zero attention to the ceremony, almost flubbing the handover of the rings. He tried to catch Julia's eye over her mother's shoulder.

And failed.

Now, during the bridal party pictures, as guests climbed aboard the vans to return to the resort for cocktail hour, Julia refused to stand next to him. He almost admired the gymnastic shuffling she did to avoid him.

Almost.

"Best man?" Roberto had elevated his style today. Instead of flip-flops, he wore slip-on sneakers. "Maids of honor and best man?"

Alex stepped away from the group. "I was Mom's maid of honor last time, so this one's just Julia."

Hope sparked inside Carson. If the sisters hated him, Alex would've shanked him with the pocketknife she always carried.

"Hi," he murmured.

Nothing.

"Julia."

She glanced up at him, and the sunset caught on her helix earring. It didn't hold a candle to the anger flashing in her eyes.

"Not here," she said. "Today's about them. Not us."

He liked the word *us* on her lips. Yes, she'd hissed it, but *us* indicated she thought of them as a unit. The "not here" meant she'd give him a chance to explain.

After Roberto gave them the signal that he'd nailed the shots, Julia clapped to get everyone's attention.

"Okay," she called. "Our ride is waiting at the trailhead."

On the van, Julia made sure to sit next to her aunt Mary.

Carson sunk into the seat next to his uncle Bill. In the movies, romantic apologies were this huge thing with boom boxes and last-minute flights and extravagant gifts.

None of that would impress Julia.

He could stand up on this bus and make a big show of an apology, but she'd explicitly said to keep the focus on their parents. She'd probably kill him for doing it with an audience, too. No, he had to adhere to her instructions, or she'd put up more walls between them.

Sometimes the only option was to do nothing.

During the ride to the resort, the driver regaled them with Maya lore. Carson alternated between checking his phone for messages, glancing at Julia, who was currently rubbing the tattoo on her forearm, and the lush Belizean forest fading into Azul Caye's bustling streets.

"Here we are," Julia said as they arrived at the resort. "Jim and Michelle have requested no formal introductions or announcements, so head in and have a good time."

The driver hopped out to open the van's sliding door. The air still carried a light sulfuric tinge, but they hustled everyone inside fast enough for it not to matter.

"Carson?" Holly caught his elbow.

"Hi," he said. "Anything wrong?"

"Not a thing. The accommodations you requested yesterday are well in hand."

"I never had a doubt," he said. "Thanks."

"You're most welcome. Enjoy the party."

He'd try. Inside the event room, the only empty seat at Julia's table was between Aunt Mary and Danny. As he pulled the empty chair out, Aunt Mary scooted backward.

"Switch with me," she said. "I'm sure you two need to discuss wedding logistics."

"You don't have to do that," Julia said.

With her back to Julia, Mary winked at him. "Of course I do."

He understood why Julia loved her so much.

After helping Mary into her chair, he sat in the one next to Julia.

She murmured, "Not here, either."

Conversation swirled around the table as they enjoyed their ceviche, which was better today than it had been when they'd sampled the menu. Soon, the waitstaff busily swapped out soup bowls for the main course. As everyone else *oohed* and *aahed* over the pepper jelly–glazed snapper or pork tenderloin, Julia gaped at the meal set before her.

A chicken sandwich with plantain chips on the side.

Alex pointed at Julia's meal. "Did you offend the chef when you chose the menu?"

Tentatively, Julia reached for a chip.

"I never offend anyone. I like simple fare better, which Carson knows." She glanced toward him. He detected a slight hesitation, but something changed in her eyes.

An opening.

"Carson, could you pass the hot sauce, please?"

That she asked *him* for the sauce instead of leaping across the table to get it herself was a sign she was thawing toward him. Wasn't it?

"Good evening, everyone," the band's singer announced. "Let's welcome the bride and groom to the floor for their first dance as a married couple."

As Michelle and Dad took to the parquet, the reggae band struck up "Love Will Keep Us Together." The first night here in Belize, when he'd checked out the club the concierge recommended, he'd known this was a must-have band as soon as they played this song.

Because Dad couldn't stop, wouldn't stop with the yacht rock.

They looked right together as he led her around the floor. Together, in love, solid. The guests applauded as the song ended and Dad dipped Michelle.

Show-off.

"The bridal party is invited to join the happy couple."

Bo and Alex took off like a shot toward the floor.

"Care to dance?" Carson asked.

"Not really." Julia dropped her napkin onto the table. "Let's get this over with."

Hmph. Maybe she wasn't thawing.

On the floor, he slipped an eager hand around her waist. "We need to talk."

"Oh, that's not true." Her touch on his shoulder was light. "We can dance silently."

Still a ballbuster. "I lied last night."

"You've lied a lot more than last night. But go on."

There was no time for anything but coming clean, fast.

"The Paramore thing. I panicked. I didn't invite anyone to my room besides you. Dad got cold feet, and I was trying to talk him through it."

"I know. Mom told me about it this morning." She stared past his shoulder. "But you didn't trust me."

"I should have. He and I have been each other's sounding boards for so long, it took me a minute to realize the only person he should've been talking to was your mom. That pattern—where he and I are each other's first confidantes—that'll take time to unlearn."

"That's the thing, Carson. You've got patterns I can't..." Julia bit her lips closed. "Never mind."

"Say it," he demanded. "Don't worry about hurting my feelings or how it looks. Just say what's on your mind."

She glared at him. Finally, direct eye contact.

Not the ideal sort, but he'd take it.

"You're a liar, Carson Miller. That first night in LA, I asked you one simple thing—did you know Michelle was my mother. You said you didn't. Danny said you knew months ago."

He faltered mid-step.

Ah, fuck. He'd been so focused on Mary, he'd forgotten he told Danny, too.

Carson searched her gaze. "I didn't want to open a can of worms. If I admitted at the engagement party that I knew Michelle was your mom from day one, then Michelle would've asked why I didn't say anything to *her*. I was hoping, since it was ten years ago, we could've treated it like water under the bridge."

"We probably could have. My mom knew who you were and gave you the benefit of the doubt. She thought you might've grown up a bit."

He blinked. "She did?"

"Yes. Carson, your desperation to make everyone like you twists you in knots. You hold on to truth that you think might make you look bad instead of trusting people to give you grace. Like the bet you had with Danny about asking me out."

Carson missed another step.

"But I honestly wanted to go out with you. Does it matter that it was part of a bet?"

"Are you kidding?" Julia closed her eyes, and a cloud passed over her face. "Of course it matters. I wish you'd just told me the truth."

"But it was ten years ago."

"We're not talking about ten years ago." Julia sighed. "We're talking about today and how you keep telling me what you think is easiest for me to hear. You don't trust me, Carson. To understand or to find my way to forgiveness. You hide and smooth and dodge and sanitize to manage people, hoping your charm erases the problem if you get caught. As much as I want you, I can't accept that, Carson. I respect myself too much, which is why this is over."

She pulled away, leaving him with his heart bleeding on the dance floor.

Twenty-Four

As she marched away from Carson, Julia fought hyperventilation. That was the most honest she'd been with any human being. She'd meant every word, but the shock that she'd let it all out without stopping vibrated in her veins.

The victory, however, was hollow, because a win for herself meant losing Carson.

Before she made it back to her table, the band kicked off Beyoncé's "Single Ladies" with a bouncing reggae beat. Oh, balls. There was only one reason to play this at a wedding reception.

"All the single ladies, put your hands up...for the bouquet toss!"

The guests laughed. *All the single ladies* equaled exactly two people—her and Aunt Mary. Maybe she could run away?

Nope. Her beaming mother snaked her arm through Julia's to drag her to the floor.

"Are you excited?" Mom asked.

"Please throw it to Aunt Mary," Julia whispered.

"It'll go where it goes." Mom faced the wall. "Ready?"

"Count with me," the lead singer urged. "One!"

"Two, three!" The crowd chanted.

The bouquet soared in a beautiful arc. Aunt Mary shoved

her into its path. The bundle thumped her in the chest, and she instinctively caught...not her mother's rose bouquet. The sweetly scented cluster of plumeria felt right into her hands.

Cameras snapped around her, but for once, she didn't care.

As she drifted back to the table, she cradled the small bouquet. It took everything Julia had not to bury her nose in them. When she arrived, Carson rose and helped her into her chair.

"I told you not to get a bouquet to toss," she said.

The plumeria smelled delicious.

"Your mother insisted, and she's the bride. The least I could do was get your favorite flowers. Oh, and this is for you. Instead of cake."

Carson slid a small confectionary box toward her. Even if it didn't have the embossed Azul Caye Chocolate Company logo swirling across the top, she'd recognize the pale blue box from across a room. She tentatively unfolded the box, and... dark chocolate, caramel, and pecans.

A bit of her heart thawed.

Sixty seconds ago, she'd unequivocally told him they were over. Now this and the flowers and dinner... Her breath shallowed. For years, she'd avoided attention. Without invitation, Carson paid attention to her in ways big and small.

What was she supposed to do with that information?

"When did you..." She scrunched her forehead.

"Yesterday between airport runs."

Julia nibbled the chocolate. "I didn't give you enough to do."

"I did plenty, but I prioritized important stuff. Like making sure you felt cared for."

"Are those Mo's turtles?" Alex asked. "Can I have one?"

"No. You're having cake." Julia snapped the lid shut. These were sentimental chocolates.

"Sheesh, okay, stingy."

She'd been called worse.

At the cake table, Mom and Jim held the knife together to

cut their first slice, then gently fed each other a bite, with a sweet kiss at the end. After the applause, the waitstaff doled out slices along with glasses of champagne.

Which meant the toasts were next.

It was her turn since Alex spoke at Mom's last wedding. Two nights ago, she'd cobbled together something personal and true-ish that didn't embarrass her. She'd written it when she was still heart-eyed about Carson, but now...

It would hurt too much.

Maybe she'd duck out and leave Alex holding the bag. How amazing would it be to do exactly what she wanted for once, even if it disappointed other people?

"Juuulia," her mother cooed. "It's time for your toast."

Before she ran away, a waiter set a glass of white wine next to her.

"Pinot grigio for the toast, miss. We understand you do not care for champagne." He nodded at Carson. "Himself made the arrangements."

Her heart thumped against her chest. "How? When?"

"Back in LA. You said you don't like champagne."

"You remember that?" She clutched her phone.

With an unblinking warm gaze, he said, "I remember everything."

She didn't doubt it. Since the moment they'd reconnected, Carson paid attention to what she liked, didn't like, things that got under her skin, made her smile, made her life easier.

This was her idea of a grand gesture, and it pissed her off.

"Why couldn't you have been *honest*?" She hissed as she rose. "We had potential."

Shadows filled his eyes. No, she wouldn't stare into the abyss of what might have been. She had work to do. Expectations to fulfill. Like always.

She shoved back from the table and stalked to the microphone.

"Hi," she snipped. "Since this is my second time serving as Mom's maid of honor, I have a unique perspective on her weddings."

The crowd tittered. Their phones came out to record the moment. Panic about being seen, caught, rose, but subsided, like high tide fading into low. This was a friendly crowd. She set her glass on the happy couple's table, then scrolled until—aha, there.

"Today," she read, "we celebrate the beautiful journey love takes, no matter how many times it knocks at your door. My mother's shown me that love is not just about finding the right person—it's also about *being* the right person. I've watched her learn, grow, and find happiness within herself before seeking it with others. In this new chapter, we see the beauty of fresh chances."

The hypocrisy of what she'd said stung her lips.

She'd clung to the old saying, *Fool me once, shame on you; fool me twice, shame on me.* Was that truly the limit? Two chances?

Even baseball allowed three strikes.

The truth was there were no rules. She should do what she wanted. Let people talk, whisper, gossip, judge. If she wasn't hurting anyone, she could do whatever the hell she wanted with her life. The smiling couple before her were a lesson—she owed it to herself to push through temporary discomfort in pursuit of what made her happy.

The only force that can stop me is me.

"Jim, we're thrilled you're a part of our lives. You're brave to marry our mother." The crowd giggled, and she took the opportunity to raise her glass. "Let's toast this lovely couple. May your journey ahead be filled with laughter, joy, love, and absolutely no sargassum. Cheers!"

She gulped, then locked gazes with Carson.

They'd settle this. Tonight, here, and she didn't care who saw.

"You're up, Carson."

★ ★ ★

As Carson approached the table, Julia shoved the microphone into his chest. He deserved that. The crowd winced at the loud *thump* and feedback squeal.

"I'm a terrible public speaker, but I'll do my best." The waiter handed him a glass of champagne. "It's an honor to stand here as my dad's best man. His bread and butter is home contracting, and it taught him—and he taught me—the importance of building strong foundations and, when needed, renovations. Together, you and Michelle have shown us that love is exciting at every stage, and I'm so happy for you both. Raise your glasses to Jim and Michelle!"

The small crowd cheered and sipped their beverages.

Carson took a deep breath. This might be his last chance to compliment Julia in public. Awkward? Yes, but the whole point of weddings was making honest, public promises.

"If I can say one more thing—some of you know this, but Julia and I went to the same high school. I had a monster crush on her, and I'd always wondered what happened to the smartest, kindest, most generous person I've ever met. So, I'm thrilled our parents found each other, and I'm glad we were able to team up to do this for them. I'll miss working with you, but I'm glad we're family now."

A smattering of applause met his words.

Julia was not clapping. Nope, she was pissed.

Before he could switch the microphone off, Julia charged toward him. The A/V equipment thumped as she snatched the microphone from him.

"No." She pointed at him.

The crowd buzzed with uncertainty, and most kept their phones on video. Roberto, the fucker, was snapping photos left and right.

"No?" he asked.

"No, you don't get to say nice things in public and la la la, Carson's such a sweetheart."

"Julia, this isn't the right place for—"

"This is *exactly* the right place." To the crowd, she said, "He was mean to me in high school. Then our parents fell in love, so for their sakes we agreed to work together. He apologized for his past behavior, and I accepted it. Then he lied to me again, and that was too much. I told him we'd be cordial, but I wanted nothing to do with him."

Prickly, unpleasant heat washed over him.

Julia turned to their parents.

"Looking at you two, though, I—" she scrubbed her face "—I realized the path to your person isn't always smooth. You might not like them the first time you meet them."

This might've been his optimism talking, but her speech sounded like good news for him.

"People can change. I have, and the least I can do is allow others that grace. It's not fair for me to be angry about a lie when I'm not willing to be honest with everyone here. And in that spirit...get your cameras ready."

Nervous anticipation swirled through him.

She curled her finger toward him, inviting him to come closer. So she could punch him more easily? He didn't care. He'd obey her wishes until the end of time.

"What are we doing?" Carson asked.

"This." She wrapped her arms around his neck and covered his mouth with hers. He caught her against him, wondering how much was too much in public but then deciding if Julia Stone didn't care, he sure as hell didn't, either.

Someone nearby—her mom?—began to clap. Soon, the whole room cheered them on.

When Julia eased away from him, her eyes sparkled.

"Does this mean I'm forgiven?" he whispered.

"Not yet." She led him from the room. "We'll get there, as

long as you promise not to lie to me, no matter how much you think the lie will protect me or my peace of mind."

"I promise," he said and kissed the back of her hand.

The resort's veranda hung a swing big enough for three. He held it while she seated herself, then joined her in the gently swaying bench.

With their fingers interlaced, she said, "I noticed things, too, Carson."

He ran his thumb along her hand's soft skin. "Like what?"

"That you're Mr. Brightside. You never allow yourself to have a bad mood."

He whipped his head toward her. "What do you mean?"

"Life's a bummer sometimes. *Rah-rah* positivity has its time and place, but last night, you could've used a helper or a sympathetic ear. I should have been a safe choice. When your dad was freaking out, I could have handled it *with* you."

He tipped his head back. "I guess we both have trust issues."

"We'll work on it. Together. Because the thing is, Carson, I've never been in love, but I feel like this could be it, and I don't want to mess it up any more than I already have."

His heart skipped a beat. "You haven't messed anything up. And, um… You told me never to lie to you, right?"

"Oh God, what now?" She covered her eyes. "Do you have a pact with the devil? Three wives scattered across the country? Wait, no, you have terrible tattoos. Is that it?"

"You have firsthand experience with my lack of terrible tattoos. And hold on—how is that equivalent to those other two things?"

"I've seen tattoos I wouldn't have doodled on a binder." She squeezed his hand. "Tell me the non-lie."

"I love you, and I'm pretty sure I always have. From the minute you didn't raise your hand to tutor me, then did when there was money involved."

She stilled. "Oh."

"It made me laugh, because every other girl at Bronson would've killed for the chance to be locked at a library table with me. The guy I was ten years ago couldn't have handled loving you. The person I am today…" He brought her knuckles to his lips and kissed them. "He's ready. And you should move to LA."

"Oh," she repeated.

Yeah, he thought that might be a lot. He reached for his phone.

"Are you seriously taking a call right now?" she asked.

"I seriously am not." He shared the project he'd created last night when she wouldn't take his calls. "My gift to you."

She answered her buzzing phone, and a giggle bubbled from her.

"Is this a project plan for moving to LA?" She scrolled through, and gasped. "And your hotel contacts?" Julia glanced up at him. "This stopped being about a job approximately ten minutes after we landed. You know that, right?"

"Yes. Doesn't change me wanting you with me in LA."

She furrowed her brow. "I still plan to permanently relocate here."

"You should, but it'll be awhile before the piers and cabanas are built. Go to LA, gain an impressive amount of experience, fall completely in love with me, and then return to Belize."

"You say that like it's easy." She fiddled with her dress's hem.

"It is." He kissed her temple. "The planner in me sees how things could unfold."

"What about you? Say all that happens—the oodles of experience, the completely falling in love. What happens to us when I move here?"

"I follow." He brought her knuckles to his lips and kissed them. "By then I'll be ready to hand the keys to someone at HQ and start a Caribbean franchise. You can see it, too, can't you?"

She closed her eyes, and the smile he'd like to see every day for the rest of his life spread across her face.

"I can." She twisted toward him on the swing. "Here's the thing."

"Another thing?"

"Yes. There will always be another thing, so get used to it." Her sapphire earring winked in the light. "Will you be my plus-one at Alex's wedding?"

"Yes." He tucked a tendril of her hair behind her ear. "I'll always be your plus-one. Even if she's getting married in those caves."

"Good." She kissed him. "Now let's go to your room."

"Our room," he corrected.

"Our room," she agreed.

Epilogue

Julia shaded her eyes as she waited by baggage claim with a caramel-and-pecan cluster from the Azul Caye Chocolate Company. After Mom and Jim got hitched, Bo and Alex exchanged vows at the courthouse to keep Bo from getting kicked out of the country.

Not super romantic, but necessary.

However, *this* weekend, eighteen months in the making, was the overdue big, fussy, over-the-top wedding. Alex's best friend, Mariele, insisted on hosting the ceremony and reception at her resort in the mountains. It promised to be more of a vacation than Mom's nuptials.

Good, because life had been a blur.

Since Mom's wedding, she'd left Ithaca for LA; scored a back-of-house job at the Ritz-Carlton, where she'd risen through the ranks; and, as predicted, fallen in love with Carson.

Eh, that was a lie.

She was in love with him from the start, but it took her ages to stop denying it. With the resort nearly complete, she'd quit her Ritz-Carlton job a month ago to start up the hospitality and guest services' back office at Stone Adventures and Resort.

They'd welcome their first guests when they launched in two months. Everything was dropping into place.

The only thing missing was Carson.

She rubbed her forearm, where a fourth gem tattoo joined the trio representing Dad, Alex, and herself. Mom's diamond was a welcome addition, and she had room for one more, right inside her elbow. Alex had filled the spot on her body with a citrine to represent Bo.

Carson's birthstone was a pearl.

"Hey, beautiful," a familiar rumbly voice said.

Julia leapt into Carson's arms. He swung her around, nearly knocking into other travelers. A glimpse of this man still sent adrenaline thrumming through her.

She glanced at his bag. "Is that all you packed?"

"You were expecting more?" He laughed and set her down.

"For someone who's moving here, yes. Here." She thrust the cluster at him. "It's been too long since you've tasted Belizean chocolate."

Carson had promoted his COO to CEO of the LA office. Danny, thank God, was staying in LA as an associate who was still receiving a boatload of executive coaching. Carson would spend his next six months spinning up an office here.

"The rest of my clothes are on the moving truck."

"Which will be here in…?"

"Four days. I have all the important stuff." He patted his oddly bulky messenger bag.

Hmph. That was a weird tone. Was he sweating?

"What's the important stuff?" she asked.

He pursed his lips. "I'd rather not say."

"Carson Miller. I demand you tell me what's in the bag."

"No." He shook his head. "I refuse. Not here in baggage claim."

She popped her hands on her hips. "You can't refuse."

"You're infuriating." He knelt, then withdrew a small velvet box from his bag. "I planned to do this tonight on the beach where we had our first kiss, but, Julia Sapphire Stone, your impatience is one of the many things I love about you. You never let me get away with anything and love me through my bad moods. You got away from me once, but I want to spend the rest of my days making you happy. Will you marry me?"

With shiny eyes, she knelt with him. "You had me at infuriating. Yes, I'll marry you."

As they kissed, she giggled.

"What?" Carson asked.

She wiped away a happy tear. "The wedding invitations will confuse people. 'Mr. and Mrs. Jim and Michelle Miller request the honor of your presence at the wedding of their children, Carson Miller and Julia Stone.'"

"We'll workshop it," he said, then rose, pulling her to him. "Now let's go home."

★ ★ ★ ★ ★

Acknowledgments

I'm sad to say farewell to my Belize Dreams world but so grateful to have shared this journey with you! The idea for these books started in the deep depths of lockdowns. I wanted to travel to places outside of my home's four walls. Researching this landscape was a *delight*, and I hope you've enjoyed the ride with me.

As always, my heartfelt thanks to John Jacobson and their frequent reminders that we *really* need to know how people are feeling in pivotal moments. Amazing collaboration and partnership, always. Your comments in the manuscript are a freaking delight.

Gratitude also to Barbara Collins Rosenberg for her guidance, enthusiasm, and support.

My Sunday writerly chats with Christi Barth, Robyn Neeley, and E. Elizabeth Watson are a cornerstone of my writing life and keep me motivated while we're rising and grinding (and drinking lots of coffee and tea).

To David, my husband, who shows up as my hero in my novels and my life—thank you for holding down the fort when I'm in the deadline cave. I promise to emerge for date nights, cocktails, and a glimpse of the stars with you, always.

I'd also like to thank my children, who are all much taller than me these days, for cheering me. One of the joys of parenting is seeing the lovely people you have become.

And lastly, a huge thank-you to everyone who reads, reviews, and posts about my books. I see you, and I'm continuously humbled and grateful. I can't wait to share more words with you!

afterglow BOOKS

Afterglow Books is a trend-led, trope-filled list of books with diverse, authentic and relatable characters, a wide array of voices and representations, plus real world trials and tribulations. Featuring all the tropes you could possibly want (think small-town settings, fake relationships, grumpy vs sunshine, enemies to lovers) and all with a generous dose of spice in every story.

@millsandboonuk
@millsandboonuk
afterglowbooks.co.uk

#AfterglowBooks

For all the latest book news, exclusive content and giveaways scan the QR code below to sign up to the Afterglow newsletter:

SCAN ME

afterglow BOOKS

The Friends to Lovers Project

PAULA OTTONI

She has a plan. But he wasn't part of it...

- Friends to lovers
- International
- Love triangle

OUT NOW

To discover more visit:
Afterglowbooks.co.uk